D0483468

NO
TIME
TO
BLINK

ALSO BY DINA SILVER

Kat Fight
One Pink Line
Finding Bliss
The Unimaginable
Whisper If You Need Me

NO
TIME
TO
BLINK

Dina Silver

LAKE UNION
PUBLISHING

This is a work of fiction. Names, characters, organizations, places, events, and incidents are either products of the author's imagination or are used fictitiously. Any resemblance to actual persons, living or dead, or actual events is purely coincidental.

Text copyright © 2018 by Dina Silver
All rights reserved.

No part of this book may be reproduced, or stored in a retrieval system, or transmitted in any form or by any means, electronic, mechanical, photocopying, recording, or otherwise, without express written permission of the publisher.

Published by Lake Union Publishing, Seattle

www.apub.com

Amazon, the Amazon logo, and Lake Union Publishing are trademarks of Amazon.com, Inc., or its affiliates.

ISBN-13: 9781503954120
ISBN-10: 1503954129

Cover design by David Drummond

Printed in the United States of America

NO
TIME
TO
BLINK

Chapter One

Ann Marie Neelan

Chicago, 2008

As I reach the attorney's office on the thirtieth floor, I'm disappointed by my reflection in the large glass panels that make up the entrance. My shoulders are slumped, and there are dark circles underneath my blue eyes. Nothing ages you like stress and sadness. I lift my chin and yank one of the door handles before seeing the word Push etched above it. A profound thud echoes through the corridor. Once inside, I can sense the receptionist's disdain.

I approach him with a rueful grin. "I'm Ann Marie Neelan. I'm here to see—"

"Please have a seat," he says.

I settle in an old leather armchair near a window overlooking Chicago's renowned Michigan Avenue and look down at my unsteady hands gripping the folders in my lap as if my life depends on them, which it does. Despite everything, my fingernails are perfectly manicured in pale pink to match my lips, and my long dark hair is pulled into a low, tidy ponytail at the nape of my neck, because I'm not allowed to fall apart. I can hear my mother's resolute voice: "Put your pearls on and fake it."

I flip open one of my folders and pretend to care about its contents. Copies of e-mails, phone records, credit card receipts. All of which I've seen a thousand times in the course of the months that led me to where I am today. Broken promises, broken vows, broken hearts—mine, anyway— and a web of lies woven so expertly that I'm ashamed to be at the center of it all. My stomach turns.

Fifteen minutes later, an intercom buzzes and alerts the reception-ist. He lifts the phone receiver and then places it back down. "Stewart will see you now."

I hurry up and out of the chair. "Oh, great. Thank you so much," I say with a smile and then disappear around a corner. I run a hand over my head, but I know there isn't a hair out of place.

Stewart Fishman is hanging up the phone and motions for me to sit down when I enter his office. His desktop is large and very sparse, save for a phone, an electric pencil sharpener, a coffee cup, and a glass paperweight in the shape of a golf ball. His skin is wrinkled and tan, and his expression gruff, but there is evidence of what was once a hand-some, youthful man. I watch as he adjusts a pair of reading glasses over his dark eyes, topped by a pair of bushy white brows, and studies me.

"You can put those on the desk." He gestures to my folders, and I do as he suggests. "So," Stewart begins, "I know we discussed your situ-ation a little over the phone, but why don't you brief me on everything now that you're here." His voice is low and comforting. All I want is to have someone else take control of my life and do my fighting for me.

I manage a smile. "My husband, Todd, moved out about six months ago, recently stopped paying the mortgage, and is threatening to stop paying the utilities if we don't come to an agreement on selling the house ASAP. I *can't* have it go into foreclosure." I pause and take a breath. "I'm sorry it's taken me so long to get in here, but it's been hard with the boys being so young. I'm embarrassed by how blindsided I was by all his lies and cheating. There was a short period of time where

I even thought maybe we could work things out." I throw my arms up and shake my head.

"So, how did you find me?" He lifts his glasses and scans a notepad on his desk.

"My therapist, Monica Farlander."

He gives a small, knowing nod. "OK, Ann Marie . . ." He looks at his notes again. "Neelan. Tell me about yourself. What's your maiden name?"

"Haddad. It's Lebanese."

He writes down the name, furrowing his brow. "I've seen that name before." He stares at the page and then looks away for a moment.

"It's a common Lebanese name," I add.

"What's your mother's name?"

"Catherine. She's from Connecticut."

He writes her name on the paper and then sits back in his chair, rests his hands in his lap, and looks me straight in the eyes. "Wait, is she a Downing?"

I'm a little surprised by his question, as people don't normally make the connection without my telling them. The Downings are a renowned East Coast dynasty, and yes, my mother is somewhat related. Her father, Albert Clarke, was the elder brother of Hazel Clarke Downing, the matriarch of the Downing dynasty. "My mom is a Clarke," I say. "Hazel Downing is my mom's aunt."

Before I know it, he leaps up out of his chair and places his hands on his hips.

I squirm in my seat. I can't afford to meet with any more attorneys at this point. Todd has already met with so many of the other good ones in Chicago, barring them from representing me. "Maybe your firm has done a Clarke or Downing divorce before?" I ask. A fair question, considering the countless number of failed Downing marriages over the past four decades. My parents being one of those.

Stewart takes a deep breath, and his eyes go wide. "Your mother was a client of mine." He starts waving a finger and pacing behind his chair.

"What?" My skin gets warm, and a lump of uneasiness lands in my throat.

"Catherine Clarke Haddad. CC, right?"

I nod.

"She was quite the beauty, that woman." He pauses, reveling in the thought of her as so many people do, including me. "And a fighter, too. She made quite an impression on people," he adds. "Do you have any idea what that family went through?" He looks away.

I'm about to answer, but he continues to speak, reliving the memory.

"What a horrible story that was." He shakes his head and sits down, placing his elbows on the desk.

"Well, no divorce is without its issues, as I'm sure you know, but I didn't think it was all *that* bad. I mean, the Clarkes and the Downings aren't in the habit of discussing 'unsavory' matters, that's for sure, but they—"

Stewart lifts a hand and points at me. "Oh my God." His eyes penetrate mine. "All this time I've wondered what happened to that poor little girl."

I eye him. "I'm not sure I know what you're referring to."

"Are you her only daughter?" he asks.

"CC's? Yes, of course." He must have me confused with someone else.

"This is incredible." He looks me over as if he's seeing me for the first time.

We stare at each other. Me, uncomfortable; him, astonished.

Stewart Fishman rubs his forehead and then briefly covers his mouth with the palm of his hand. His eyes become glossy. "I can't believe you're the little girl."

Chapter Two

CATHERINE CLARKE HADDAD

Chicago, 1970

On top of the dining-room sideboard was a photograph from our honeymoon in Italy. We'd gone to Rome, Florence, and then Venice. Gabriel was pictured standing in Saint Mark's Square—arms outstretched liked a human perch with a pile of birdseed in each hand and a mass of fluttering, ambitious pigeons on each arm. I couldn't help but smile when I lifted it for a closer look. I placed the frame back down and finished dusting.

Our first few months of marriage had been challenging. We'd eloped at city hall after dating only a couple of months, disappointing both our families and, worse, enraging my mother. Not long after, we left my childhood home in Greenwich, Connecticut, for Gabriel's new job in Chicago. Mother begrudgingly drove us to the airport and would hug only me, not my husband, goodbye.

He and I met in Greenwich during the summer of 1970, which I was quick to term "the summer of disappointment" when my parents didn't show up for my graduation from Mount Holyoke. They were traveling with friends on the Orient-Express at the time and sent my two eldest sisters to be with me instead. I cried for a good hour on the train ride home but never confronted my mother. We just didn't talk about things like that in our family.

A good portion of my childhood had been spent trying to get my mother's and father's attention. At first, I began by excelling in sports. My freshman year of high school, I ranked fifth in the state for girl's tennis, yet my mother attended only one match the entire year. When that didn't work, I switched to rebelling. I gave up tennis for smoking weed and staying out past curfew, but all that did was validate her indifference toward me. Once my priorities were back on track, I would've bet my inheritance that graduating from college might have garnered some significant interest on her part, but I would've lost.

She viewed emotional weakness as being unappreciative. If I'd told her how disappointed I was that she'd missed graduation, she would've chastised me for making her feel bad.

But things turned around pretty quickly.

One morning, early in the summer, two girlfriends and I rode our bikes to Tod's Point, an incredible spot located on a peninsula jutting out into Long Island Sound with walking trails, kayaking, and beach access. On days when we'd tire of the snack bar at the Belle Haven Club, we'd drive out to the Point with a picnic basket, but that day we were all stuck with bicycles. We exhausted the morning by gossiping and sunning ourselves with baby oil when I spotted a man leaning against the concession stand, looking very out of place. The first thing I thought was that my mother would've made a derogatory comment about his appearance. The second thing I thought was how attractive he was. He was smoking a cigarette with his arms crossed and a Labrador puppy at his feet. Standing about six foot three with thick black hair, he had caramel-colored skin, mirrored sunglasses, and wore a very small bathing suit for a man of his size. His short-sleeve button-down shirt was hanging wide-open, revealing an ample amount of chest hair. There was nothing about him that screamed "prep-school graduate," and I couldn't have been happier.

"Those suits are very popular over in Europe," my friend Pamela said.

"Maybe he thinks this is a nude beach," Caroline added with a snicker.

"Too bad it's not," I said, leaving my gaze on him.

Then, as it often happens when people stare at each other, he sensed me. I willed it to happen, and it did. I was taking my time uncoiling the chain from my front bike tire when he turned and faced me. He pushed his glasses up onto his head, and Caroline squeezed my arm. "He's looking at us," she said.

"He's looking at me." I quickly slid my feet into a pair of white Keds and placed my kickstand back down. I wore a light-blue sleeveless terry-cloth cover-up that accentuated my long legs. "Wait here for a minute," I said to my friends, and walked in his direction. A breeze carried the scent of a nearby barbecue, and as I got closer to him, I could hear the squeals of little children splashing in the water. He was grinning by the time I reached him, and my heart was pounding at the same pace the puppy was panting.

"Can I help you?" he asked with a trace of an accent I couldn't place, and flicked the cigarette butt into the sand.

"I was going to ask you the same thing." I tilted my head. "I've spent my entire life here. You're the one that looks out of sorts."

"Do I?"

I bent to pet the dog. "Is she yours?"

"For the moment," he said. "Her name is Sheba."

"She's so sweet. I love dogs. We have three beagles at home." Sheba nipped at my fingers until I stood. "What brings you to Tod's Point?" I asked. "I haven't seen you here before."

"And you've seen everyone else that's ever been here before?" He narrowed his eyes.

"Maybe I have."

"Maybe you've been too busy with your own group of friends. Perhaps spending your entire life here, as you say, has made you indifferent when it comes to meeting new people at the beach?"

I shook my head. "Not many new people around here, mostly locals."

"I see, and you came over to me because you know I'm not a local?" He lowered his chin. "You don't look like the beach police to me." He raised an eyebrow and looked me over from head to toe in a way that I'd become accustomed to from men, and even some women.

"I came over because I wanted to." I shrugged and blushed a little.

He let out a heavy, robust laugh that drew a few stares from people standing nearby in the soda line. "I'm flattered."

I squared my shoulders and extended my hand. "I'm Catherine Clarke, but my friends call me CC."

"It's nice to meet you Catherine. I'm Gabriel." He stood up off the wall he'd been leaning against, took my hand, and kissed the back of it. "Please let me know, as we get better acquainted, of course, when I, too, may call you CC." His voice was deep, and his eyes were dark. He could have told me he modeled for *GQ* magazine, and I would've believed him.

"I look forward to it."

"Do you live around here?"

I nodded. "Yes, Belle Haven. It's a little neighborhood within Greenwich. Not too far."

He glanced at Caroline and Pamela, who were staring at us like spectators at a tennis match. "That's quite a bike ride from here," he said and then reached forward and brushed some sand off the front of my dress. The gesture ruffled my nerves and made my heart race. I wiped my brow and smiled.

He pulled his hand back, and our eyes locked. There were dogs barking in the background and bicycle bells ringing in the distance. I could still smell the food from the grill behind the concession stand.

"We usually drive, but none of us had access to cars today," I added.

"Girls from Belle Haven without cars of their own?"

"So, you're familiar with the area?" I laughed. "A travesty, I know. We all have too many siblings."

"I'd offer you a ride, but I don't have the room." Gabriel checked his watch. "I have an appointment later, and I really need to get cleaned up. It's in Belle Haven, as a matter of fact." He met my gaze. "I hope to see you again."

I crossed my arms. "Likewise."

He lifted the puppy, serenaded by the sound of the waves lapping offshore, and walked toward the parking lot.

"Sander wouldn't be too happy to see that grin on your face," Caroline said when I came back to where she and Pamela were standing.

"Sander had his chance."

Pamela placed her hands on her hips. "You and he are through?"

"Through," I said and turned my attention to the parking lot, but there was no sign of my new friend. "There's something very familiar about that man."

"Maybe he was our limo driver last weekend in Manhattan?" Caroline cracked.

I slapped her on the shoulder. "You're so rude."

She just laughed. "Maybe he's Sander Crawley's limo driver."

I rolled my eyes. Sander Crawley and his family were the epitome of Greenwich perfection. The term *old money* was almost never mentioned without the Crawley name uttered in the same sentence. He was everything my mother hoped one of her daughters would wed. In fact, if I had a dime for every time she reminded me that his family came over on the *Mayflower*, I'd have been able to afford my own ship.

Sander and I had been high school sweethearts and had lost our virginity to each other after the senior prom, in the pool house on his parents' estate. He was a kind, good-looking, impeccably polished, thoughtful boy whose etiquette and good manners could rival those of

Prince Philip. But I would always think of him as just that: a thoughtful boy. Never a man. We decided to see other people after college, and
he confessed to me that my own mother had tried to fix him up with
my sister Margaret when she'd heard we broke up. He and I had a good
laugh. It's cruel to say about a nice person like Sander, but he was a dime
a dozen in Greenwich. If a man met the approval of my mother, chances
are I was likely to reject him. There was nothing more I needed to know
about country clubs and golf games. I longed for someone to talk to
me about places I'd never been and things I'd never seen. I didn't need
to spend the rest of my years in Connecticut drinking Bloody Marys at
9:00 a.m., sipping clam chowder at noon, and playing tennis until 5:00
p.m., only to come home for an hour nap and wake up to a pitcher of
martinis while my kids were being fed by someone else. These opinions
of mine were precisely what my mother viewed as unappreciative.

~

Two hours later, I was sitting in my cousin Laura's house, down the
road from my family's home on Field Point Drive. She and I were the
same age, and Laura had just graduated from Dartmouth, like most
of our relatives. And despite having four sisters of my own, I felt the
closest to Laura. She'd suffered through my high school heartaches;
she'd helped me forge my mother's signature after I'd been suspended
for cheating on an exam. She'd been the one who took the blame when
Mother found marijuana in my pocketbook. And she was the only one
who truly understood what it was like to have parents like mine, who
were more interested in their next martini than their next of kin. When
you're young and cared for—clothed and fed with the proverbial roof
over your head—you never question your circumstances. And when
you're privileged, you're simply chastised for dreaming about anything
that might threaten the status quo. Mother's insistence that I live my life
according to her plan, coupled with her lack of compassion for anything

I wanted, left me with little to do but challenge her at every turn. Given the opportunity to talk with each other about our lives and struggles and joys and feelings, I think Mom and I would've gotten along swimmingly. She was fun and gregarious and loved a good time, like me. But when it came to dipping below the surface and discussing emotions and opinions, it simply wasn't done. She considered it painfully gauche to listen to anyone's hardships. Least of all her own daughters'.

Laura and I had been sitting in her family room off to the left of the foyer, with its high ceilings and enormous wrought-iron chandelier. In the center of the main wall was a stone fireplace with mahogany shelving on either side that showcased rows of books and framed family photos, while the back of the room was anchored by a bay window and a window seat overlooking the yard. I was sprawled across a couch, flipping through *Cosmopolitan* and reading an article predicting the popularity of go-go boots, when Gabriel walked through her front door.

"What on earth?" I nearly spit out my iced tea. "What is he doing here?" I lowered my tone to a whisper while Laura continued to page through another magazine.

Laura eventually looked up and followed my eyes to the front entry. "Who?" she asked and then turned back to me.

Gabriel was talking with the housekeeper who'd let him in. He hadn't noticed us, as we were slightly out of his eyeshot.

"Why is he here?" I asked.

She shrugged. "I have no clue. I think he's a friend of my father's. He mentioned someone was stopping by, but he told my mom he wouldn't be staying for dinner. That's all I overheard."

"Your father's friend? Do you know him?"

She slapped the magazine down in her lap. "Do you?"

Just then, my uncle David met Gabriel in the foyer and led him out of view. I snatched the magazine and covered my face.

"What's the matter with you?" She laughed and took it back.

I sat up and turned around, trying to get a glance out the windows behind us that overlooked the limestone terrace, but there was no sight of them. "We met today at Tod's Point. What do you mean he's a friend of your father's? How old is he?"

"I don't know. Not as old as my dad, if that's what you're worried about," she said. "He's here for some sort of summit. He's a doctor or medical salesman or something. I don't know." She waved an unconcerned hand. "I think his father knows mine somehow through the club."

I rolled my eyes. "How else does anyone know anyone around here?"

She went back to reading her magazine, and I leaped off the couch and scurried to the bay window, where I had a better vantage point standing on the seat cushion. Gabriel was out back with his hands in his pockets, looking very relaxed. I thought about how hot it had been earlier at the beach and how I'd willed him to notice me. I tried it again from behind the glass, but he and my uncle walked out of view before I could wield my mind controls.

Just as I was about to hop down off the window seat, I heard a man's voice.

"CC?" My uncle questioned my bare feet on his upholstery.

I stepped down and scratched the back of my head.

"She was seeing if the pool cleaners were still out there," Laura interjected. "We were going to have a swim."

Gabriel hadn't said a word, but I could sense his astonishment as though it were another person standing beside him. Feigning disinterest, I let my eyes wander everywhere else in the room but his direction.

"I'd like you to meet Gabriel Haddad," my uncle David began. "He's Serine Miller's brother."

Serine Miller was an elegant and clever Lebanese woman who was married to one of the largest and most successful restaurateurs in the area. I never saw her without full makeup and jewelry. Her forearms, covered in gold bangles, announced her presence before she was ever seen, like a cat with a bell on its collar. She and her husband, Michael Miller, owned four restaurants in Manhattan, two in Greenwich, and were considered local culinary royalty. They single-handedly had converted diehard fans of clam chowder and lobster rolls to Middle Eastern foods such as hummus, baba ghanoush, and falafel.

"Nice to meet you," Laura said, and he nodded with a smile.

I cleared my throat and took a few steps forward, imagining Laura's eager eyes on me from behind. "We met at the beach this morning," I said, smiling the instant my eyes landed on him again. He was curiously good-looking in a very "European way," as Mother would say, yet his features were angular and faultless. He was wearing navy linen slacks and a white dress shirt with the sleeves rolled, exposing more of his naturally tanned skin. Almost Waspy and just on the verge of fitting in . . . but not quite. Perhaps that's what was so intriguing about him. It was exciting to be around someone different. Someone who'd quietly landed himself in the middle of my world, much like a grenade before it explodes.

Uncle David couldn't have cared less. "I see. Well, the pool cleaners left about two hours ago." He rolled his eyes and started to exit. "If you two would ever look up from those magazines," he mumbled on his way out.

"We meet again," Gabriel spoke, bending forward in somewhat of a bow.

Laura got up off the couch. She and I were both tall, and yet he still towered over us. "Care to join us for a swim?" she said.

He turned to her. "Thank you, but I have to be getting back to my sister's place. Perhaps you two would like to join us for dinner?"

"CC and I are having dinner at the club with some girlfriends," she said.

"Perhaps another time, then." He gave us a nod.

"What happened to your puppy?" I asked. "Sheba?"

"I bought her for my nephew. She's with him now."

My aunt Harriet yelled for Laura to come to the kitchen, and Gabriel took it as a sign that he should leave.

"I'll walk you out," I offered.

We walked through my aunt and uncle's foyer, past the double staircase, and out onto the gravel driveway where a white Corvette was parked. As soon as our feet hit the stones, he reached for a pair of sunglasses dangling from his shirt pocket and put them on.

"Nice car," I said and loosely ran my fingertips over the hood.

"It belongs to my brother-in-law, Michael." Gabriel opened the driver's-side door with the key. "Perhaps you'd like to go for a ride sometime?"

I swung my arms gently. "I'd like that very much. I would also have liked to join you for dinner tonight. Thanks for the invitation."

"How can I compete with the Belle Haven Club? I know your family has always enjoyed it there."

The comment about my family eluded me as I rambled on. "I can taste the entire menu with my eyes closed. In fact, I was weaned off baby formula with their Bookbinder's soup, but we're meeting some girlfriends we haven't seen in months . . ."

He laughed and crossed his arms. "You don't remember meeting me before, do you?"

I remained still for a moment before shaking my head. "No, where?"

"At your club. You were just a teenager then, maybe sixteen or seventeen," he said, studying me. "You were quite outgoing. I could hear you laughing from across the room. And who could forget that hair of yours? It's like sunlight."

He placed his hands in his pockets and leaned against the hood of the car. "It must've been five years ago. I was a guest of a guest—if you will—of your mother and father's." He looked up, thinking for a moment. "A yacht party of some sort." He shrugged.

I was taken aback. "You know my parents?"

"I've met them only once, and it was a long time ago. My friend Shep, Tom Sheppard, was the connection. Tom and I met one summer when I was here visiting my sister. His parents know your parents."

"Did you recognize me at the beach this morning when I came up to you?"

"Yes."

I raised a brow. "Then why didn't you say anything?"

"I was enjoying your inquisition too much."

"And I'm supposed to believe that you remember me and my hair"—I yanked the ends—"from all those years ago?"

"There are some people in life you just never forget." He grinned.

Gabriel's compliment floated between us and then scattered as soon as I heard the crunch of gravel from behind. "We better get inside," Laura said, shielding the afternoon sun from her eyes with her hand. "Nice meeting you, Gabriel."

I looked up at him. "I'm in the book. Your sister, Serine, also knows my family quite well."

He nodded and understood. "I can't wait to tell her I met the beautiful Catherine Clarke twice in one day."

I watched as the car drove off, and then Laura came up and dragged me inside by the elbow.

That was the day everything changed. Every course my life had been primed to take had vanished in that moment. I was supposed to marry one of my own: a Catholic Ivy League graduate—the son of a club member with a twelve handicap and a summer home in Provincetown. Any version of Sander Crawley would suffice. Certainly not a Lebanese man ten years my senior who had a home in Beirut and wore cologne to the beach.

Chapter Three

CATHERINE

Greenwich, 1970

A week later, Gabriel called to ask me out on a date, and as the evening approached, my anticipation grew. My sister Colleen lent me her bright yellow minidress, which had a belt that sat low on the hips. The color was a little much with my blonde hair, but I thought he'd get a kick out of me dressing like sunlight.

At 7:00 p.m., I walked into my father's office, gave him a kiss on the top of the head, and walked out. He was nose-deep in a vodka gimlet and the evening paper, and as far as he cared, any one of his five daughters could have breezed in and said goodbye.

At 7:15 p.m., the doorbell rang, causing the dogs to bark and run through the foyer with boundless excitement and curiosity. When I opened the door, Gabriel was standing there with a bouquet of yellow tulips. "For you," he said and allowed our beagle trio to perform due diligence with their noses. One they were satisfied, they all bolted outside onto the driveway.

"These are my absolute favorite, thank you," I said, taking the tulips.

"Your cousin Laura told me."

I took the flowers from him just as Mother walked up behind me with a cigarette teetering on her bottom lip and a martini in her hand. She was silent at first.

"Mother, this is Gabriel, who I told you about. Tom Sheppard's friend."

He took a step forward onto the slate flooring in our entryway and went to shake her hand, but she did not offer it to him, just gave a nod. I took his hand instead and handed her the flowers. "Please put these in water for me."

She forced a smile as I headed out the door and into the warm evening air.

"Lovely to see you again, Ann Marie," he said to Mom, nearly knocking me off my platform sandals by using her first name.

Gabriel had the Corvette again that evening. "I apologize for the mess," he said, referring to a pile of laundry in the tiny back seat.

"Please don't bother. I adore the scent of damp beach towels."

He drove a short distance to Steamboat Road, a popular little street that jutted out like a thumb into Greenwich Harbor, and pulled up in front of Manero's Steakhouse.

"Have you been here before?"

I almost had to laugh. "Are you kidding? Nick Manero has been pinching my cheeks for decades. Hopefully, he'll give me a reprieve since I'm on a date this time."

"Hopefully not," Gabriel said.

The restaurant was buzzing with activity, and we were greeted by a hostess and seated immediately. The place was located across the road from the water, and the interior was made up of wood-paneled walls with bright red vinyl chairs at each table and sawdust on the floor. Waiters flew around with crisp white dress shirts and long black aprons tied in the back as they served up hundreds of filet mignon dinners each week—including an appetizer, Gorgonzola salad, garlic bread, fried onions, dessert, and coffee, all for $12.95. Locals and visitors alike flocked to Manero's for the filet dinner, and we were no exception. I'd been going there with my family for many years, but that night was the first time I remember enjoying myself so much.

Gabriel ordered us shrimp cocktails and manhattans to start.

"Sorry about my mother," I said. "She's a tough nut to crack."

"I'm used to it."

"She's wary of everyone," I added.

"Everyone who doesn't look like a Downing."

His comment caught me off guard, but I placed my napkin in my lap and maintained my composure. "Well, I see you've done all your research on me, but I'm a Clarke, not a Downing."

"The Downings are your family, too," he said as the drinks arrived.

"If you're so taken with them, then what are you doing wasting time with me?" I took a sip and stared at him over the rim of the glass. "I have no shortage of Downing cousins I could introduce you to."

He laughed. "Oh, I am quite taken with you. That's why I bothered to do my research."

My father, Albert Clarke, had two sisters, Hazel and Harriet.

Hazel had married a man named Patrick Fitzgibbon Downing, a.k.a. "Fitz," who was a Connecticut senator and son of a well-known businessman. My father's other sister, Harriet, had married Fitz's brother, David. The Downing family had lived in the Belle Haven neighborhood for generations. Between them, Hazel and Harriet had nine children— my cousins—who received a great deal more attention than my four sisters and me because of their prominent last name.

"Laura, who you met today, for example. She's a Downing, as you know." I typically preferred to surround myself with people who were unequivocally unimpressed with my lineage, but they were increasingly harder and harder to find. I was mildly disenchanted when Gabriel admitted to knowing my parents because it meant he'd have preconceived notions about how I was raised and what my expectations were.

"I hear your uncle Fitz is thinking about running for president in a few years."

"So I've heard," I said and changed the subject. "How long will you be staying in Greenwich?"

"Just through the end of the summer. Only about two more months, and then I will be transferred."

"To where?"

Gabriel lit a cigarette, exhaled smoke into the room, and shrugged. "I'm not certain yet, but it looks like Chicago, most likely."

"What is it that you do?"

He took a sip of his cocktail and leaned in. His eyes narrowed a bit before he began to speak. He was handsome, for sure, and there was a fascinating contrast between the darkness in his eyes and the lightness in his smile. But there was something precarious about him that captivated me most of all. The deep, loud tone of his voice and the way he threw his hands in the air as he was telling a story. The way he held his shoulders back and his chin up, and the way he smiled at me and no one else. And the way he came into my life as a bit of a mystery. I knew very little about his past and what had led him to the beach that day at Tod's Point, but I couldn't wait to uncover everything there was to know.

"I work as a consultant for a pharmaceutical company based in Beirut. I come to the States when new drugs are introduced in my category, every couple of years or so. Once the physicians and hospitals are acclimated, and the training teams in place, I head back to Lebanon."

"So, you're only in the States for a short time?"

"I expect to be in Chicago for at least two years, maybe longer."

"I see." I looked away.

The waiter brought our appetizers, and I lifted my head to peer out the open windows. It was my favorite time of the day, when the faint chatter of seagulls accompanied the setting sun.

After dinner, we drove to Tod's Point, where we'd met a week earlier. We sat talking in the car for a while until the sun was fully retired. Then he grabbed a towel from the back seat, and we went for a walk on the sand. He was a little too boisterous and crass at times, and his manners were somewhat lacking, but he captivated me with stories about growing up in a much different place. He mentioned a home in the mountains of Lebanon, a younger brother who struggled with learning disabilities, and a father who had left them at an early age. From what I could tell, he didn't see his mother or brother much, but he and Serine, who had moved to America as a college student and never looked back, supported them both financially.

His figure was lean yet protective, with wide shoulders and strong arms. His legs were muscular and scarred, not riddled with tan lines from tennis socks. I could barely contain my smile as I sat with him, fretting over saying the wrong things or sounding horribly boring by talking about my relatives and Greenwich all evening. He'd traveled the world, spoke three languages, had two degrees, and all I'd ever accomplished was being born into the right family.

When we finally picked a place to sit, he took the towel that had been draped around his neck and laid it down. Once we were both off our feet, he didn't hesitate to kiss me. His approach was bold yet tender, and I lost myself completely with him. My limbs loosened, my lips parted, and I used every inch of my body to prove to him that we were a match. That I was his equal. That he should adore me and treasure me while he had the chance because he would miss me when he left, and he may never have a third chance to meet Catherine Clarke in one lifetime.

The flame from Gabriel's lighter illuminated his face as he lit a cigarette and then exhaled the first drag. He blew smoke from his lungs and ran a hand through his thick hair. It was already an hour past my curfew, but what twenty-one-year-old college graduate should have a curfew, anyway? I couldn't tell him it was time for me to go home. I simply wouldn't. He could sleep on the beach all night if he wanted. He wouldn't have to go to church the next morning and serve cheese sandwiches to the parishioners afterward. He could walk up and down

Greenwich Avenue the next morning and sleep on a park bench and drink manhattans all along the one-mile stretch if he chose, because he had that freedom. Freedom to talk three octaves above everyone else in the restaurant and be indifferent to their stares, freedom to live where and how he wanted, and freedom to do as he pleased and not simply what was expected of him. Freedoms that I longed for.

"What about you, Catherine?" He looked directly at me when I spoke and focused on my lips as I answered him. "What will you do with yourself once the summer is over?"

I crossed my ankles and brushed some sand off my lap. "I may decide to go to graduate school."

"More school means you don't have a plan."

I tilted my head and sighed, enjoying the sound of the waves breaking against the rocks for a moment. "My plan is to be a reporter for a magazine or a newspaper. I have an English major, but I was thinking that another degree in journalism . . ."

"Another degree won't help you. You need experience. School cannot replace real-world experiences. While you'll be wasting time with more classes and football games, your more ambitious colleagues will be starting their careers and leaving you behind."

I huffed a little at him chastising me, although he was probably right. "I asked my father about talking to the editor of the *Greenwich Times*, and he said to send him some test articles."

Gabriel shook his head. "A real professional who is committed to her trade doesn't send her father in first. You should go to the editor yourself," he scolded, waving his hands as he spoke. "Is he hiring you or your father?"

I was silent for a minute and then kissed him square on the lips. "You're right. I've been guilty of wasting these weeks since graduation."

He dragged his hands through the ends of my hair as I pulled away.

"Thank you for being so blunt with me," I whispered, elated that he hadn't scoffed at my choice. "Mother thinks it's a useless career, reporting about other people's business, although that's precisely what she does at the club all afternoon."

He lowered his gaze. "Promise me you'll go in and talk with the editor in person." He paused. "If that's what you really want."

I crossed my heart with my finger. "I promise."

Gabriel and I held hands and kissed our way back to his car. Looking back, it might seem as though things were moving fast, but when I was knee-deep in it, time stood still for me. I'd never felt so grounded and comfortable with someone before. He made me believe I could be a writer if I wanted. He made me believe there was more to life than the prestigious Belle Haven bubble I existed in, and he made me fearful of a future without him.

When I came home later that evening, the yellow tulips had been tossed onto my bedroom floor.

Chapter Four

ANN MARIE

Chicago, 2008

As I come to life after a restless night's sleep, my therapist's voice rings in my head along with my son's cries through the baby monitor. "Every morning, write down five things you're grateful for," she would say. Hurriedly, I sit on the edge of my bed and grab the pink spiral-bound notebook she forced on me a month ago. Unlike my mother, I loathe writing in journals or anything else for that matter. I open to yesterday's page.

1) My health
2) My boys
3) Our home
4) My mom
5) That revenge is possible

I grab a pen and try to write quickly before Luke wakes Jimmy and Ryan, and I have three cranky kids on my hands.

1) My health
2) My boys
3) Our home
4) My mom

5) That revenge is possible

Luke gets quiet as soon as I enter his room. The lights are dim, and he's standing clutching the bars of the crib, his hair a sweaty mop of sticky golden locks. The room smells of lavender and poop.

"Hi, sweet boy," I whisper, and lift him out, kissing his cheeks. "Momma's here." He buries his face in my shoulder as I carry him to the changing table. I lay him down and reach for a clean diaper as he eagerly begins chewing his foot. Once he's in a fresh pair of footie pajamas, I carry him downstairs to the kitchen, latching the child gate behind me at the top of the stairs. Our home is nestled on a cul-de-sac in Wilmette, a suburb about fifteen miles north of downtown Chicago. When I was pregnant with Ryan, we had an apartment in the city, and we'd drive up every Sunday for months, going to open houses and looking for the perfect home. I cried tears of joy when we found this one, a yellow Cape Cod with a cedar shake roof and a covered wraparound porch, two weeks before my water broke.

Todd knows how much I love this house, and that only makes him more enthusiastic to sell it. I spent months picking out paint colors and cabinet pulls and carpet weaves. I gave birth to two more beautiful boys and had countless holiday parties and birthday parties over the years in this house, only to find Todd naked and underneath his equally nude coworker on the five-hundred-thread-count sateen sheets I'd ordered for the guest room. Even worse, I'd decorated that room especially for my mother.

My mom lives in Connecticut and doesn't visit too often, but when she does, my heart is full and my home feels complete. Like the frayed strands that make up the fabric of who I am get snipped and tailored back to perfection. The summer I left for college, it was hard for me to leave her. She and I have always been very close, and after I graduated from Purdue University in Indiana, I had a choice. Go back to Greenwich, move back in with my mom, and hope to find a job in Manhattan. Or follow Todd and my heart back to Chicago, where most of my new Midwestern college friends were headed. But by that time I was smitten with Todd, so it wasn't a difficult decision.

We'd met at a fraternity party my sophomore year. He was tall and good-looking, with wispy sandy-blond hair, and he was ambitious as all hell. Todd was an only child, and if there was something he wanted, he couldn't conceive of not getting it. His teeth were white and his eyes were green, and he had me charmed out of my clothes and into his bed the first night we met—a detail I'd left out when gushing to my mother about him.

She supported my decision and me, as she always has. That's why it's important for me to have a comfortable place for her in my home. She loves the color yellow, so I have two lemon-colored swivel chairs upholstered in linen tweed, under the window in the guest bedroom. On the opposite corner is a desk that belonged to my grandmother so Mom can sit and read or write before bed. The sheets have since been burned, but everything else is as she likes it.

It's never been a drama-free relationship between us; we have our disagreements like any mother and daughter, but she's my biggest supporter and my biggest critic rolled into one, and I can't imagine not having her as a sounding board.

My chest tightens when I think about discussing the divorce with her. The hardest phone call I ever had to make was telling her about Todd, and how horribly cliché the demise of my marriage is turning out to be. She burst into tears when she found out he'd been cheating on me with so many different women. I think she'd rather I have a third eye in the center of my forehead than have a man disrespect me that way.

As I'm thinking about her, I realize she hasn't returned my phone call from two days ago.

"Mooooooom!" Jimmy screams from the top of the stairs, just as I'm getting Luke's bottle. "I can't find my gym shoes!"

"I'll be right there." I look around for a spot to put Luke. *Where on earth has the high chair gone?*

"Mom!" I can hear Ryan now. "Jimmy woke me!"

I shift Luke onto my other hip and hand him his bottle. "Oh, Ryan, you have to get up anyway. Could you please help Jimmy find his shoes?"

"No! He woke me."

"Please, honey," I beg, and locate the high chair by the bay window in the family room. "How on earth?" I mumble to myself. After rolling it back to the kitchen, putting Luke in the seat, and placing the chair smack-dab in front of the television, I grab a coffee mug from the cabinet and feel a tug on my sweatpants.

"I'm starving," Jimmy says, shoulders slumped and clearly defeated by morning hunger pains.

I place the empty mug on the counter. "Do you want some eggs?"

He shakes his head no.

"I can make them scrambled with cheddar cheese?"

"No."

"How about cereal?"

"I don't want cereal."

I take a breath and look at the clock on the microwave. *Six thirty-five a.m.* "Have some cereal."

He shakes his head again and crosses his arms for good measure.

"Do you want some apple slices with peanut butter?"

"No."

Luke drops his bottle, so I go to retrieve it. "Well, Jimmy, for someone who is as starving as you say you are, you're certainly rejecting lots of delicious options."

"I want pancakes."

Luke points at the television, squealing, trying to engage me with the singing backpack that has him enthralled on today's episode of *Dora the Explorer*, but all I can muster is a quick smile in his direction. "I don't have the mix. We ran out over the weekend, and I haven't been to the store."

"I want pancakes." He begins to cry, which gets Luke's attention away from the TV. Nothing seems to fascinate my boys more than one of their own brothers in tears.

I kneel in front of Jimmy. "I'm not going to have you crying over pancakes. That is unacceptable. I've offered you eggs, cheesy eggs, apple slices, and cereal. So pick one of those foods, and go sit down at the table." I ruffle his hair.

He huffs and stomps his foot before grumbling, "Cheesy eggs."

I glance at my coffee mug, wishing it would magically fill itself with a warm foamy latte as I pull a nonstick pan from the drawer beneath the stove. Our house has been on the market for two months, and now that the school year has recently started, it's impossible to keep the place clean and presentable. Today some potential buyers are coming at 11:00 a.m. for a second showing, and my Realtor has insisted I have it sparkling like the Chrysler Building. I think about purposely flooding the basement as a deterrent instead, but imagine no less than a four-hour tongue-lashing from Todd if I do anything to screw this up.

Had I ever thought about it before, I would have assumed that having a spouse (the Cheater) cheat on you would give you (the Cheatee) at least some sort of leg up in the divorce proceedings. You know, as a bit of a consolation prize. But that's not the case. No one gives a shit which role you play, and in my case, least of all Todd. It's a funny thing, having your spouse cheat on you and then make you feel like you're the one who's done something wrong. He's constantly questioning my parenting, constantly berating me about keeping the house clean, and continues to come and go as he pleases without ever giving me notice. Even though he moved into an apartment, as long as we own this house together, there is nothing I can do to keep him out. The only way for me to have any peace from him is to sell the house and move, or buy him out of his half, which would be a little more than $400,000.

I feel the urge to write in my goddamn pink notebook, but I just don't have the time.

Ryan walks in the kitchen and trips over a box of LEGO bricks, sending them flying like confetti and causing Jimmy to laugh uncontrollably.

~

6:42 a.m.

Once everyone is dressed, fed, teeth brushed, lunches packed, faces wiped, and shoes tied, I wave goodbye to my still-empty coffee mug, and we all pile into the minivan and head for school. Ryan is in second grade, and Jimmy is in all-day kindergarten this year, so Luke is the only one left at home during the day. A widowed neighbor of mine, Edith Stern, has begun sitting for him in her home three mornings a week. All I have to do in return is drag her garbage bins to the curb on collection day and bring her fresh pumpernickel bagels from Barnum & Bagel every Monday. She's a retired schoolteacher with six grandchildren of her own, but they all live out of state. She dotes on my boys when she has the chance, which, if I had my way, would be more often.

"Come, come." She waves a toy rake in the air as I stand in her driveway, pulling Luke out of his car seat and realizing he's still in pajamas. My head is throbbing from caffeine deprivation.

"Good morning, Edith! How are you today?" I shout, always assuming the woman is hard of hearing, although she's never once told me she was.

"I'm looking forward to seeing my friend. We have a lovely fall morning and lots to do in the backyard. Lots!"

Luke curls his sweet little face under my chin but keeps his eyes on her. His routine is to play shy upon arrival, then throw a fit when I come to pick him up later. I love this woman for making him want to live with her. Once on the ground, he takes her hand, and the three of us walk into the foyer. He isn't as verbal as he should be for his age, which leads me to blame the divorce for his shortcomings and everything else that is wrong—and normal, for that matter—in my children's lives. Typical things like Ryan struggling with reading, or Jimmy throwing a tantrum at recess, all come flooding back to the divorce. It's the landing pad for everything these days. My therapist, Monica, charges $110 an hour to convince me otherwise, but so far she has failed to do so.

"Sorry we're late. Jimmy dropped his water bottle in the car, and it rolled under one of the seats and took us almost ten minutes to find." I wipe some sweat from my brow. "But we did manage to locate every lost McDonald's french fry, so there's that. You'd be surprised at how completely void of mold they—"

"Say goodbye to Mommy and give her a big kiss," Edith interjects. Instead, he gives my leg a side hug and allows me to kiss the top of his head.

"Thank you. I have to run home, clean the house, get dressed, and then head downtown. I have my second meeting with the divorce attorney."

That piques her interest. "What time?"

"Eleven thirty."

"Anything happen with the boy that took you out on a date last week? The one from the Internet?"

"God, no." I shake my head.

Despite my knowing that there's nothing less attractive than a thirty-six-year-old woman going through a divorce, with three small children and a stalled marketing career, I've recently begun dipping my toes into the cesspool that is online dating. Yet no matter how thin I am, how much makeup I wear, or how much Botox I get, nothing can mask my reality. The gem of a suitor that Edith is referring to met me for drinks last week, showed up an hour late, and told me the only reason he'd agreed to go out with me was because I have sons. "Girls are crazy bitches," the guy said.

Edith gently latches onto my forearm. She's a tiny woman, maybe five foot two, and I have easily four inches on her, but she's emotionally larger than I am in every way. Her demeanor, her confidence, her pride. "Love will find you again. Pretty young thing like yourself." She squeezes my arm. "You'll be just fine."

God, I love when people tell me that. I press my lips together and give her a hug. One day, maybe I'll believe it. "I certainly hope so," I say, and look down at Luke, who is still holding her hand and staring up at me with his big brown eyes and no choice in life besides doing exactly what he's told. All I want is to take him home, snuggle in bed together, fall asleep watching *The Little Mermaid* with his mop of curls against my face, and stay there until the proverbial sun comes up for all of us.

"I may be taking a very short girls trip soon. I know it's the worst possible time to leave town, but my friend and our neighbor, Jen Engel, has been begging me to join her," I say. "I'm considering going if my mom can come in and stay with the boys for the weekend."

"Sometimes there's never a good time, so you should go and enjoy yourself when you have the chance. If I can be of any help, just let me know."

"Thank you."

Even though the image of Todd humping another woman in my home is still fresh in my mind, the fact that I'm even considering a weekend away from my kids means I'm making progress.

The day I walked in on them was a Saturday afternoon. Todd and I had planned to take the boys downtown to the Shedd Aquarium to meet up with some friends. I had packed the double stroller, picnic lunch, snacks, water bottles, pacifiers, portable DVD player for the car, and filled the tank for what was to be a fun family day. At the last minute, Todd had bowed out because of work.

"It's fine," I'd said, gritting my teeth, not wanting to disappoint our boys or the other family. "We'll just go without you."

Traffic turned out to be a nightmare, and it had taken us forty minutes just to get from Old Orchard Road to the junction. Even though I'd remembered extra juice boxes and Goldfish crackers, I'd forgotten an extra change of clothes on the one day Luke decided to have explosive diarrhea in his car seat.

Needless to say, I had to call my friend and tell her we wouldn't make it, cursing myself for not rescheduling in the first place. By the time I got home, every single one of my kids had had no fewer than three nervous breakdowns each. Ryan and Jimmy because the trip to the aquarium had been canceled, and Luke because of the obvious. There's only so much a stack of McDonald's napkins can do in a pinch. I'd pulled in the driveway and told the boys they could get out of the car, but they had to stay in the garage and keep an eye on Luke until I got back. When I'd walked into the kitchen, I'd known something was amiss.

There's a certain sense to a home when it's empty, and I could tell immediately it wasn't. I grabbed the cordless phone and dialed "9," then "1," then hovered my thumb over the "1" as I climbed the stairs. When I heard noises coming from the guest room, I knew. I stood in that doorway a good forty seconds before they noticed me.

"Holy shit," was all Todd said, and later admitted to having sex with at least five other women over a twelve-month period after connecting with them on Facebook. After hours of amateur investigative reporting on my part, I discovered that he worked with two of them and had gone to high school with the other three. At first, I blamed myself, like maybe if I'd been more sexual with him, he wouldn't have cheated. Maybe if the kids didn't occupy so much of my time, he wouldn't have cheated. I wallowed in self-pity and promised to change if he would give us a chance, but it didn't matter. He'd grown tired of crying babies and a tired spouse and a cluttered home. He lost all appreciation for his family and the things that matter in life. His ego prevailed over all of us.

I cry as I drive away from Edith Stern's house. Nothing outlandish. No runny nose, no convulsions, no squawking bird noises, just my typical I've-failed-everyone-in-my-life-especially-my-children-and-haven't-had-an-ounce-of-caffeine-in-thirty-hours cry.

Once I'm home, I brew a pot of coffee, vacuum the floors, pick up the toys, and make the beds. When I'm done, I fill my mug and dial my mother's number.

"Hello?" she answers.

"Hi, Mom. I left you a message on Monday."

"Huh," she says. "I thought I got back to you. How are you, honey?"

Just as I'm about to speak, the floodgates open. She lets me cry for a moment until I catch my breath. "I'm just having one of those days."

"What's going on?"

"Nothing. Everything. I'm scrubbing this place like Little Orphan Annie, trying to sell this house, and yet I have no idea where we're going to live. The boys have so many friends in the neighborhood, and I want them to stay in this school district. I'm going to have to go back to work, and after doing the math, I'll make just enough money to pay for day care, assuming any company wants to hire someone who's been out of the workforce for eight years." I sip my coffee and wipe my face. She was silent. "Mom?"

"I'm here."

"I wouldn't blame you for hanging up on me."

"I'm going to come stay with you."

"I'm fine. The Mexico trip isn't for a few weeks, and I'm feeling horribly guilty about leaving with everything going on."

"A few days by yourself might do you some good. You know I always say that the sun heals everything. I want to be there for you, regardless. I should've gotten on a plane a long time ago."

The knots in my shoulders loosen a bit, and my neck relaxes forward. "I would really love to see you," I say. "I have another meeting with the attorney today." I rub my forehead. "I can't believe I haven't talked to you since I met with him last week. That's what I was calling about."

"How did it go?"

"Does the name Stewart Fishman ring a bell?"

She doesn't say anything.

"Mom?"

"It does, yes."

"He said he was one of your divorce attorneys," I say. "Can that possibly be true?"

"Did he say anything else?"

"Actually, he seemed to think you had one of the worst cases in his entire career. Tragic, he called it. I wasn't sure if he had you mixed up with another client."

I hear a soft sigh through the phone. "I think maybe he does."

"That's what I was thinking."

"Is there any way you can reschedule your meeting with him?" she asks.

I lift my head. "Why would I do that?"

"There are some things I need to tell you."

Chapter Five

CATHERINE

Greenwich, 1970

After our first date, I saw Gabriel Haddad every single day. Sometimes just for a cup of coffee, sometimes for dinner, and sometimes for whatever we could accomplish in the front seat of a Corvette. If I'd ever been happier in my life, I had no recollection of it. I caught myself smiling and laughing when no one was around. Writing his name on pages in my journal and nothing else.

Six weeks into our relationship, Gabriel led me through the doorway of a hotel room at the Stanton House Inn on Maple Avenue. I'd told our housekeeper, Jessie, I was sleeping at Laura's that night—something I did at least twice a week—so there was no reason for her to question me.

The room was quintessential Greenwich. Pink-and-green bedding matched a set of lime-colored throw rugs covering large square sections of the hardwood floors. There were rose-covered curtains, striped wallpaper, and a fireplace on the back wall. A combination of wicker and pine furniture was carefully placed throughout the room, and a watercolor painting of the Long Island Sound hung above an upholstered headboard.

Gabriel placed the key on a dresser once we were inside. "You look beautiful," he said.

A stack of folded towels lay on the end of the four-poster bed, and a pitcher of water and two tumblers sat on the nightstand. By the windows were a pair of swivel chairs with a side table in between, and atop that were two crystal flutes and an ice bucket with a bottle of champagne. I placed my purse on one of the chairs.

Gabriel uncorked the champagne and poured me a glass. There was an obvious dance going on between us. He would pace the room, making small talk about work and friends he meant to visit in East Hampton before heading to Chicago, where it had been settled he'd live. Occasionally, he'd pause and kneel in front of me and kiss my hands before pacing the room some more, guzzling more of his drink, telling me about his week, and refilling our glasses.

"I have some exciting news," I said, my head tingly after finishing my second glass.

"Oh?" He sat on the bed.

"I'm going to be writing a weekly column for the *Greenwich Times*."

His face lit up. "Well, well, well. That is wonderful news. Good for you!" He cocked his head and clapped.

"Thank you." I placed my empty glass on the side table.

"What will it be about? What is your topic?"

"So far, just some local stories. Places to shop, popular outdoor cafés and pubs. Things of that sort. Gotta work my way up to the grittier stories—like most popular dog breeders in Lower Fairfield County."

He snickered. "You should be very proud of yourself."

"I am, thank you," I said and stood. Little did I know that I would never write even one article.

Reading my body language, he walked over to me.

Gabriel placed his hands loosely on my cheeks, kissed my lips, and leaned his body into mine. I gently pulled away.

"Can we lie down?" I whispered.

"Of course," he said and took my hand, but not before kissing it. "You, my darling, are in charge of me tonight."

We lay down on the bed, and he bent over and placed his lips on my neck. A whiff of his cologne proved more intoxicating than the champagne. We stared into each other's eyes as his hand slowly went to the hem of my skirt. My breathing intensified, and my body tensed when his hand found its way underneath. It was not the first time a man had been there, but it was the first time I was eager to give myself to anyone so completely.

I was a rule follower, a mostly good student, a girl who strived to make her parents proud, or at least hold their attention for five minutes. The minute I found passion in the form of Gabriel Haddad, I latched onto it with every ounce of my being. I risked everything I'd ever had to hold on to that sensation, to trap it because I'd waited patiently for it, and I was not going to leave it behind for anything. I grew up feeling strong, yes, but ordinary more. As the eldest daughter, I was replaced almost every other year with a newer, shinier girl, forcing me into the role of caretaker and example leader without my consent. Gabriel made me feel confident and independent and wanted.

"Are you OK?" he paused to ask.

I nodded with conviction, both thrilled and terrified. In only a few weeks, my heart and soul had become his puppets. When I was with him, I could barely focus on anything else, and when I was without him, all I could think about was how long I had to wait to be with him again. When would he pick up the strings and bring me to life again? We were as inseparable as his work—and my mother—allowed, but it was never enough for me. And poor Laura—we'd had so many plans to visit the Cape and travel to Boston to visit friends, and I'd bailed on all of them. I'd become one of those miserable lovesick women. Having Gabriel's attention made me feel like I could conquer the world.

I took a deep breath, lifted my skirt, and placed my hand firmly on his for a second before removing it and curling my arm next to my ear. He read my expression and slid his fingers under the fabric of my underwear, watching my body respond to his touch. Quickly, he pulled away, removed his shirt, and stood beside the bed wearing only his shorts. "Please." He held out a hand. "Stand up."

Gabriel removed my camisole and then gently spun me around and unhitched my bra, letting it drop to the floor. He stepped closer and wrapped his hands around my body from behind, placing them between my breasts as my heart continued to beat at an embarrassingly rapid pace.

The anticipation was wonderfully agonizing. His hands slid from my chest to my waist. "Lie down," he instructed while kissing the nape of my neck.

I lay on the bed again and watched him remove his shorts before kneeling over me. I shimmied out of my skirt and then my slip and helped him slide my underwear off. Gabriel bent forward and took one of my breasts between his lips. My breath intensified, and I tightened my grip on his shoulders, closing my eyes. He tenderly squared my waist, then kissed his way from my chin to my chest again and down to my stomach before sitting up. I let out a small breath and clutched the sheets with my hands as he moved himself inside me, gently at first, and then harder after seeking permission with his eyes. He lowered his mouth on my breast and steadied himself as he tended to every part of my body. My limbs relaxed, and he increased his speed until we collapsed together.

My nose searched for a trace of his cologne, and I nearly wept when I found it.

Afterward, he covered me with the sheet and fetched a glass of water.

"I love you, Catherine Clarke," he told me. "More than I can express with just those words, this room, and this night together. More than I can say with my lips and my body and my heart." He sat on the edge of the bed and touched my hair. "I hope you know that."

"I love you, too." Tears were running down my cheeks. "So much."

Four weeks later, we eloped and moved to Chicago. We'd been in the city only a few months when I found out I was pregnant.

Chapter Six

CATHERINE

Chicago, 1970

After I finished dusting the apartment, I sat by the window listening to the "L" train whiz by the corner of Armitage and Sheffield, watching pedestrians scurry about the street corner beneath me. Our two-bedroom apartment was on the top floor of a three-story walk-up in Chicago's Lincoln Park neighborhood, about a mile and a half west of Lake Michigan. There was parquet wood flooring throughout, with bright green and metallic geometric print wallpaper in the kitchen and bath. I'd purchased a matching emerald velvet couch for the main room and a bamboo dinette set when we'd first arrived.

It was unseasonably mild for early December in the Windy City. My glass of iced tea was nearly empty, and I'd forgotten to get lemons at the market, which made me long for an iced tea from the Belle Haven Club. Strong, tart, and best of all, made *for* me and served *to* me along with a saucer of lemon wedges. Thanksgiving had come and gone and turned out to be a colossal disappointment. I'd promised Mother—and Laura—we would come home to Connecticut, but Gabriel was unable to take any additional time off work due to the honeymoon, and he forbade me from going alone in my condition.

Since it was the first major holiday without my sisters and parents, he tried to lift my spirits by taking me to the Pump Room, located in Chicago's Gold Coast neighborhood inside the Ambassador East Hotel. For years, the upscale restaurant's Booth One was a celebrity hub for the likes of Humphrey Bogart, Lauren Bacall, Marilyn Monroe, and my favorite singer, Frank Sinatra.

We sat under crystal chandeliers and ate steak Diane and Cherries Jubilee, made tableside. It was a lovely evening, but there was a part of me that felt horribly isolated. I was surprised by how much I missed being in my flannel pajamas on the couch in my family's home, listening to Mary Grace and Patricia argue over walking the dogs or fetching Mother another vodka gimlet, and begging Jessie to make a dessert other than pumpkin pie for once.

Christmas was to be my saving grace. Gabriel promised me two weeks at home. He would come for a few days, but I would take the train early and stay through the New Year and celebrate with my sisters. I smiled at the thought of it even though I dreaded the idea of leaving him for so long.

Gabriel worked from 8:00 a.m. to 6:00 p.m. most days and was too tired to go out after work unless he had a business dinner, in which case he'd muster some mystery energy—that he could never find for me— and stay out until past midnight. I begged Laura and my eldest sister, Margaret, to come visit. I'd written to both of them and promised I would get us a room at The Drake hotel, a Chicago landmark famously perched on the edge of Lake Michigan, and we could spend a weekend shopping. But Margaret was enjoying her senior year at Boston College, and Laura had taken a job at a law firm in Greenwich where my uncle David worked. Juggling everyone's schedules proved futile.

I glanced at the clock on the kitchen wall above the stove. It was 11:00 a.m., and Gabriel would be home from work at 6:00 p.m., expecting dinner on the table. That evening I would serve roast turkey breast with steamed carrots and instant mashed potatoes, but first, I had something very exciting planned—my first official assignment as a writer.

As soon as we'd arrived in the city, Gabriel had encouraged me to apply at the two largest newspapers, the *Chicago Tribune* and the *Chicago Sun-Times*. Within four weeks, I had an interview with an assistant features editor at the *Tribune*.

Once the day of my interview arrived, on my way to the building, I found my reflection in the window of a retail shop and applied some lipstick. A light coral Revlon shade. "Never wear red when you want to be taken seriously," Mother always said.

I squared my shoulders and pushed through the revolving door of the Tribune Tower. A lobby receptionist directed me to the elevator banks that would take me to the twelfth floor, where a second receptionist asked my name.

"Catherine Clarke Haddad, here to see Mrs. Rushton."

Behind the desk were four rows of narrow tables, each with about five typewriters on them. Some had people vigorously pecking away and flipping through notepads as they tapped their cigarettes into ashtrays. A smoky haze filled the air, and the walls were in desperate need of some color. The whole place reminded me of the recreation room at a psych ward I visited as part of a Junior League excursion in college.

"Right this way, Catherine," the receptionist said.

I followed her down a long hallway to a tiny windowless office. A lovely young woman, no more than five foot one, stood and offered me her hand. I had to bend to greet her. "Abigail Rushton," she said. We shook. "Please have a seat."

Abigail was a clever-looking gal. She wore a royal-blue tunic with matching pants, hair very straight and parted severely down the center. On her face was a pair of black-rimmed glasses with thick lenses that made her lashes appear three-dimensional when she looked directly at me.

I did as she suggested and sat opposite her. "Thank you so much for meeting me."

She lifted the résumé and article I'd sent her off her desktop. I could see they'd been creased in the mail. "It's what I do." She smiled. "So, Ms. Catherine Clarke Haddad."

"Please call me CC." I smiled back at her.

She scratched her chin. "You may not believe this, but I think I went to Dartmouth with your cousin Henry Downing," she said, still grinning. "As soon as I saw that you were from Greenwich, I figured, how many Clarke families are there in Greenwich besides the ones related to the Downings!"

Despite my aversion to playing the Downing family name game, I couldn't help but appease her. "Why, yes, he did go there. What a small world." I folded my hands in my lap.

She leaned in and winked. "I'm a married woman now." She fluttered the fingers on her left hand. "But I must confess that Henry was quite the looker!" She smiled with her mouth wide open that time.

I giggled. "Henry and his brothers are blessed in the looks department, yes."

She reached for a chain-mail cigarette case and offered me one.

I shook my head and placed my right hand on my stomach. "I'm trying to cut back, thank you."

"Are you expecting?"

I nodded.

"How exciting. Why on earth do you want a job?"

It's true, my sisters and I were raised to be debutantes and wives. Education and occupation were minor priorities. I didn't even look for a job when I first came back from Mount Holyoke because Mother had snubbed her nose at the thought of my becoming a writer. I spent my time having parties and going to parties and shopping for a husband, but Gabriel changed all that. He pushed me to recognize my worth and realize there was value in the expectations I had for myself. Rebellious as being with him was, he gave me a reason to live my life as I wanted, not as my mother dictated.

"As you see"—I pointed to my résumé on her desk—"I have a degree in English, and I've always wanted to be a writer, specifically a reporter. I was planning on getting my graduate degree . . ." I looked down at the gold band on my hand. "Well, not everything went as planned." I paused. "I've kept many journals over the years and thought maybe one day I could tell my story." I blinked. "I know that sounds proud, but I've been blessed with an interesting life—not just charmed—and family, and have chronicled much of it in my own words. My own voice. Not everything is always as perfect as it seems."

I was nine years old when I'd learned about my father's first affair. Mother was at the hospital, having just given birth to Mary Grace, while my other sisters and I were back at home. There'd been a wicked spring storm that night in April, with thunder and lightning trying to outdo one another for hours. After one particularly loud crack, I ran into my parents' room and found a woman sitting on top of the bed. She turned when the door opened, covering herself with her hands, and froze. A moment or two later, I noticed my father was beneath her. Seconds after that, he was screaming at me to leave the room and not come back. From my bedroom window, I could see that one of the many trees in front of our house had been struck and had fallen across the driveway, blocking any cars from entering or exiting. Maybe thirty minutes after that, a taxicab pulled in, up to where the tree had fallen, and someone got in and drove off.

When I'd turned away from the window, I'd nearly choked on my own breath when I realized my father was standing in my doorway.

"Stay in bed from now on, and do not say anything to upset your mother," he'd said and then closed the door.

I wasn't exactly clear on what had happened. It all felt very wrong to me, but at the time, I was sure there was a reason for it. My journal entry that next day read: *There was a really bad storm and a lady in the house.*

The second time I found out my father was having affairs was much worse.

"I see," Abigail said. "Well, I read the article you sent, of course. It was good, but I think you could do better. Don't hold back with this *voice* of yours. As you say, you have an impressive East Coast lineage that our Midwest readers would find quite intriguing." She leaned in, sensing my battle between being my own person and resting on my laurels. "Don't fight who you are, CC. You must know that it's fascinating to people. You're an authority on many things by association."

I crossed my legs. "I can see that, yes."

She lifted the article and waved it gently at me. "You can still be humble, if that's who you truly are, but write from here"—she tapped her heart—"and people will respond to you. You don't have to write what you think people will like. Just write what *you* like, and readers will find what's relatable to them, and if it's not relatable, it will be that much more interesting."

"Thank you for that. I would love the opportunity to do so."

She put my article down. "OK, then. Let's get your feet wet with something festive, given that the holidays are soon upon us. How long have you lived in Chicago?"

"Just over three months."

"We're doing a lot of seasonal pieces right now. Have you been to the Walnut Room at Marshall Field's?"

I shook my head no.

"Perfect place for a socialite to start!"

And with that, I had my first assignment. Writing an article about lunch at the Walnut Room during the Christmas season. Two weeks after my meeting with Abigail, I had my reservation booked.

I'd never been to Chicago before moving there, but I was somewhat acquainted with Marshall Field's and its renowned Walnut Room, and

I was thrilled to have been given such a task. I woke up the morning of December 5 determined not to waste another moment holed up in that apartment. Next year I'd have a baby by my side and not a lot of time to focus on much else, so that afternoon, I would enjoy lunch at the Walnut Room and pen my first article for the *Tribune* with my very own byline. Plenty of women were attempting to have babies and careers, and I was determined to be one of them.

More than a retail shop, Marshall Field's was a Chicago institution. The grand dame of department stores. I pulled my bright blonde hair into a low bun, penciled in my brows, tied a scarf around my neck—one that matched my pale-blue sweater set—put on my pearls, and paired the look with some navy slacks and loafers. In my canvas tote was my wallet, lipstick, compact, two pencils, and my writing journal.

A valet opened the door when I reached the expansive four-block-wide building. "Welcome to Marshall Field's, madam." He nodded and repeated the greeting to some other women entering behind me. I floated through the first level, inhaling the fragrant scent of perfumes and powders and lotions and anything else a woman might desire to make her feel even more feminine and glamorous than she already was. I paused at one glass counter and sampled a hand cream that filled my nose with the bouquet of a dozen roses.

I made my way to the elevator and rode it to the seventh floor. When the doors opened, I nearly tumbled backward with surprise when I saw Sander Crawley standing before me. He was wearing a dark suit with a narrow tie, a tweed overcoat, and carrying a matching fedora in his hand. He tipped his head when he noticed me and took a small step backward.

"What on earth?" My face lit up, and so did his.

We locked eyes until he placed his hand on the door to prevent it from closing. "You might want to exit the elevator," he said.

I laughed and stepped out. We hugged and then I offered him my cheek, where he planted a kiss. "How lovely to see you here, and what a surprise."

"I'm in town with my aunt Violet and cousin Martha. She's touring Northwestern University."

"Are they here with you?" I glanced behind him.

"No, they're at the hotel. I'm here picking up some Frango mints and perfume for my sisters back home."

I crossed my arms. "Such a gentleman you are."

"How about you?" he asked. "Are you alone?"

I shifted my tote from one shoulder to the other. "I'm writing an article for the *Chicago Tribune*. East Coast girl lunches at the world-famous Walnut Room for the first time." I pulled out my journal and showed him. "I've been hired to do a features column for them."

"That's incredible. Good for you." He smiled. "I hear additional congratulations are in order, Mrs. . . . ?"

My marriage to Gabriel was anything but predictable. The Greenwich gossip hounds had been barking for weeks afterward, according to what Laura had told me. "Haddad." I said my new last name proudly. There was a part of me that was genuinely pleased to be relieved of the name Clarke and all the societal pressures that accompanied it, yet there would always be a part of me that would never quite shake the awkwardness that came with a shotgun wedding. It just wasn't what "we" did in our family. I decided not to mention the baby.

"Well, Mr. Haddad is a lucky man." He winked.

"You have always been too kind."

Sander checked his wristwatch. "It was a pleasure running into you. I hope that you're happy and enjoying the change of scenery here in Chicago." He leaned forward and kissed my cheek again. "It certainly sounds like your career is on track. I hope you have a very merry Christmas, CC."

"I'll be home for the holiday, actually. Will you be around?"

He nodded. "Good luck with your article."

"Thank you, Sander. Please give my love to Martha and your aunt."

Seeing Sander was another reminder of how often I thought of Greenwich since I left, which was ironic since all I ever did when I lived there was dream about being anywhere else. It was in that moment, watching him disappear when the elevator doors closed, that I made a promise to myself to never look back. I would be back home for Christmas and New Year's, and that was enough. After the New Year, I would leave country clubs and clambakes behind and focus on my writing career, my husband, and our child.

I walked into the restaurant, and a young man showed me to my table. The glow from the colossal Christmas tree in the center of the room was magical, breathtaking. The tree's décor that year was "country living," and all the ornaments were themed as such. Green upholstered chairs and crystal sconces on the walls and columns that proudly stood throughout the impressive space accented the room's walnut paneling. Each table had its own lamp, omitting the need for bright overhead lighting and lending a tranquil intimacy to the grand room. Once my waiter approached, I placed my order for chicken potpie, the dish that had started a culinary revolution, from the bit of research I'd done. According to legend, a store clerk working in Marshall Field's millinery department overheard two women customers complaining that they were hungry, but there was nowhere close by to eat. The store clerk, wanting to do anything she could to keep them shopping, offered them the potpie that she'd brought with her that day for herself. That clerk's name was Mrs. Herring, and Mrs. Herring's Chicken Potpie was still the most popular item on the menu nearly one hundred years later.

Back at home that evening, I played my favorite Frank Sinatra album and nearly danced my way through preparing the roast turkey and instant mashed potatoes. At 6:00 p.m., the door to our apartment opened, and Gabriel came home in an even better mood than I was. He lifted me off my feet and pressed his lips to mine when he found me in the kitchen. "Hello, my love," he said and smoothed the back of my hair. "How was your day?"

"It was incredible. I filled twelve pages of notes on the Walnut Room, with three on the food alone."

He looked at me questionably. "The Walnut Room?"

"For my article."

He threw his head back. "Yes, of course."

I turned to stir the potatoes and added two tablespoons of butter. "I ordered their famous chicken potpie."

"How do you feel?" he asked, and bent to kiss my stomach.

"I feel great." I hugged him, my heart full.

Gabriel placed his briefcase on the dining table, and I handed him a glass of Scotch. He stood behind me and kissed the back of my neck as I stirred the butter into the potatoes, and then he took a seat. "I've had some fantastic news today. I couldn't wait to come home and tell you," he said.

I wiped my hands on my apron. "What is it?"

"Come." He waved for me to come closer, so I stood in front of his chair, and he took my hands in his. "Start packing, my darling."

My eyes went wide with enthusiasm.

"In two weeks, we are moving back to Beirut."

Chapter Seven

Ann Marie

Chicago, 2008

"You're scaring me," I say to my mom. "I can't reschedule my appointment with the attorney. I've waited too long as it is."

"I don't mean to scare you."

"What's going on? Does this have something to do with my father?"

My parents had split up when I was very young, and I'd lived with my mother my whole life in Connecticut until I'd left home for college and never came back. Mom has always been tight-lipped about the relationship, never wanting anyone in her family to discuss him with me, good or bad. Needless to say, he's been a mystery. Every once in a while, I'd get a Christmas or birthday gift in the mail, but those stopped many years ago. I would cringe and stammer when kids at school would ask me about my dad. The majority of my childhood was spent pretending I never had a father and coping with that void. Especially with my mother and my four aunts being around me at all times. There was an overwhelming female contingent, and asking them about my father was off-limits.

"Just stick to the topic of your divorce, and please don't tell Stewart you've mentioned his name to me."

"Why?"

"Please, Ann Marie. I have a royal headache this morning." Her voice is stern, and I don't press her.

Just as I hang up the phone, my stomach drops as I hear a key in the lock on the front door. I walk to the foyer, and a second later the door flies open as Todd storms inside. He's standing there looking like he doesn't have a care in the world, dressed in jeans and a short-sleeve Polo shirt, with a fresh haircut. It kills me that he looks good. I can barely look him in the eyes because I'm still uncomfortable hating him.

"Can I help you?" I ask.

"Doubt it," he says, and runs past me up the stairs. My face goes flush with anger as he casually struts back down a few minutes later with a suitcase in his hand.

"I've asked you not to barge in like that!" I scream, grateful that the boys aren't home.

"It's my house, too," he scoffs, and looks behind me into the family room. "I thought you were going to clean this place up for the showing?"

I shake my head. "Just get out." I don't even bother to ask why he needs a suitcase because it doesn't matter, and I won't believe him anyway.

Todd rolls his eyes. "With pleasure." He exits and purposely slams the front door so hard that the light fixture in the foyer shakes.

I stand there alone again for about three minutes, shaking like the light above me but too angry to cry.

I get in the car thinking I can't go on much longer like this. Once I reach the city, my friend Jen texts me as I'm parking the car in the attorney's lot.

Good luck today, and make sure your mom can come in town so we can go to Cabo and do tequila shots and then vomit because we're getting old and can't hold our liquor.

I smile before tossing the phone back in my purse.

Now that I'm an official paying client, the receptionist greets me with added vigor. And refreshments. "Good morning, Mrs. Neelan," he says.

"Please call me Ann Marie," I say. "Mrs. Neelan has stopped taking my calls and refuses to acknowledge that she raised a cheating SOB." I smile.

"And you can call me Thomas." He winks at me. "Your shoes are the shit, Ann Marie."

I glance down at my blue patent-leather pumps. "Thank you."

"Mr. Fishman will be ready for you in about ten minutes. Would you like something to drink? Snapple?"

I shake my head. "No, thank you," I say, and take a seat in the leather armchair by the window and text my mom.

I'm going to need a set of black pearls to match the circles under my eyes.

She replies, I think I have an old set from your grandma.

I laugh out loud. Love you, Mom. Can't wait to see you.

Stay strong. We've been through worse, she writes. And please don't worry about anything I've said. I'll explain later.

OK. Hope your headache feels better soon.

Thank you, she answers.

Whatever she has to tell me can obviously wait if it's waited this long, and I can't afford to stress about one more thing these days. Sleep has become as rare as peace of mind. Yet while I'm afraid for my future, for my sons' futures, I find fear to be a great motivator. The things that keep me awake at night are the concerns and worries about how they will grow up and deal with the truth behind the demise of their parents' relationship. How will they react when they grow into men and learn what their father did to me? To us? Will they become cheaters? Will they have hate in their hearts? The truth always comes out, and I'm still struggling with the burden of understanding why and how these things happened to me.

I can't help but assume that my own parents' relationship was riddled with aggression and betrayal. "It was a different time," my mom would say whenever I dared to ask her about it. "People know better these days." Now that I'm in a position of raising children as a single mother—just as she was—I'm going to hold her to a better explanation.

Somewhere between today and the last time I was standing in this waiting room, I turned a corner and am determined make things right for my boys and myself. I don't want to hold on to the revulsion I have for Todd. I want to rid myself of the shame and hold my head up again. Each day I inch a little bit closer to the edge of confidence.

"He's ready for you," Thomas tells me.

Stewart is in his office, and this time there are two other attorneys with him. The first is a woman about ten years younger than I am, and it looks as if she passed the bar and leaned how to ride a two-wheeler just this morning. Her short skirt and long hair make me think she'll be sleeping with one of the married partners within a year. Thanks to Todd, that is where my mind goes now. The second guy is closer to my age, wearing a light-blue dress shirt, navy twill trousers, and wing-tip shoes. His thick round neck is spilling over a plaid bow tie that's begging to be loosened.

"Ann Marie, I'd like to introduce you to two of my associates. This here is Noah Goldman and Amanda Dorneker."

"Nice to meet you." I shake their hands.

"Please, everyone, sit," Stewart says, and gestures to a round table in the corner of his office. "I'm obviously your lead attorney, but Amanda and Noah will be assisting me. The good news about that is that they're both fantastic attorneys in their own right, and they charge one-third of my hourly fee." He raises his brows. "We've reached out to Todd's attorney and don't have much encouraging news to report, other than he's agreed to pay the electric and the gas."

I take a deep breath. "What a prince."

"It's a starting point," Stewart says.

Noah fumbles through some papers. "So, your husband is claiming he makes very little money and is unable to afford unallocated support, which includes your child support and alimony. He's also showing a tax return that would only make him liable for one-fourth of what we were asking for in child support." He looks at me, and I say nothing. "I know you're selling the house, and there's a little bit of equity there, so we're going to see if he'll allow you to keep all of the proceeds from the sale in exchange for alimony, at least."

"He can afford both. He makes thirty thousand dollars a month."

Amanda speaks softly. "We're going to hire a forensic accountant to do a little more digging."

All I can think is that a forensic anything cannot be cheap. Todd runs a moving company with four locations. When he first started, I used to help him do the books, and many people would pay him in cash. I went to great lengths at the time to hide those transactions and bump up our expenses to make it look as though the business barely broke even. "He doesn't report most of his income, as I'm sure you can guess." Amanda is taking notes. "I was actually being generous by asking for the minimum child support required from him. How does he expect us to live on a fourth of that?"

I exchange glances with Noah and Amanda, but they say nothing. "Stewart?"

"Like I said, we're at the beginning stages. We'll uncover whatever he's hiding and make things right. We're far from over."

That can't be cheap, either.

I stand, cross my arms, and begin to pace. "I don't want this to drag on forever. I can't have him continue to come into the house whenever he pleases."

"Well, he's legally entitled to access the home because he's still on the title."

"I know the law, but it's disruptive for me and the boys. Can we at least get him to agree to forfeit his right of entry until it sells? He's the one that put us in this position. At the very least, he could show some compassion. It's beyond unnerving for them to have him pop in and out unannounced. They have no structure and no promise of seeing him or not."

"We asked him that, and he declined."

I throw my arms in the air. "What do I get to decline? Can I decline having to be here with all of you this afternoon? Can I decline the invoice that's going to come from a forensic fucking accountant?" I bury my face in my hands. "Please forgive me. I honestly hate profanity. Todd just brings out the worst in me, and I can't seem to express my thoughts where he's concerned in any other way."

Stewart stands up and places a hand on my shoulder. "No need to apologize."

I wipe beneath my eyes. "Do I need permission to leave the country?"

"With the children?"

"No, with a friend."

He smiled. "No, you fucking don't."

Chapter Eight

CATHERINE

Chicago, 1970

I was still grinning like a fool and thinking about goddamned chicken potpie when he finished his sentence. "What?" I asked.

"I'm being transferred back to Beirut. They have an immediate position for me and want me there before the holidays." His tone was eager. "This is a dream come true for us."

I stared at him, stunned. "You're not serious." I shook my head. "We've only just gotten settled here. This is our new home."

Gabriel frowned. There was disappointment on both of our faces. I stood in the kitchen waiting for whatever he was going to tell me next, and at the same time not wanting to hear one more word about it. My head was still shaking when he pulled a chair out from the table and told me to sit.

"I know it's sooner than I ever thought it would happen . . ."

"Years sooner!" I nearly laughed.

He took a breath. "It's going to be beautiful. You and me, back in my country, together. The two of us in the place that I love the most. You are going to be so happy there."

I sat, speechless.

"We are leaving in two weeks." His tone changed.

I looked into his eyes and saw irritation. "I'm not going there," I blurted. "I've only just begun to get comfortable here. I'm staying here." I clutched my stomach. "I'm not having my baby in Lebanon."

Gabriel slammed his fist on the table, shocking me and rattling the silverware. I closed my eyes when he did it a second time. He stood abruptly, causing his chair to fall backward onto the floor.

I kept my head down and my eyes on my lap while he paced the kitchen, pulling his hair and mumbling something to himself in Arabic. "Our baby, CC. Our baby!"

I stayed still when he pulled his chair upright and sat back down.

"It is our baby, and we're a family now." His tone was softer, and he placed a finger under my chin. His dark eyes were fixed on me, searching my face for any indication that I might be relenting. I was taken aback by his aggression, but regardless of my devastation in that moment, we could always find solace in each other.

I flinched a little when he kissed my forehead. "I'm sorry. I'm so sorry. I should never have come home and surprised you like that. I should've known this would be a big adjustment for you." He looked away for a second. "I was just so thrilled when they called and told me today. Please understand. I did not mean to upset you." He kissed me again. "I never want to upset you."

When Gabriel would speak about the prospect of moving to Beirut, it was always more of a "one day" probability. One day we'll buy a house in the suburbs. One day we'll get a cocker spaniel. One day we'll have three children. One day we'll move to Beirut. My brain couldn't conceive of it happening before all those other things.

"Is this a new blouse?" he asked, trying to distract me.

I nodded.

"It looks beautiful on you."

I forced a smile. "I bought it today at Marshall Field's."

"How nice."

I folded my hands in my lap and hesitated before saying anything that might upset him again. "You know how much I've been looking forward to spending the holidays in Greenwich."

He tilted his head to the side. "My darling, I know. I'm sorry for the timing, but we must go together. I cannot leave my new bride behind." He searched my face again for some reassurance that I understood where he was coming from, but instead I began to cry. Gabriel sighed and left the room.

We didn't speak of it again until two days later when I confessed how nervous I was to break the news to my mother.

"You're a married woman, CC. She will have to understand," he said.

"I know, but it doesn't make it any easier."

"Who is more important to you, your husband or your mother?"

"That's not fair. You're both important to me, but you know how we were all looking forward to being together for Christmas."

He threw his arms up. "And what about what I'm looking forward to?"

Mother had begged me to come home in March so that her ob-gyn could be the one to deliver the baby, who was due in April. She didn't trust anyone in any vocation who practiced outside of the state of Connecticut. Even less if they weren't at least three degrees of separation from a member of the Belle Haven Club. Telling her that I'd be having my baby delivered in Beirut, Lebanon, would be akin to telling her I'd become a Charles Manson follower.

Eleven more days.

I kept a countdown on a piece of paper and began the process of packing everything I'd just unpacked a few months earlier. I would call Mother the next day, giving her ten days to fret over everything. Growing up with a strict Catholic background and four younger siblings, I learned early on to give her the least amount of time possible when it came to digesting bad news. And to make sure she had at least three gimlets in her before doing so.

The next morning, I sat near the window and snuck a few puffs of a cigarette before dialing. One long drag gave me the bit of strength I needed to endure the number of times the phone rang before anyone answered.

"Someone pick up," I mumbled to myself.

"Hello? Clarke residence."

My ears rejoiced at the sound of Jessie's voice. "It's CC," I said. Jessie was a true southerner who had been displaced at some point in her young life and wound up working for my mother when she was newly married. She was a proud African American woman who wore a white, pressed uniform every single day and made a fierce pitcher of spiked lemonade for parties. Growing up, Jessie's room in the annex was a safe place to escape, and she often served as a sounding board for my four sisters and me. Many times she would act as a neutral go-between with Mother and us. She'd take time to listen to our gripes and gave great real-world advice when those gripes were categorically First World complaints. I always valued her opinions, and when she was cross with me, I'd move mountains to get back in her good graces.

"Oh, my girl. How are you feeling? I'm thinking about you every day, you know."

"Thank you, Jess. Is Mother nearby?" I asked. "I need to speak with her."

"Let me find her for you." The receiver made an initial thud and then a few more as it inevitably hung, bouncing against the kitchen wall. I could picture it dangling inches above the yellow vinyl stool that was reserved for phone calls and matched the tiny pineapple print on the wallpaper. A huge chunk of which was missing from years of wear due to my sisters and me putting our feet up on the wall.

The phone was jostled again before I heard her voice. "You there?" she asked.

"Hi, Mom."

"So good of you to call. How are things in Chicago? Have you had a big snow yet?"

"Not even close. The weather has been very mild. Quite nice, actually."

"Have you settled on a parish? Father Patrick asked about you last week after Wednesday-morning Mass. I presume his recommendations were good?"

Thanks to Mother's insistence, Father Patrick of Saint Mary's Parish in Greenwich—where I'd spent every Sunday morning of my childhood—had made some calls and set up appointments for me in Chicago so that Gabriel and I could have a proper place of worship. I had only just settled on Holy Name Cathedral the week before.

I took another drag and blew the smoke through the window screen. "They were good. And yes, I've put a thank-you note in the mail to him."

"Very glad to hear that," she said. Mother would continue to ask me about myself, how I was feeling, about the church, the apartment, the weather, but never about Gabriel. It was as if I'd packed up and moved to the city alone and impregnated myself.

"I have some news," I started. She must've dreaded every time one of her daughters began a sentence that way.

"Oh?"

My throat tightened. "Gabriel has been transferred to Beirut." There was a long, disapproving silence on the other end, and the words were as difficult for me to speak as they were for me to believe. I yearned for her to comfort me. "Mom?"

"I'm here."

My eyes began to well up. "Please say something."

The day I left for college, my mother had stood at our front door beneath the outdoor lantern that hung from an enormous steel chain. It had been drizzling outside, and she puffed a cigarette as I stood in the driveway, embracing my sisters and saying goodbyes. Once everyone else had gone inside, Father had his driver bring the car around, and then he'd handed me some cash and told me to phone when I needed more.

"Darling," Dad had called to her, and she'd waved from where she was standing. "Are you going to say goodbye?"

"It's raining." She'd crossed her arms as if to shiver. "Call when you get there, CC."

I could have gone to her and embraced her that day; I wanted to. But I'd never done that before, so why would I have done it then? Instead, I'd gotten in the car with the most vacant feeling I'd ever had. I'd longed for her warmth, and all I could think was that she was stuck at home with my father and maybe she longed for some compassion as well. Maybe she envied me because I got to leave.

Talking with her on the phone that day, I experienced the same emptiness.

"I don't imagine that you're going with him, are you?" she asked.

"Of course I'm going with him. He's my husband, and we're having a baby." She needed constant reminders. "What would you have me do?"

"I would have you come home. You are not going to have your baby in a foreign country with doctors who don't even speak our language. I will not allow it!"

"Please don't make this any more difficult for me than it already is. I'm going to need so much help. We're due to leave in ten days—"

"Catherine! Ten days?" She was nearly panting. "How long have you known about this? How could you spring this on us?" She always included the entire family when she was exceptionally furious.

"Gabriel just told me only a few days ago. He found out at work and came home happier than I'd seen him in a long time." My voice cracked. "I'm so scared, Mom. Please, I could really use your help." Something I rarely asked for.

I could hear her sigh on the other end. I knew she'd rather pretend she was in control of the situation than listen to me cry for much longer. "We will work this out. Uncle David has some business connections over there. He's the one who knew Gabriel to begin with. I will ring Serine and see to it that she recommend a physician and contact some family for you." She paused. "Please tell me you'll still be able to come for Christmas."

I shook my head as if she could see me. "I don't think so." There was no hiding my tears at that point.

"OK, OK, all right. Take a breath. Don't get all upset. I'm going to make some calls, and I will get back to you. I still think you should be allowed to come home for the holidays. We've many plans with family, and I was counting on you being a part of everything." Again, she neglected to include my husband. Perhaps that was why he was less than eager to spend the holidays with her in Greenwich.

"I've been looking forward to seeing everyone more than anything in the world."

"Then that settles it. You will come home and then meet him in Beirut."

I wiped my eyes. My family did not discuss much in the way of emotions. If I was cross with my mother or father, I simply kept my anger to myself. My sisters and I did not dare to confront our parents and challenge their decisions, no matter how frustrating. My parents did not sit us down if they knew we were displeased with something. We were expected to follow rules and keep quiet. The mere idea of being given a platform for our grievances simply did not exist in our home. But I was married, and those rules did not apply to me any longer. I think that was the hardest pill of all for my mother to swallow.

"It's not going to happen. We've already talked about it, and he wants us to be together, and to be honest, I don't really want to travel there on my own without him." I took a deep breath.

"Your father is not going to be pleased."

"Hopefully, he will understand," I said.

"I don't know how much more of this I can take. This is a great deal of Gabriel to ask."

I sighed. "He knows, Mother, and he loves and appreciates me."

"I certainly hope so."

Ten days later, we left for Lebanon, but not before I submitted my article on the Walnut Room. Abigail Rushton encouraged me to do so, even though I would never see it published.

Chapter Nine

CATHERINE

Beirut, Lebanon, 1970

As we flew in from above, the city's buildings resembled a crowded cluster of white beehives nestled closely together on the edge of the Mediterranean Sea.

We landed two days before Christmas, and the air was a damp sixty degrees Fahrenheit. A driver named Walid greeted us in Arabic and then in English as we walked out of the airport before taking our bags. He was a small man and moved around as quick as a fox. His driving was erratic, yet on par with everyone else's. I craned my neck to see if there were any dividing lines on the streets.

"How do people know which lane to stay in?" I asked Gabriel.

He smiled and held my hand. "They get used to it. It's organized chaos."

Palm trees stood on the water's edge, begging to be noticed against buildings and makeshift markets everywhere. Balconies were littered with people, some leaning way over to talk to neighbors below. I could hear their voices shouting as we passed. It was a beautiful, bustling city with an energy reminiscent of the French Riviera. The drive was just shy of twenty minutes from the airport to Rue Clémenceau, where Gabriel's apartment was. The Clémenceau district was somewhat of a diverse cosmopolitan area at that time, home to Christians, Muslims, and Jews alike, and just blocks from the esteemed AUB, American University of Beirut.

Walid came to an abrupt stop in front of a charming old building that looked like it could have stood on Bourbon Street in New Orleans, with its round, ornate balconies protruding from the front. It was tightly nestled between two other buildings that were similar yet less flamboyant. All three had a bevy of Christmas lights and other various decor—such as large pine wreaths—dripping from the terraces and doorways. I could smell them as soon as I exited the car.

"We are home." Gabriel turned around and kissed me.

Not long before, that word had meant only one place for me: my family home in Greenwich. The idea that this was my third home in seven months was inconceivable. And the fact that I couldn't call upon a friend or cousin to commiserate with, let alone speak the language, was terrifying. I took a deep breath and rested my hands on my stomach.

Walid jumped out to get our things from the trunk.

Cars and buses were whizzing by fiercely, preventing me from exiting the vehicle. And the honking! Gabriel jumped out the passenger side and then opened the back door. "Come this way." He extended his hand and helped me out onto the sidewalk.

I shivered a little. "What is everyone honking at?"

"It's the service cars. They are like shared cabs. They honk to get attention and let people know they are around."

I shook my head.

"Can I get you a sweater, Miss?" Walid asked as he began to rummage through my tote bag.

I took the bag from him. "I can manage, thank you." I wore a pair of black slacks and a long-sleeve cotton crewneck T-shirt in a dark eggplant color. On my feet was a pair of black loafers.

"Of course. Please let me know if you need anything." He nodded and smiled, revealing numerous missing teeth.

I smiled back, clutching the tote to my chest.

Gabriel came up from behind and kissed my neck as Walid watched. "He's going to drive you anywhere you need, OK?" Gabriel told me, and then spoke to Walid in Arabic. "We can get settled, and then he can take you to the market if you like."

A mother and her four children walked past us on the sidewalk and entered the building. The last one, maybe two years old, stumbled behind the pack, dragging a stuffed penguin. The woman waved enthusiastically to Gabriel and welcomed him with her smile, but she didn't stop for any introductions.

"It's been a long day," I said to him. "Maybe tomorrow."

He and Walid exchanged a few more words I couldn't understand, and then Walid drove off, but not after telling me in English to have a wonderful evening.

"He seems lovely," I said. "But I don't want to trouble him."

"It's fine, my dear. It's what he does. And you will find that everyone will be able to talk to you. Around here, most people will speak English and French and, of course, Arabic—which you will learn—but there will always be someone who speaks English." He studied my face. "Don't worry, OK?"

I nodded.

He took my hand, and we walked up three flights of stairs to Apartment 310. Gabriel unlocked the door and helped me drag what bags we could carry on the first trip into the foyer, and then he went to open the balcony doors. The horns from the service cars filled the apartment, along with bits and pieces of conversations in Arabic from people standing near the curb who were smoking and catching up with one another. The white curtains hanging on either side of the doors billowed, coming to life from the breeze as if they'd been holding their breath during his absence. The living room was a simple mix of white-and-cream furniture with one large Oriental rug that covered a small portion of the marble flooring. There were two paintings on the walls, both depictions of the beach and the ocean that added some color to the room. It had the look of a bachelor pad, a little sparse and dispassionate but comfortable.

He slipped an arm around me and pulled me close. "What do you think?"

"I think it's very nice."

"I love you, and I want you to love it here," he said and then pulled away, waving his arms about. "You change anything you want. Anything!"

I laughed and remembered how much I adored him. Every part of him that I fell in love with months ago was exaggerated in his home. His smile, his deep voice, his affection for me and his country, and the ease with which he expressed his emotions to me and the rest of the world. I felt all of it in his embrace.

"This is a tight community. This neighborhood and these buildings, they are like family to me, and they will treat you as such." His eyes were serious. "Those who know me will do anything for me, and I for them. You will see."

"OK."

"I know how things were back at home for you. You will be able to have those relationships here, too. You just have to open yourself up to them."

"OK," I said again, and we hugged.

"I will get the other bags," he said, pulling away and darting back down to the street where we'd left them.

I walked to the edge of the glass doors overlooking the street, where Gabriel was chatting with a man below. The air was filled with the scent of baking flour and spices. I didn't step outside because there were people just next to us on their balcony, and I didn't want to intrude.

A moment later, there was a knock on the door. I rushed to it, thinking Gabriel had been locked out. But it was the tiny little girl with the penguin that I'd seen waddling behind her mother earlier.

"Why, hello," I said, and she quickly thrust a round, pizzalike dough at me. "Thank you." I giggled.

She stared up at me like a little fawn with heavily lashed brown eyes. "Thank you," she repeated.

Her mother laughed from across the hall. "You are welcome!" the woman shouted, coaching her on the correct response.

I lifted my head. "How kind of you," I said to her mom.

"Manakeesh," she said, pointing to the dough. "It is *Manakeesh.* I remember Gabriel likes his like my husband, Sammy, with a little bit of cheese and meat and lots of extra thyme."

Gabriel's voice could be heard from the stairwell below. "You spoil me, Brigitte!" he hollered, carrying bags in both hands. She leaned in to kiss his cheek when he made it to the top.

"It is my pleasure," she said, then looked back at me. "I am Brigitte, and this is Reema." The little girl beamed at the mention of her own name.

"Nice to meet you. I'm Catherine." We loosely shook hands.

"We have heard a little about you but are excited to know more." She pulled a card out of her apron. "It's a wedding card. Many of the ladies were very happy that Gabriel has found someone to love, and many of the ladies were not so happy!" She laughed some more and winked at me.

He and I exchanged smiles. "Well," I said, "I hope not to disappoint anyone. Thank you so much for this."

"We have more good news," Gabriel started. "I am going to be a father."

Brigitte clasped her hands over her mouth and then embraced both of us. "How blessed you are!" she squealed. "Come, Reema!" she yelled, but the girl did not move. She stood staring at my hair. Then her mother yelled something in Arabic, and the girl ran back into her apartment.

Gabriel wiped his brow and closed the apartment door behind us. He was home. He was speaking the language, greeting the neighbors, talking about his favorite foods, boasting about his baby on the way, and rummaging through drawers and cabinets, knowing exactly where everything was.

I walked to the balcony again and stepped outside. It was not my first time out of the United States, not even close. I'd traveled before, vacationing with my family in the South of France, visiting Laura at boarding school in Switzerland. Heck, Gabriel and I had honeymooned in Italy only a few months ago. Oh, no, I was not naive to international travel, but previous excursions had all been under the guise of a vacation, with the promise of returning *home* on the near horizon. And there it was again, that word. I wrapped my arms around myself, never feeling so out of place in all my life.

Chapter Ten

Ann Marie

Chicago, 2008

"If you can get a treadmill in here, I could kill two birds with one stone," I say to Thomas, Stuart Fishman's receptionist and my new best friend, then place a Grande, no-foam latte on his desk.

He lifts the cup. "This better be nonfat."

"It's free, drink it."

"I literally cannot even talk to you if you didn't watch *Lost* last night."

"I had a dream that Sawyer saved me from a burning movie theater and had to use his shirt to put the flames out. Does that count?"

Thomas rolls his eyes.

"I watched it," I say. "Can you believe Juliet outed Sun like that about the affair? I can't stand her."

"She's such a bitch. I hate her and Jack together," he says while I take a seat in my favorite leather armchair.

"When this divorce is over, I will own this chair, and I intend to leave here with it," I say.

"Have at it." Thomas waves a hand in the air.

About ten minutes later, I'm sitting in a conference room with Amanda and Noah.

"Stewart is in court today," she says. "Leaving us to be the bearers of a new challenge."

"Is that legalese for bad news?" I ask.

A look passes between them. "Todd is trying to go after your trust fund," Noah says and leans forward. "We are confident he has absolutely no claim to it, but we just wanted to prep you."

"What? How?"

"He's claiming that the funds in your trust, and even a portion of the boys' trusts, should be made available to him."

My eyes go wide with disbelief. I've already dipped into those funds to pay for these attorneys and a stack of bills that Todd left me with. My breathing intensifies, and I have to grit my teeth to suppress a scream. "He does not get any of that money."

My mother comes from a wealthy family but doesn't have a ton of money at her daily disposal. It's always hard for people to understand that, especially Todd. When we were first looking to buy a house, he'd constantly ask why my mother couldn't help fund a more expensive place for us, despite the fact that we paid close to $900,000 for our home. He even dared to bring up my father. "How could they leave us with all these student loans?" he'd ask, meaning his loans, not mine, as if my mother should be responsible for clearing his debts. Mom's family had money, but it was old money, split among many family members and tied up in a trust. She was given a monthly allowance to live on for many years, and was generous to no end with gifts for the kids and me, but once I graduated college and married Todd, she was through providing for her daughter, as most parents should be. There was a healthy trust set up by my mom for the boys and me, and my biggest fear was that Todd was going to try and claim some of that money for himself.

"Todd will have to kill me first," I add, causing both Noah and Amanda to pause. "I mean it."

Amanda spoke up. "Like I said, we're confident this is some sort of attempt to upset the apple cart, or delay proceedings. We don't want you to worry about it. No judge in his right mind will even consider this, but we obviously have to keep you in the loop and do our best to prepare."

Going after money that my mom saved for the boys and me is the last straw. I begin to pace, and I can feel myself teetering on the verge of insanity. I raise my voice. "If he wanted to enjoy those funds one day, he never should have . . . ," I start, and then pause to refocus my energy. "Those trusts are off-limits." I fix my eyes on Noah. "Todd knows exactly what he's doing and what buttons to push with me, and this ends here and now. Are we clear?"

He nods.

"Please let him know that I will go for full custody if this isn't dropped by the end of the day. I will put every one of his sluts on the stand, prove he's a sex addict who's unfit to parent his kids, and I'll spend this *trust fund* of mine suing him for everything he has. Tell him he'll be so broke, he won't be able to afford his online porn subscriptions anymore. That should silence him."

They both avert their eyes and take notes.

"Does my mother need to know about this?" I ask. "Please tell me she's not being served with some bullshit papers."

Amanda shakes her head. "No, she doesn't."

"OK, because that's a call I'm not prepared to make."

I walk out of the building and into a cool afternoon breeze. I have about two hours before I need to grab the boys from school and pick up Luke from Edith's house. If I were in another state of mind, I might walk across the street and treat myself to lunch on Michigan Avenue, but instead I pay the twenty-eight dollars it costs me to park downtown and head home.

When I pull in the driveway, I'm thankful that Todd's car is nowhere in sight.

I open the freezer and rummage through stacks of food-storage containers and Ziploc freezer bags, ghosts of my proactive and organized past. I grab one of the bags with something that resembles chicken breasts, but it's wrapped in foil, so it's true mystery meat at this point. I flip the bag over, hoping that I'd had a Sharpie nearby the day I packaged it. No such luck. Upon further inspection, I notice an ice storm of freezer burn has taken place inside the bag, so I toss it in the trash. That goes on for another four bags and containers until I shut the freezer and sit at the kitchen island.

The fridge is decorated with the boys' artwork. There are potted plants on the patio with lifeless foliage and American flags that I've been ignoring since the Fourth of July. The glass patio doors are smeared from the neighbors' dog, which stops by every morning and licks them clean. One of the recessed bulbs above the stove has been out since before Labor Day, and the clock on the microwave has been flashing *2:37* for weeks—reminding me that I've let time stand still around here and am not allowed to celebrate one more holiday until I put the others to rest. I get up to check the pantry for a bottle of wine.

"Thank God," I say to myself and pop it in the fridge for later.

The way I see it, I have two choices. I can flounder around feeling sorry for myself, wallowing in freezer burn and self-hatred until all the bulbs in my house are burned out and my home is literally and figuratively the darkest place on earth. Or, I can keep my chin up and fight. Fight for my boys, my money, my pride, and myself.

I grab my cell phone and call my mom. "Hey," I say when she answers.

"Hi, sweetie, how are you?" Her voice is tired.

"Did I wake you?"

"No, I was just thinking about going to the market and getting some juice for the morning."

I smile at what is surely her biggest decision for the day. "I thought you play tennis on Tuesdays. Are you feeling OK?"

"Just a little headache. I normally do play today, but I played a doubles match this weekend, and I'm still beat. How are you?"

"Well, I met with the attorneys again." I hesitate. "But I'm good; it went fine. I was wondering if you've given any thought to coming and staying with me and the boys for a week?"

"Oh, right."

"I was thinking that you could come in on a Wednesday or something. We could have a few days together, and then I could go away with Jen for the weekend," I say.

"That will be nice. I'd be happy to watch them for you. I know you could use a weekend to yourself."

"Amen to that."

"How has Todd been?"

I pace my kitchen. "He's a miserable prick."

She sighs.

"He comes over to the house unannounced, just to torment me." I feel myself falling into the self-pity abyss. "It's fine, though. I'm going to be fine. I actually think Ryan is on my side because he never asks to call his dad and say good night anymore. He waits to see if Todd will call him." The idea of my kids losing contact with their father seems all too familiar and sad.

She doesn't say anything.

"Mom?"

"Sorry, honey. Your boys will always be on your side."

"I sure hope so," I say. "So, if you're up for coming in and watching them, we'd all love to see you."

She doesn't respond again.

"Mom, are you there?"

"I'm sorry, yes, I heard you. That's fine."

"You sure you're OK?" I ask.

"I'm fine."

After hanging up with her, I text Jen.

Looks like we're on for Mexico. My mom is going to come in. Not quite sure I'm ready for it, as I travel with lots of baggage! And I don't mean the kind you zip up.

She answers quickly. I'm bringing a tankini and a shot glass.

I place my phone down and grab a floodlight bulb and the step stool from the garage. I change the light over the stove and then look through both bottomless junk drawers until I find the manual for the microwave and reset the clock. Next, I take a garbage bag outside, uproot the dead flowers, and toss them in the bag with the plastic flags. As for the neighbor's dog, he makes the boys happy, so I can live with a knee-high blurry mess on the glass for a while.

Once I finish, I have about ten minutes before I have to pick up the boys. I run down to the basement, grab my suitcase, take it to my bedroom, and leave it out on the floor. Quickly, I toss in a bathing suit and flip-flops. Just seeing it there will give me all the motivation I need to get through the next few weeks.

Three days later, a large cardboard box shows up on my front stoop. It's addressed to my mother.

"Did you order something for the boys?" I ask when I get her on the phone.

"No, it's for us."

"Should I open it?"

"Sure, but promise me you'll wait until I arrive to go through them."

I slice open the box. Inside is a pile of her journals. I lift the first one out, thinking I'm not going to be able to keep my promise.

The leather is soft from years of wear, and there's a rubber band holding the pages together. I slide it off, open to a random page in the center, and am puzzled by the heading: *Our first Christmas in Beirut.*

Chapter Eleven

CATHERINE

Beirut, 1970

It was still dark when Gabriel's alarm clock rang the next morning, and I vaguely remembered him saying goodbye to me before he left. I lay there for a while, staring at the white ceiling and thinking I should get up and unpack before showering. By the time the sun came up, I was dressed and ready to go to the market. Christmas was the next day, and Brigitte had invited us to have dinner with them and a couple of other families in the building. Gabriel had not hesitated to accept the invitation when Brigitte's husband, Sammy, had come to our door the night before.

I grabbed my wool coat and purse and skipped downstairs to find Walid waiting at the curb, leaning against a Volkswagen Beetle with a newspaper and cup of coffee in his hands. He quickly folded it up when he saw me. "Where to, Miss Catherine?" His toothless smile was quite charming.

I stopped when I reached the end of the walk. "You didn't have to come today," I said. "Did Gabriel send you?"

Walid glanced at my stomach and then patted his own. "He doesn't want you walking far."

"Thank you, but I'm just going up to the market and the patisserie. I've been told that they are only three blocks away, and I'm really looking forward to the walk, having never been here before."

"Permit me to accompany you, then?" He pointed to his feet.

I sighed in the subtlest way possible. "Yes, of course." I'd desperately wanted to be alone and unburdened by an overzealous local who was hired to be my shadow and make conversation. Little did I know at the time, Walid would become one of the most significant people in my life.

We walked for a few blocks, and I was eventually pleased to have my own personal tour guide. The streets and sidewalks were busy, but free of trash and debris. They looked as though they'd just been swept clean, and I never saw them any other way. Walid and I passed several pushcarts along the way selling fruits and vegetables and meats, which they would boil or grill for you right on the cart. "Picked fresh today from the mountains. You will not find fresher than these," Walid assured me as we stopped to inhale the warm scent of smoked foods filling the air above the sidewalk.

"Gabriel and his family have a home there, in the mountains. I'm looking forward to seeing it," I said.

"Yes." He nodded with enthusiasm, as he did everything. "Beit Chabab."

"How do you say it?"

"Beit Chabab," he said, slower. "I will drive you there." He grinned.

"Oh, no, not today."

He laughed at me. "No, it would be almost two hours today. Another time. When Gabriel is ready."

Many of the people who lived in Beirut had roots in the mountains. They spent time in the city, but went "home" to the mountain villages where their ancestors had been for many years. Each village had something for which it was renowned. One was known for olives, one for soap making, and Beit Chabab was a well-known bell foundry—crafting church bells for Christian communities in Lebanon and overseas.

Gabriel had never said much about it other than his mother lived there with his younger brother, who was born with severe learning disabilities, and she hadn't left the village in forty years. I knew very little about her other than that she was Lebanese and spoke no other language than Arabic. His father had left when Gabriel was very young, and he had very little memory of him. Once Gabriel's father was gone, his maternal grandmother had moved in with the family to help until she passed.

I walked into a bakery and was welcomed by the smell of fresh flour and a pleasing mix of cinnamon and other spices I could not identify. Walid waited for me outside. "Hello, I would like to get some dessert . . ." I paused, testing the English of the girl behind the counter who looked about my age.

She spoke perfect English with a thick French accent. "What would you like?"

"What would you recommend bringing to someone's home? We will be guests for the holiday." My brows were raised. "Maybe something traditional?" I asked.

She shrugged, her lids heavy and bored. The bakeries opened very early in Beirut. "Maybe some cake and ice cream. We're known for our *bouzet ashta*. It's rosewater ice cream with mastic—like a little bit gummy paste—and pistachios."

I hadn't heard of gummy ice cream before, but she seemed confident in its classic appeal. "I will take some of that, please. Enough for twelve people."

She packed the ice cream and a few pastries into bags, which Walid promptly took from me when I exited.

By the time we returned to our building, I was famished. "Let me put these things in the freezer, and then I would like to buy you lunch."

Walid began to shake his head.

"And I won't take no for an answer. Gabriel said there is a falafel stand on the other corner, and I simply must eat, as you know."

Walid insisted on running all the groceries to the apartment while I waited outside. When he returned, we walked in the opposite direction to a kiosk on the sidewalk. He was always a half step behind me. "Are you married, Walid?"

His head bobbed. "Yes, yes, of course, ma'am."

"Please call me Catherine. You are my first friend here." That made him chuckle, as did most things I said. "Tell me about your family."

"My wife, she is beautiful like you. Well, not such white hairs like you, but she is beautiful and she works at the university, so our kids can go there. We have one son, who is eighteen, and our daughter is nineteen." He paused. "I also look after my wife's sister's daughter, who is eight. She lost her parents in a car accident many years ago."

I stopped walking. "I'm so sorry for her."

He smiled and shrugged and waved his hands. "It's OK, it's OK! She is with us now. Very happy and smart girl."

The shelves behind the man working the food stand were filled with baskets of *Manakeesh* in different varieties, emitting a fresh doughy aroma that reminded me of Jessie's homemade biscuits. There was a long line of people waiting; some looked like American students from the university nearby, and some looked like locals. I'm not sure what I looked like, other than out of place. When we finally reached the counter, I thought I might faint from hunger. I ordered three *Manakeesh* for Walid to bring home to his family, two falafel sandwiches—one for him and one for me—and a chicken *schwarma* plate for us to share. We sat on the spotless curb and devoured it in seconds. The chicken was juicy yet crisp around the edges, and was served with a side of hummus that was drizzled with a healthy portion of olive oil. I think I went through no less than ten napkins.

When we returned, little Reema was alone in front of the building, blissfully playing with some dolls. "Thank you for spending so much time with me today," I said to Walid, and handed him the bag of warm *Manakeesh*. "Please bring this home to your beautiful wife, and tell her I can't wait to meet her."

He leaned forward and took the bag. "Thank you," he said earnestly.

"You're welcome!" Reema shouted from behind.

Chapter Twelve

CATHERINE

Beirut, 1970

It was Christmas Day, and the overseas ringtones were long and drawn out. I sipped a bowl of chicken broth I'd made as a snack before dinner because my pregnancy came with hunger pains every ten minutes. My ears perked up when I heard my sister Margaret's voice. "Hello?"

"It's me, it's CC. Merry Christmas!"

"Same to you! How are you? I've been hoping you'd call." She muffled the receiver, and I heard her call out to my sister Colleen before returning to the phone. "What's it like there?"

"It's nice. Our apartment is clean and a little dull—lots of white everywhere—but Gabriel has promised to let me change things around. First thing will be painting the kitchen a light green, I think. How about you guys?"

"We're all getting ready for brunch at the club. You just missed Mom. She dragged Mary Grace over to the neighbors to borrow a pair of tights. Dad's had three Bloody Marys with Uncle David in the salon already, and Colleen and I are plotting our escape to meet up with Jack and Craig Denny behind the caddy shack. Mom will be too smashed later to notice. Not much has changed. We're going to that new place,

Gulliver's, tonight. They have a disco there, and we're meeting up with a huge crowd and some friends from the city. Now that Colleen is eighteen, she doesn't need a fake ID anymore."

I was a little envious. "No jelly-bean trail?"

She laughed. "Of course we did the jelly-bean trail! Just 'cause you abandoned the family doesn't mean the rest of us have to suffer."

Every year for as long as I could recall, my sisters and I would wake up Christmas morning to find my parents on the orange floral divan in the four seasons room that overlooked the yard, sharing a pitcher of Bloody Marys and a pot of coffee. Jessie would be in the kitchen preparing her famous holiday casserole consisting of eggs, ground sausage, chopped onions, and easily two pounds of cheddar cheese. She'd make four of them, and we'd reheat platefuls for a week.

While my sisters and I were eating breakfast, Mother, in her housecoat, would lay trails of jelly beans, one for each of us, that led to our Christmas stockings. It initially began as a ruse so that she didn't have to hang the stockings by the fireplace. When I was five years old, my parents stuffed Margaret's stockings and mine, hung them with care, and went to sleep. Around 3:00 a.m., a spark from the dwindling fire flew out onto Margaret's stocking, caused some minor damage, and forever changed the mantel on Christmas morning. As a result, Santa invented the jelly-bean trails to guide us to the new location. Mom or Dad or Jessie would set out trails of jelly beans leading from the fireplace, through the family room, winding in different directions—one trail for each daughter as the family grew—and then we'd spend the morning walking through the house like it was a minefield until it was time to find our stockings. As silly as it sounds, my sisters and I looked forward to it every year.

"Did you get new underwear in your stocking?" I asked.

"You know I did."

I smiled. "A journal?"

"Yes. Which I will place on my shelf right next to all my other empty journals. You're the only one who ever uses those things."

"And five bucks?"

"Believe it or not, you picked the wrong year to move away. We each got ten dollars and some candy. I stole Patricia's Charleston Chew a few minutes ago."

"Maybe you got ten because I left."

"You might be right. Thank you," she said.

Missing all my favorite traditions left me a little heartsick, but the holiday was almost over for me in Beirut, as it was eight hours later, so I was determined to make some new memories for Gabriel and myself.

"Are you feeling good, with the baby and everything?"

I looked at my stomach whenever anyone mentioned the baby. "I am. I feel good. Mom was able to get me the name of a doctor here, so I'm going to have my first visit with him next week after the holidays."

"Wow, April seems so far away. Are you getting fatter?"

"Not too bad yet. Mostly looks like I had a big lunch." Gabriel walked into the kitchen, where I was sitting at the table, and grinned when he saw me. "I should probably get going because we have dinner plans with our neighbors," I said to Margaret, but Gabriel shook his head. "Please give my love to everyone."

"Will do, CC. Merry Christmas."

I placed the receiver on the phone base. Speaking with Margaret brought a huge smile to my face, but when I hung up, my smile faded and left me uneasy. I really missed my family and had no idea when I would see them again.

I turned to Gabriel. "Hi," I said, and he planted a kiss on my lips. "Why'd you shake your head?"

"Our plans have changed." He took my hands in his and sat.

"Oh? I was looking forward to spending some time with Brigitte and Sammy and the girls. And, of course, my newest friend, Reema." I tilted my head. "Won't they be offended if we cancel at the last minute?

I promised Reema some *bouzet ashta*." I butchered the pronunciation, and he laughed.

"You can bring it to her before we go to my cousin's."

"Your cousin?"

He let go of my hands and sat back in his chair, lighting a cigarette. "He's like a cousin to me. Very prominent family. They live in Ras Beirut. He's a member of parliament. There will be many other political families there and some American professors and their students. When he called to ask me, I knew you would feel much more at home there."

"What's his name?"

"His name is Danny. Danny Khalid." Gabriel stood and blew smoke into the air.

"And you talked with Brigitte?" I asked.

"I talked with Sammy, of course. He is fine with any choice we make. They have a very full house as it is." Gabriel walked out of the room for a second and then returned as I was clearing my broth from the table. I could feel him come up behind me, though he hadn't made a sound. "Darling?" He placed an arm around my waist and pulled me close. I nearly dropped the bowl in the sink.

I leaned back into him. "Yes?"

"Close your eyes."

I closed my eyes, and he kissed the back of my neck. "Turn around, but don't open your eyes."

He placed his lips on mine and then reached for the palms of my hands, kissing them and sending shivers through me. "I have a present for you."

I smiled. "Can I see?"

"Not yet." He took me by the hand and led me to the bedroom. "Don't peek," he said and began to unbutton my blouse. "Promise?"

"I promise." Goose bumps covered my chest and arms as he slid my shirt off and then removed the rest of my clothing. My hands were resting on his shoulders when he knelt and kissed my belly and then lifted me onto the bed, where he kissed every other part of me as I relaxed beneath him, eyes tightly shut, skin tingling, ears ringing, and the essence of his cologne tickling the inside of my nose.

"Don't break your promise," he said as we lay entwined, trying to catch our breath. He dragged his fingertips between my breasts, which stilled at his touch when I felt something draped loosely around my neck. My hand went to it.

"You can open your eyes," he said.

I lifted the gift off my skin and sat up. It was a gold chain with a tear-drop emerald the size of a quarter hanging from the center. "Gabriel," I said, eyes wide. "I don't even know what to say. This is magnificent." He sat, naked, and went behind me to assist with the clasp.

"I love you, Catherine Clarke."

I leaned back into him, our bodies warm and bare. One kiss was all it ever took to remind me how much I loved him. I felt the sting of joyful tears. "Please hold me," I implored. "Thank you so much." I wrapped my fingers around the pendant and folded myself in his arms.

"I want you to be happy here," he whispered in my ear.

"I'm happy wherever you are."

~

An hour later, we walked outside, hand in hand, and Walid was waiting at the curb to drive us to the home of Danny Khalid. I smacked Gabriel on the chest. "You did not make him come out on Christmas!"

"He's fine with it."

"I'm so sorry to disturb your holiday with your family. We can easily get a taxi," I said to Walid as he approached, causing Gabriel to let go of my hand.

"It is my honor." He bent forward a little and opened the passenger door.

Gabriel stopped me and abruptly grabbed my bicep. "Do not disregard me like that in front of him, CC." He squeezed so hard, my knees buckled.

"You're hurting me." I met his eyes.

"I have hired him, and that is it. There is nothing more to be said, and he certainly does not wish to think you don't want him here, or worse, are disagreeing with what I've asked him to do." He let go.

"OK. Of course."

The Khalids' home was stunning. Built with a wine-colored brick exterior, it had three archways—each with its own ornate wreath—that lead to a cherry-red front door. A servant let us in and took our coats, which reminded me of the holiday parties my aunt and uncle would throw. There was always a coat check, regardless of how big or small the guest list. The foyer was long and wide, with marble tables on both sides, and a crimson carpet running the length of the room, leading guests to a ballroom. To our left was a five-piece orchestra, and to our right, buffet-style tables filled with delicacies, both traditional and American, as guests kept telling me when they found out where I was from.

"We have hot dogs and hamburgers for you and our American friends!" Danny boasted after embracing me. "You are good with that?"

"Of course I am. Thank you for having us."

"And New York cheesecake!" He elbowed Gabriel. "My professor friends who teach at the school, they are always going on about the cheesecake." His excitable demeanor reminded me of a wealthier and more sophisticated version of Walid.

"Well, now that I'm here—and with child—they will have to fight me for it," I joked. "Cheesecake is my favorite."

Danny threw his arms in the air, said something in Arabic I did not understand, and proceeded to hug Gabriel and lift him off his feet. Once Gabriel was back on the ground, Danny took my hand.

"Many congratulations to you, Catherine." He smiled at Gabriel. "How truly wonderful for you." He put his hands in a prayer position and bowed to us. "I wish you many blessings."

"Thank you very—"

"Yasmine!" he yelled over his shoulder.

A slim woman in a long black sleeveless dress glanced over at him. Her hair was slicked back and pulled into a tight knot. She had a cigarette holder dangling from one hand, and her dark eyebrows were arched to perfection, reminiscent of the Evil Queen in *Snow White and the Seven Dwarfs.*

"Come." He waved to her when she did not move.

I shifted uncomfortably in my heels and touched my pendant. I could see her apologize to the group she was with before slowly heading over to us.

"You know Gabriel," Danny said, and she gave my husband an odd look. "And this is his very beautiful new wife, Catherine, who is carrying their baby!"

She stared at my hair first, as most people did, especially in a country where natural blondes were scarce. Then her eyes landed on my emerald, then made their way down again, pausing at my belly, and finished at my shoes. I would've felt less self-conscious standing there naked.

"We should have them for dinner, yes?" Danny was still talking.

"We are having them now," she said coolly.

Unfazed by his wife's indifference, he went on. "You will come again, maybe next week or after the New Year. Have you taken her to Beit Chabab yet?"

Gabriel looked uncomfortable at the question. He drew me close, sensing my discomfort. "We just got here a few days ago. We've hardly left the apartment."

"You will enjoy it there, in the mountains," Danny said. "Maybe you can introduce Catherine to some of your American friends?" he suggested to Yasmine. "Make her feel welcome."

"Danny." She said his name in a tone that sounded innocent enough, but he recognized whatever annoyance was behind it. We all did. "I was just in the middle of a conversation over there."

"It's fine. Please don't worry about it," I said. "I've got plenty of friends."

That got her attention. "I won't worry about it." She turned to my husband. "Congratulations on the baby."

"Thank you, Yasmine. Wonderful to see you both again, and thank you for hosting us tonight."

"What are two more people?" She made a dismissive gesture with her hand and slithered back to where she was standing before.

I looked at Gabriel, trying to convey what I was feeling with my expression, but he just kissed me.

"Lovebirds," Danny said and embraced us both. "Go eat and drink and be merry together." He walked away and was immediately greeted by someone else.

"I hope to never see that woman again," I said to Gabriel.

"Neither of you were very friendly to each other."

I turned to him and crossed my arms. "Don't even pretend you did not notice how inexplicably rude she was. And for what?"

He put an arm around my waist and pulled me in as if a hug would fix everything.

"I mean it," I said. "Danny is lovely, but if he forces her to invite us to dinner, please decline or go without me."

Two things made me rummage through boxes that night looking for my journals. The first was the fact that Margaret had reminded me how much I loved—and missed—writing in them, and the second was my disdain for Yasmine Khalid. My journal entry that night read in part: *Just met the most awful woman on the planet.*

Chapter Thirteen

Ann Marie

Chicago, 2008

The boys and I walk in the house after going to the grocery and immediately hear noises coming from upstairs. "Wait here," I say to them and slam my keys on the counter.

At any other juncture in my life, I would assume there's a thief in the house, but not anymore.

"Where the hell do you think you're going?" Todd screams and startles me as I find him standing in our bedroom—my bedroom—unannounced and uninvited, with my black halter-style bikini in his hand. The master bedroom has white walls, white carpet, and white bedding with a pale gray stripe. The only real color in the room comes from the bright red sweatshirt Todd's wearing.

I glance at my open suitcase on the floor. "What are you doing?" My blood is boiling.

"Answer my question," he says.

I snatch the bathing suit from his hand. "Get out of here!" I scream.

"What's the suitcase for?"

"Get out." My temples throb. I point to the hallway and move aside, but he doesn't budge.

"You know you can't take the kids anywhere without my consent."

"Get out, or I will call the police." Just as I threaten him, Ryan appears in the doorway. Slim, yet tough, little Ryan with his big blue eyes and white-blond hair. Gifts from my mother's gene pool, no doubt. He's only seven years old, but his expression is stern and mature.

"Stop yelling," he says with the voice of a fallen angel and crosses his arms. He can sense the hostility between us, and my knees buckle with guilt.

I take a deep breath. "Honey, please go back downstairs right now," I say to Ryan in a soft voice.

"No," Todd interjects. "Let him stay where he is, and tell him you're going to call the police on me."

"Mom?" Ryan questions me, but I ignore him.

My hands are shaking, so I cross my arms. "Get out of here, now," I say to Todd. And just as he's about to respond, Ryan speaks up.

"You better do what Mom says," my son tells him.

Todd glares at me, and then, for once, does what he's told without making our child suffer through more drama. I almost commend him on his courtesy, but I decide not to. Once he's out of the room, I slam the door shut and follow him down the stairs, where Jimmy and Luke are now standing.

"Are you staying for dinner?" Jimmy asks excitedly. "Mom's said she's cooking something really good."

I sigh and look at Todd, pleading with my eyes. Hoping he'll say the right thing and not make me look like the asshole, but my pleas go unanswered.

"I'm sure your mom won't let me. Sorry, dude."

"Mom?" Jimmy calls out to me, but Todd's already heading out the front door.

"Please keep your brothers inside," I say to Ryan and follow Todd outside.

"Do you care about your children at all?" I ask, walking behind him.

He stops and turns to face me. "Fuck you."

"It's an easy question, so answer it." My voice is calm, and I look him in the eyes. "Because everything you are doing says otherwise. Do you think that little stunt doesn't go unnoticed? Do you think their little heads are in their happy place now, as they deserve to be? Or do you think they're doing their best to grin and bear something they know nothing about? Something they are not equipped to handle, and something that will irrevocably change who they are. Forever."

"I can come and go as I please. They like when I come by, so screw you. I needed my dress shoes anyway. I still have things in this house."

I throw my hands up. "Then you've answered my question. You only care about yourself."

Todd turns and walks away. "I hope you don't think you're going anywhere with those kids. I'll make sure my attorney knows about this."

"And I'll make sure to sign them up for therapy!" I shout.

"Is everything OK?" Ryan asks when I'm back inside. Jimmy and Luke just turn and go back to watching TV.

I drop to my knees and put my arms out. Ryan comes running to me for a hug.

"Everything is fine," I say into his ear. "Dad needed his dress-up shoes, but I didn't know he was upstairs, so I got scared a little when he surprised me." My pulse is racing.

"Oh."

I let him go. "So, I'm going to do a nice thing for Daddy and make sure all of his clothes and things—whatever he might've left behind— are in one big pile in the garage." I smile like the crazy lunatic I've become.

For the next two hours, I empty every drawer, cabinet, and closet in the house that might contain something of Todd's. In the garage, I lay out a tarp on the side where his car used to be and throw all his belongings on top of it. Then I snap a picture of the pile and text it to him. Easy access to your things from now on, I type. Stay out of my bedroom.

Once I'm through, I pour myself a glass of wine and make dinner for the kids. Nothing *really good*, as promised earlier. Kraft Macaroni & Cheese with a side of Goldfish crackers, and steamed broccoli that none of them eat. I clean up the kitchen when they're through and treat myself to a feast of congealed macaroni and cold broccoli florets.

At 9:00 p.m., the boys are asleep. I pour myself another glass of wine to temper my headache and walk upstairs to my bedroom. I reach for my phone and dial my mom's number.

"Hello," she answers. "I tried calling you earlier."

"I saw. I'm sorry. It's been a day," I say.

"What happened?" she asks.

"Honestly, I feel like the more I tell you, the less you'll want to take my calls."

She makes a breathy sound on the other end. "Tell me what's going on. I mean it. I want to be here for you."

I take a sip of my wine. "So, today, I stopped at the grocery after picking Jimmy and Ryan up from school, and I had Luke with me all day because Edith's grandkids are in town to celebrate Rosh Hashanah. I was feeling all domestic and creative, so we all picked out a rotisserie chicken, and I was going to make the boys my fancy pepperjack chicken quesadillas. But when we walked in the house, I heard a bunch of noise upstairs. I actually hoped I was being robbed, because it would've been better than finding Todd in my bedroom. Anyway, I completely forgot about the groceries and the boys, and spent the entire rest of the afternoon running around the house gathering his belongings and tossing them into the garage." I pause to take a breath. "Needless to say, we all ate cardboard food for supper."

"He's an ass," she says.

"I put a tarp under all of his shit, which I thought was quite generous."

"You should've left it on the front lawn."

"Too cliché," I say.

"Then you should at least put that spoiled rotisserie chicken at the bottom of the pile."

I smile at her cleverness.

"There has to be something you can do to stop him from coming over," she says.

"Yes, I can sell this house, or buy him out."

"Still no offers?"

"Nope," I say.

"What do you think is the biggest issue?"

"I have no clue. My Realtor says we're priced too high, so we lowered it a bit, but I think buyers can feel the bad karma in here."

"There's not bad karma in there," Mom says.

"Bad karma and a pile of crap on the garage floor. Oh well. Thanks to you, I have a trip to Mexico to look forward to." I haven't admitted to peeking at her journals yet, because I haven't let myself get past the confusion from the one page that read, *Our first Christmas in Beirut.* It's still sitting on my nightstand while the weight of those words is sitting heavy on my chest. She has never told me anything about my father and her visiting or living in Beirut. I know that he is Lebanese, of course, but I never knew she went there with him. And now she's chosen to box up her most intimate thoughts and send them to me. Why now?

"Thank you for listening. I mean it."

"Don't be silly," she says.

"I know you have some things to tell me, Mom, and I just want you to know that nothing will ever change the way I feel about our relationship."

"You went through the box, didn't you?"

I place my free hand on her journal. "I'm just looking forward to hearing what you have to say." Which is true, but I'm also a little scared. "I love you, Mom. Good night."

As I hang up the phone, my thoughts turn to Todd. There was a time—after learning about his affairs—that I thought I could forgive him, and I hated myself for it. I've spent days and nights since then trying to figure out why I was so scared of losing him, scared of being alone, scared of disappointing my family and living with the failure and humiliation. My therapist, Monica, says many people can't cope with the loss of control, but there's a voice in my head that's telling me it goes deeper than that.

When I first began online dating, Monica said I was trying to prove to myself that I was still desirable to men after Todd's rejection. That when he left, he took a piece of me with him. But what if that piece has always been missing? And what if that piece is sitting next to me on my nightstand? Is there something that happened in my parents' marriage that parallels what's happening in my own? Did it happen in Beirut, of all places?

That night, I make a promise to myself: it's time to let go of the anger. I take my hand off Mom's journal and reach under my bed for the pink spiral-bound notebook Monica gave me. I grab a pen and write five things I'm grateful for.

1) My boys

2) My mom

3) My health

4) Our home

5) My willingness to forgive

The next morning, I get a text from Todd saying that he's going to come pick up his things from the garage over the weekend, and that his latest girlfriend is pregnant.

I take the pink spiral notebook and toss it in the trash.

Chapter Fourteen

Catherine

Beirut, 1971

On a warm and sunny day in late March, there was a knock on my door.
I braced myself with one hand on the table as I wobbled onto my feet,
very pregnant by then. Little Miss Reema was standing barefoot with
her purse in one hand and dragging her favorite penguin in the other.
"Hi, sweetie. Am I late to get you this morning?"

She nodded.

"OK, well, come on in, then. We mustn't keep our guests waiting."
I looked up to see the door to her apartment ajar, but Brigitte was not in
eyeshot. "I'll leave the door open in case your mom is looking for you."

For two months, I'd been watching Reema three mornings a week
so Brigitte could work part-time for the local butcher, who lived in the
building next door. I used to watch her from the balcony, trying to bribe
Reema each morning to come to work with her, and Reema would plug
her nose and scream because she couldn't stand the smell of raw meat.

"I'd be happy to watch her for you," I'd offered one morning once
I caught up with them in the stairwell.

Brigitte had laughed. "You will end up wishing you weren't pregnant with your own after a day with this one!"

"Don't be silly." I'd smiled at the little girl, almost three years old by then. "I think it'd be wonderful practice for me."

Brigitte rolled her eyes.

"What?" I'd placed my hands on my hips. "I'm quite the resourceful woman, as you know."

Brigitte had become a trusted and valued friend in a very short time. I'd used some connections I had with a friend from Greenwich who had an old colleague on the board of the university to get her husband some additional work. Sammy had a company that did construction, and the university board had granted him a huge project in one of the student housing wings. It meant a great deal of extra money for their family, and I was thrilled to be able to help. Another time when Brigitte's mother was very ill, I had Mother's doctor research and recommend the best person in Beirut for her to see after many failed attempts at the local clinics. Once she had been properly diagnosed, Gabriel was able to work with the physicians to get her a break on the necessary prescriptions. "It's what we do," I'd told her when she'd thanked me. "If you're like family to my husband, you're like family to me."

"Reema is a handful," she'd said.

I'd waved her off. "You think all your girls are handfuls, but they clearly only misbehave when they are with you." I'd looked down on Reema. "Isn't that right?"

She'd nodded.

I'd knelt to her level. "Would you like to spend some time with me?" I'd asked, grinning.

She'd nodded again.

"It's settled, then. You know how bored I've been sitting around here waiting for this baby to come."

"What about your volunteer work at AUB? Sammy said you were helping grade exams or something like this."

"There's a young professor from my hometown in Connecticut. His name is Randall Cunningham; our parents are acquainted. He teaches a course on investigative journalism. He allows me to read papers from time to time, and I help with some of his scheduling. It's mostly a way for me to access the amenities on campus. My father set it up for me." I'd paused. "But looking after her won't intrude on any of that. I make my own schedule, and Randall is just happy to have the extra help."

I didn't make any money working for Randall. I was simply happy to have the diversion. Besides, my husband made a good living, and my father would mail me cards every month with a short note and little spare cash inside. So I was never in need of a job.

Brigitte had shrugged. "You are my own personal angel." She'd waved her index finger at me. "And that baby of yours is truly blessed."

I'd smiled. "And what would I do without you?"

"You would manage just fine."

But that wasn't true. The first few months had taken a toll on my relationship with Gabriel, and when I assumed I had no one to confide in, Brigitte turned up. One evening after a particularly loud argument between us over my long-distance phone bill, Brigitte called me the next morning.

"Hello?" I answered.

"I'm making some white coffee. Would you like to come over and join me for some?" White coffee was invented in Beirut and consists of boiled rosewater or flower water sweetened with sugar. She insisted I drink it during my pregnancy and warned me off caffeine, many years before doctors began cautioning their own patients. I eventually fell in love with the warm, fragrant concoction.

"Thank you, but I'm going to go to the market soon."

"Please, I insist."

That day she confessed to overhearing several other arguments between Gabriel and me. "You are too feisty," she claimed. "And you are loud, too."

I laughed. "Too feisty and too loud? And you're just noticing that about me? I thought that was my charm, no?"

"You needn't argue back so much," she said, her brow furrowed.

"I'm not very good at keeping silent when I don't agree with him."

She sipped her drink. "Lebanese men expect a certain amount of respect."

"So do American women."

She blinked.

"I'm sorry that you heard us. That's embarrassing and not how I was brought up. My mother would die to know the neighbors could hear me fighting with my husband." And that was the truth. I knew my parents had their fair share of arguments, but never in front of my sisters and me, and certainly never in front of anyone else. This was largely due to my mother refusing to take the bait. Even when my father would angrily snap at her for saying something naive, or chastise her for her frivolous spending, if there was company present, Mother would smile and flutter her lashes as if she hadn't a clue as to what he was referring. But I know she must've been dying inside. I know I would have been.

The funny, and often frustrating, thing about my relationship with Gabriel was that our arguments were like foreplay and often concluded with lovemaking. Sometimes it was the only way to hold his attention.

I rubbed my forehead. "I'll make sure that we're much more discreet next time."

Brigitte smiled and placed her hands in her lap. "Why must there be a next time?" She was older than I was, maybe by fifteen years, and our relationship vacillated between friend and mentor. I was grateful to have her as both. "You are young and beautiful and newly married . . . and pregnant . . . and I know about American women and women's liberation that is going on over there, but I only want good things and peace for you and Gabriel. And the baby." She reached across the table and rested her hand on mine. "Beirut is a wonderful place. I have lived here all my life, and I'm used to the customs. But you will learn that women do not have many rights here, and foreign women even less. There are many important things you should know about how it will affect your child."

I drew a breath. "Like what?"

"For example, I have four daughters and no sons, as you know. Because of that, if something were to happen to Sammy, his wealth would go to his brothers—everything—not to my girls and me. We would have to rely on Sammy's brothers—one who is single and a drunk, and one who is married and lives in Greece—to care for us. We'd have no claim to anything, including this home, which my husband has worked for his whole life to provide for us."

That night I couldn't sleep. I lay awake listening to the gentle tick-tock of Gabriel's wristwatch on his nightstand. What if I had a baby girl inside of me? I couldn't imagine something happening to Gabriel and being at the mercy of his brother, whom I've never even met. My father would never allow that to happen, but what if his hands were tied? And how long could I rely on my family for everything? I'd nearly pushed my mother to the brink of a nervous breakdown as it was.

Unable to drift off, I went and sat on the balcony. The truth was that I'd lived in Beirut for three months, but I'd never committed to actually *living* there. My perception of life in Beirut was temporary, noncommittal. I always assumed I'd be back home one day in the States with a house in Greenwich down the road from my parents, and Gabriel would be with me. But he'd actually never promised me that. Brigitte's words shook me to my core.

The next morning, I began to watch Reema three days a week and host tea parties for her stuffed animals. Penguins, mostly. She even gave me one of them for my baby.

"I'll make sure the baby gets this penguin when he or she is born."

Reema smiled proudly.

We'd walk to the beach and build sand castles, and I'd treat her to whatever she wanted from the patisserie on the way back home. I refused to accept any compensation from Brigitte other than rosewater and homemade falafel in return for my work. And from that day on, any money that my father sent me went into a secret envelope in the back of my lingerie drawer. Gabriel didn't blink an eye when I told him my dad had decided not to send me monthly allowances anymore. All he did was restrict the number of phone calls to the States if he was going to be paying for them.

Chapter Fifteen

CATHERINE

Beirut, 1971

"Push again!" the head nurse, Robin, bellowed. My hands were gripping the edges of a pillow placed atop my chest. "You're doing great, Catherine," she assured me through the moans and groans and wails that were flying out of my throat. My birthing team at the American University of Beirut Medical Center was all Americans. My mother had handpicked the doctor, and he had a staff of residents and medical students whom I will never forget as long as I live. I was alone and in labor for twelve hours before my daughter decided to grace us with her presence. One of the residents was by my side at all times, chatting with me and encouraging me and feeding me ice cubes. They even made certain my makeup bag was within reach.

With their help, I gave birth that day, April 6, 1971, to a baby girl, ten days before she was due. She had dark hair like her father, but I instantly recognized my own face in hers. I was beaming with joy when Gabriel was brought in from the waiting room. He had yellow tulips in his hand and a cluster of cigars sticking out of his shirt pocket. Seeing the elation on his face made everything perfect.

He placed the flowers on a table and then kissed my forehead and lips over and over until I began to laugh. "May I?" He reached for the precious bundle in my arms.

"I'd like to name her Ann Marie, for my mother," I said.

"Of course," he agreed, his eyes fixed on hers. "Beautiful sweet girl. My tiny Ann Marie. I love you so much." Gabriel gently placed his lips on the baby's cheeks and held them there with his eyes closed.

The staff left us alone with our daughter. Gabriel could not contain his grin. "Everyone at the building is going crazy waiting for news. Brigitte was ready to tackle me if I did not call her as soon as I heard."

My eyes were heavy, and my heart was light. Beirut was the last place I ever had imagined giving birth, and yet I was pleased to be there in that moment. "I can't imagine ever being this happy again in all my life."

Gabriel leaned over, Ann Marie still cradled in his arms, and kissed me. It took all the energy I had left to lift my head and kiss him back, and then I was officially drained.

Nurse Robin knocked as she entered. "How is Mom doing?"

"She is spectacular," Gabriel answered for me. "My golden-haired queen."

Robin looked at me. "Congratulations to you both."

"Thank you," he said to her without lifting his eyes from mine. "What can we get you?" he asked me.

"Maybe just some water."

He looked at Robin, and she poured me a cup from a pitcher across the room. Then she took Ann Marie from him. "I will take her to get some shots, have a bath, and feed her a bottle. Don't worry about a thing." She arranged the swaddling blanket around Ann Marie's chest. "Get some rest, and I'll bring the baby back in the morning when you're ready for her."

"Thank you," I said. "I need to call my parents," I told Gabriel when she'd left. "I asked the hospital. It will go on our bill, but I promise to be quick. I can't wait until we get home."

"Of course," he said.

I couldn't help but smirk. "I should have a baby for you every day with how accommodating you're being."

Gabriel stretched the phone cord to the bed, and I dialed my home number. It was 10:00 p.m. in Beirut, so 6:00 a.m. in Greenwich. The call was sure to awaken everyone but Jessie.

"Hello, Clarke residence," she answered hurriedly on the second ring.

"It's me," I said.

"You OK, CC?"

"Just very tired."

"I bet you are. Walking up all those steps you tell me about is not good for my baby."

"It's not the steps, Jessie."

"What is it, then? Don't tell me you're still looking after that little girl. I told your mom to tell you that was too much for you. Did she tell you that was too much for you? And why are you calling so early? You want to give us all a good scare? Your mom nearly ran downstairs without her face paint on."

I missed Jessie and Mother both so much. "I'm tired because I had my own little girl tonight."

She let out a boisterous squeal, and I could picture her expression. She would adore Ann Marie as much as anyone. I swallowed a lump in my throat when I realized I had no idea when Jessie and my family would meet my daughter.

Two days later, we left the hospital, and Walid dropped us off in front of the building on Sunday afternoon. The sun had just begun to set. Reema and her sisters shouted and waved from their balcony as soon as they saw us. Minutes later, Brigitte burst through the front entrance, weeping as if the building was on fire.

"We do love our little girls around here!" she yelled. She squeezed my face with her hands and kissed my cheeks as soon as she reached me. "Let me see her."

Gabriel reached inside the car for the basket Ann Marie had been transported in. She was swaddled and quiet, with her eyes open. Brigitte immediately lifted her out and held her. "This is a beautiful baby, and I know a thing or two about babies."

I tilted my head and gazed at my daughter. "Thank you, Brigitte."

Gabriel handed Walid a cigar, and they began to converse.

"We will head upstairs," I said. "Can you bring my bag in?"

He nodded and blew me a kiss.

"Thank you, Walid, for the ride."

"My pleasure, Miss. And my wife would like to bring by a gift this week, if that is all OK with you."

"Of course, but that is not necessary—"

"She will be glad to receive it," Brigitte said to him. We walked ahead. "Don't tell me people don't bring baby gifts in America. Let the man and his wife do a nice thing." She rolled her eyes at me.

"Don't give me that look. I'm a mother now, so you'd better stop treating me like one of your children."

She laughed and began to speak in Arabic to my daughter.

The next day I greeted more people than I knew lived in the building. Gabriel and I would have enough food to feed us through three more pregnancies. I had to beg Brigitte to take some for her family, and Reema and her sisters would sneak over for cookies every day after school. Mother called me every other night that week and allowed me to talk with Jessie as long as I needed, on her dime. She was beside herself that I'd named my daughter after her, although I had to find out through Jessie how much it really meant to her. "She called everyone in the club directory and told them about the baby," Jessie had whispered to me one time when she'd answered the phone before getting Mom on the line. "And she's ordered no less than ten embroidered items from the shop in town with the baby's name on it."

It was an emotional time for me those first few weeks. The previous summer, I'd been a young, single college graduate, smoking weed and partying with Laura and my sisters, talking about starting a career . . . but making the newest disco our top priority. Then, in the blink of an eye, I was in love and married to a man I'd known for only a short time, living in a foreign country with a newborn in my arms, and trying to function on a schedule that had me waking up every couple of hours throughout the night. Humility came at me like a flash flood. I struggled to keep my nose above water by putting someone else's needs before my own. I'd barely been married long enough to make Gabriel a priority, let alone carry the burden of someone's entire existence on my shoulders. In the middle of the night, I'd sit with Ann Marie in my arms as she'd drain her tiny bottle of formula and stare up into my eyes. Her trust in me was overwhelming. I'd sit there night after night, making promises to my little girl, wishing I could remember my own mother cradling and caring for me the same way.

I promise you'll have no curfew when you're twenty-one years old.
I promise I'll always hear your side.
I promise to let you follow your heart.
I promise you'll wake up to jelly-bean trails on Christmas morning.
I promise to attend your college graduation.
I promise you'll never question my love for you.

Ann Marie was a delight, and Brigitte and our other friends in the building were warm and wonderful, but they were not my family. I wanted my family to meet my daughter, and I didn't feel right asking anyone to fly to Lebanon. Nor did I ever think I would have to. My mother had offered one time to come visit me, the day I'd come home from the hospital, but I insisted she and Dad shouldn't have to do that, and she hadn't brought it up again since. I'd been fine for the time being. Gabriel came home from work early every day at the beginning, and I hated to pry his daughter out of his arms to put her to bed at night. It was a happy time, and one I remembered fondly, mostly due to the baby and embracing motherhood.

But there was no masking the fact that I was still a young independent woman, much to my husband's dismay. We'd go out to dinner every Saturday night and walk to a local restaurant with Ann Marie in the stroller, but Gabriel and I spent very little time together—just the two of us—and the idea of going to a dance club became as likely as a good night's sleep.

Six months later, everything changed.

Chapter Sixteen

ANN MARIE

Chicago, 2008

"It's a good day," I say to my friend Jen on the phone. "No, it's a great day." The November air is crisp and cool, but the sun still shines brightly without an ugly winter fog to contend with.

"I'm so happy for you. For us, really. But no one deserves a weekend away more than you do," she says.

Jen is one of those awesome women. When she isn't working, she runs a neighborhood book club so her friends can drink wine and stick their husbands with the children for a few hours. She has five kids in the school district, so she has the scoop on every single person in the community. She yells and honks at other parents in the pickup line when they're on their cell phones and not moving forward, and she volunteers at a local animal shelter and guilts everyone she knows into adopting a pet. Her youngest child is a close friend of Ryan's, and she's always offering to take him in when I need some extra help.

"What day is your mom coming?" she asks me.

"My mom arrives today, so that gives me two days to get her acclimated with the boys and the house and their schedules before we leave Saturday morning."

"Well, don't worry about soccer and tae kwon do. I have both of those covered. Howie can run carpool while I'm away. We didn't buy him a car last year for nothing," she said of her eldest son. "And Ryan can sleep over here on Saturday or Sunday if he'd like. That could take some of the pressure off your mom."

"Thank you for everything, Jen. I mean it. Especially for encouraging me to go. I can't tell you how much I'm looking forward to it."

"Me too. Make sure your mom has all my husband's contact info. I'll talk to you later."

We hang up the phone, and I finish making the bed in the guest bedroom. Mom likes a high thread count, so I ran to Bed Bath & Beyond yesterday to make sure she'd be willing to visit me again in the future. A couple of years ago, I'd helped get her settled into a new condo not far from her cousin Laura and Laura's husband. She's not an enthusiastic flyer, preferring to stay home and socialize with her family and close friends in Greenwich.

I've had the boys with me all day, so I wasn't able to get her from the airport. At about 6:00 p.m. I see a Town Car pull into my driveway. "Nana is here!" I yell to the boys, but they can't be bothered to look away from *SpongeBob SquarePants*. I shake my head and run out the front door. Seeing even a glimpse of her makes me wish she lived closer. The driver is already at the trunk retrieving her bags. She stands on ceremony and waits for him to open her door. God, I love this woman. I slowly approach the vehicle, giddy with anticipation, and then she gets out. She is regal and immaculately dressed, with her blonde hair in a tidy bun. Her slacks are creased, her pearls are polished, but something is amiss, and I sense it immediately.

She smiles at me.

"Hi, Mom." We embrace. The scent of her perfume, Chanel No 5, puts me in a state of childhood euphoria. Even now, when I'm walking through a department store, I will stop at the fragrance counter just to spray it in the air so I can be with her for a moment.

"Hello, my darling, how are you?" she says, tired.

"I'm good. How was the flight?"

"I was able to upgrade to first class, so all crises were avoided."

"Thank the good Lord for that." I roll my eyes.

She laughs and reaches for her bag.

"I'll get that," I say.

She stands straight and looks at me. It takes just an extra second or two for her to respond, but the delay is troubling. "OK, thanks," she says.

I lift her canvas carry-on onto my shoulder and grab the handle of her rolling bag. "Are you all right?" I ask.

She places a hand on my shoulder as we walk to the front door. "Of course. I'm fine. Just a little drained. Traveling always makes for a long day, even when you're not going very far."

Mom goes to the boys while I take her things upstairs. I'm so thrilled to have her with us—almost as thrilled as I am at the thought of sipping margaritas on the beach—but something doesn't feel right. There is a strange pit in my stomach. I take my phone out of my pocket and text Jen.

I don't think we're going to Cabo.

Once Mom and I tuck the boys in, we each grab a light coat and take a glass of wine out on the front porch. I'm convinced something is wrong with her other than traveler's fatigue, but she insists I stop asking.

"Tell me about you. I'm worried about you," she says, and we each take a seat in one of the two white Adirondack chairs.

I let out a colossal sigh, one that I would only burden my mother with, and take a sip of wine. It's a clear sky above us with a full moon and a smattering of glittery stars accompanied by the occasional airplane. "I don't know how you did it," I say. "Divorce is so hard. Tell me how you managed."

"Oh, my sweet girl. It breaks my heart to hear you say that."

"I don't mean to upset you."

"I know, and you will pull through this stronger and better than ever." She pats my leg and then buttons her coat.

"If it were just me, I would sign whatever papers he wanted me to sign and get a job and sell this house and move the hell on with my life." I take a breath. "But my babies are still so little, and they don't deserve this. They didn't ask to be a part of this mess. When I look at Luke, just barely two years old, I want to cry. How could Todd have done this to us? How could he be so callous?"

"I wish I had answers for you, but I don't know why men cheat," Mom says and crosses her legs. "Sometimes they're unhappy with their lives, sometimes they're unhappy with their wives, and sometimes they just think they won't get caught."

"I think about that every day," I say. "That maybe my marriage would still be alive if I'd never come home early from the aquarium. That Todd would still be driving Ryan and Jimmy to soccer on the weekends, still giving Luke a bath after work, still screwing women on the side, and then kissing me good night." I shrug. "I'll never know how long it was going on before I found them." I shiver at the thought.

"Do you really want to know?" she asks.

I nod. "I kind of do. I feel like I deserve to know if he ever loved me."

Mom places her glass on the small wicker table between us and rubs her eyes.

"Let's go inside," I say. "I can tell you're not feeling well."

She lifts a hand. "I'm fine." She positions herself so she's facing me. "I know I haven't been entirely up front about what your father and I went through. I also know that my own parents had a complicated marriage. But in both twisted relationships, there was love."

I smile.

"And I'm so disappointed in the choices Todd has made, but I know that he loved you."

"How do you know?"

She leans back in her chair. "Because when the two of you first met, he used to look at you the way I look at you. I remember the first time you both came to Greenwich for a visit during your senior-year spring break, and he was smitten. You both were." She leans over to give me a hug. "A mother knows."

My throat goes tight, and I have to hold back my tears as we embrace. "I love you, Mom," I say into her ear.

"You'll find someone who looks at you that way again, I promise," she says, but she never found it again after my father. There were times when my mother would date when I was growing up, but she never made much effort. I recall her cousin Laura trying to play matchmaker a couple of times, to no avail. There was a gentleman who was a widower, a member of the Belle Haven Club, who had taken Mom to dinner a few times until she stopped returning his calls. Whatever happened in her marriage obviously made her hesitant to fall in love and be vulnerable again. I'd be lying if I said I couldn't relate. Being deceived by the man I'd trusted with my heart and my children has been the most frightening experience of my life. So I thought.

I pull away from her, and she startles me with a gasp. "It's a full moon." She points, and we look up at the sky. "I think that means your mother knows best."

"I think you're right."

～

Mom has some relatives who live in the Chicago area, not far from where I live in Wilmette, so the next day I invite some family and friends over for pizza, including Jen and her kids.

"I can see where Ann Marie gets her natural beauty," Jen says to my mom.

She blushes. "Thank you."

"Jen is Wonder Woman," I say to Mom. "She volunteers for every damn thing, runs the block party every summer, carpools my boys, and works in advertising sales for the *Chicago Tribune*."

Mom's face lights up. "The *Chicago Tribune*? I almost worked there myself a lifetime ago."

"No kidding?" Jen says.

"In fact, I wrote one article for them when I was pregnant with Ann Marie." She pauses, and the memories of what might've been glow behind her blue eyes. "There was a young gal named Abigail who was taken with me and my family. She hired me on the spot after reading only one sample article I'd written for the *Greenwich Times*."

I raise a brow and interject, "You did?"

Mom nods proudly. "It was nothing but a holiday fluff piece, but I still have the article back home in a drawer."

Jen chimes in, "That's funny. The editor's name is Abigail. Was it Abigail Rushton?"

We look to Mom for her response, and it takes an extra second or two, like the day before outside in the driveway.

"Yes," Mom says with a shred of enthusiasm, the most I have seen from her in twenty-four hours. Even Jimmy's portrait of her in solid red Sharpie—he likes monotones—didn't elicit such a reaction. "Oh my, Jen. You've made my day. She is the head editor?"

"Editor in chief," she says.

"I don't expect she'll remember me, but would you send her my love? I can never thank her enough for her kindness back then."

"I absolutely will."

Jen helps me serve the food and then clean up while the rest of the people visit with each other in the family room. When we're about through with the dishes, I peek my head around the corner and notice my mother sitting quietly with her hands in her lap, not being her talkative self. Once everyone is gone, I tuck the boys in and rush back downstairs, hoping to bend her ear for a while, but she's gone up to bed.

That night, I can't fall asleep. Images of Mom sitting quietly on the couch as the kids and guests conversed around her are haunting me. She's always the loudest in the room, and she was eerily reserved tonight. Jen was doing her best to convince me to go to Mexico, and despite Mom's insistence as well, I know something is wrong with her that requires my attention. I feel it in my gut.

The next morning, after Ryan and Jimmy are off to school, I invite my cousin Rory over for breakfast because she wasn't able to make dinner last night, and prep her before she comes inside. "I know I haven't seen my mom in a couple of months, but she seems off to me," I tell Rory at the door. "I'm supposed to leave for Mexico this weekend, and I need another opinion."

Rory steps inside. She's my aunt Margaret's eldest daughter, and she lives with her fiancé in the Lincoln Square neighborhood. "I can look in on her when you're gone. How long will you be in Mexico?"

"Just four days."

"She'll be fine," Rory tries to reassure me. "It's weird when we start to realize our parents are getting older."

"Just come in the kitchen." I yank her hand.

Mom is sitting at the small square table near the window, lost in thought and looking out at the yard.

"Rory is here, Mom," I say, and she turns to face us.

"Hi, Aunt CC." Rory kisses her cheek.

"You look beautiful," Mom tells her.

The three of us chat for a few minutes while she and Rory catch up, and then Mom excuses herself to go to her bedroom.

"I hate myself for asking this," Rory starts, "but do you think she's on something? Like, maybe taking some pills she shouldn't be taking?

Painkillers or sleeping pills, or some bad prescription?" She looks at me. "I can see what you mean about her not being herself."

I reach for Rory's hand and give it a squeeze. "I'm going to talk to her. Can you sit with Luke in the front yard? Just make sure he doesn't chase any squirrels into the street."

I knock on my mom's door. "Can I come in?"

"Of course," she says.

I take a seat next to her on the bed. "Do you feel OK?"

My mom clasps her hands together and looks at me. "No, I don't."

Chapter Seventeen

CATHERINE

Beirut, 1971

The first time I caught Gabriel lying to me, he'd been away for a week on a business trip to Paris. When I tried to phone his hotel, they had no record of him ever staying there or booking a reservation. Upon his return, he claimed he'd given me the wrong name of the hotel. An innocent and believable mistake, but I knew he was lying. When I threatened to check with Walid to make sure he'd driven him to the airport, Gabriel disconnected our phone service for a week. I had to sneak over to Brigitte's apartment just to place an order with the butcher.

The second time was a month or so later. Gabriel had called at 5:00 p.m., saying he was at the office and would be home by 7:00 p.m. for dinner. At 10:00 p.m., he walked through the front door, claiming an impromptu dinner meeting, but my gut told me he was in Beit Chabab and couldn't get back because of traffic. The next morning, I simply asked Walid how the drive to the mountains was, and he replied, "It was a long one yesterday."

When I accused Gabriel of having a mistress up there, he flew into a rage and tossed a pitcher of water onto our terrace. Shards of glass flew everywhere, and neighbors could be heard swearing and screaming up at us in horror. I'd never seen him so angry. My hands were trembling, and I slipped on a pair of shoes and ran outside, apologizing in French, English, and Arabic for my clumsy grasp on the handle. Another innocent and believable mistake. I didn't dare tell Brigitte what actually happened, lest she think it was my fault for being too feisty and loud. I expected an apology from him, but the next day it was like nothing had ever happened, and it reminded me of what was once the worst night of my life.

I was sixteen years old the second time I caught my father cheating on my mother. It was a Saturday night in September, and Mom was in Manhattan for the weekend, visiting a friend. Dad had been at the club all day, drinking Scotch and smoking cigars, and my sister Margaret and I were at a party at the house of Tim Foley, a neighbor in Belle Haven whose parents traveled every weekend. The weather was warm that night, so a group of kids were in his backyard, huddled around a bonfire and smoking weed. There was always lots of pot to go around. A little after 11:00 p.m., Margaret said she wanted to go home, so I said goodbye to her, and she walked home. Not twenty minutes later, she came running back to Tim's house, screaming at me to come home, and trying to catch her breath. I thought she'd been hurt.

"Dad is arguing with some woman out by the pool!" she said.

We ran home and slowed down as we got around the back, past the guesthouse and to the pool deck, where we stopped behind some bushes.

"I don't hear anything," I said.

"When I came into the house, I heard them arguing, and it took me a few minutes to realize they were outside." She craned her neck.

We made our way farther past the wall where we were hiding so that we could see the entire deck of the pool, but it was empty. "Look." I pointed across the lawn to the cabana. "There's a light on."

Margaret tugged on my arm. "Let's get out of here."

"No. We're going to the cabana."

"No, we're not! He'll kill us if he thinks we're spying on him."

She and I stared at each other under the dim spotlight hanging from the top corner of the wall. "We don't know he's in there."

Margaret looked like she was about to cry. "I'm going to bed," she huffed and walked off.

I began to walk to the cabana and then ducked behind a lounge chair when I saw them emerge. It was completely dark outside, except for the lights from the pool and a few spots on the edge of the house. The woman's blouse was unbuttoned, and her bare breasts were exposed. She was obviously drunk and hanging all over my father like a needy toddler, kissing his neck with her arm draped over his shoulder as he fastened his belt. I almost vomited. And then she gave him a playful smack and said something I couldn't hear, but it angered him. As soon as he pushed her away, she smacked him again. That time he smacked her back, hard. The women tumbled off her high heels and hit her head on the edge of the pool. I could've heard the crack from Tim Foley's house, had I still been there.

I gasped and covered my mouth, then slid back behind the guesthouse. My father stumbled over to her and called her name. "Lola," he said, but she didn't move.

I watched my father, with a tumbler of Scotch in his right hand, tap her body with his foot and then swear under his breath. Moments later, he walked inside, leaving her there.

In my sixteen-year-old mind, I remember thinking I wanted to push this horrid woman in the pool and watch her drown. How dare she disrespect my parents' marriage like that! And who invited her, anyway? I hated her for lying there motionless with her tits hanging out. It wouldn't be right for little Mary Grace, who was eight at the time, to wake up and see some strange woman passed out next to the diving board the next morning. *What was he thinking leaving her there?*

I snuck in through the service entrance and ran up the back stairs. I was just about to wake Margaret when I saw a Belle Haven security car pull in the driveway, followed by a Greenwich Police car. Two men got out of each vehicle and walked to the back of our house. Father was nowhere in sight.

Quickly as I could, I scurried back down the kitchen stairwell and slammed into my father as he was walking up.

"What in God's name are you doing?" he said.

I caught my breath. "I'm . . . I was getting a Coke," I said, but he couldn't have cared less. He was more annoyed that I'd knocked into him and spilled some of his drink. He walked right on past me with the signature sound of ice cubes jingling against the sides of his glass.

I froze on the steps, thinking I might be seen if I walked to the window. I couldn't even imagine how he was going to explain this mess to my mother. I leaped down the remaining stairs and ran through the house to the back patio doors that overlooked the pool. It was dark in the house, so I stayed close to the drapery, hoping I wouldn't be noticed, but that didn't last very long. One of the police officers, a very tall man with bright orange hair, looked up as the other three men gathered Lola by her feet and under her arms. He was a striking figure, towering over the others, standing about six feet seven inches. Without meaning to, I willed him to look at me. In an instant, he was staring at me, studying me. And if I were any average sixteen-year-old girl other than a Belle Haven brat, he'd pity me. I took a step backward into the shadows, but he didn't take his eyes off mine, even nodded to make sure I knew that he saw me.

In the morning, Lola was gone, and there was never any mention of her. Not another visit from Belle Haven security, not from the ginger giant, and certainly not from Lola. It was as if nothing had ever happened.

After I accused Gabriel of having a mistress in the mountains, he forbade me from going there.

"If you have nothing to hide up there, then why haven't we been to visit?" I pressed him.

"My home there is not for you right now."

"What the hell does that mean? I've heard you talk about it for a year. It's a two-hour drive from the apartment, and you promised to take me there."

"I'm tired of arguing about it," he said. "I have never promised anything about that house."

I sighed and relaxed my tone, opting for a different approach and hearing Brigitte's advice ringing through my head. "Can you see where I'm coming from? If I had a second home that was important to me and my family, and it was only a short ride away, don't you think you would want to go there?"

He just stared at me.

"I know you'd be very curious if I treated it as some sort of a secret," I added.

Gabriel slid a pack of cigarettes out of his shirt pocket and walked to the balcony. When he was through, he found me in the kitchen, brewing some water for tea.

"It's a very special place, and one day I will take you both there. When I am ready." He dismissed me and went to make a phone call.

In the bathroom, I gazed at myself in the mirror. I knew all too well that men, loving husbands and fathers, could easily keep secrets from their wives with zero guilt. I also knew what those secrets could do to their families. My mother wasn't naive. Just because she never caught some floozy stumbling around the pool deck doesn't mean she didn't know they existed. I mean, she never told me she knew my father was a cheat, but as I got older, I could tell. It was in her eyes. The way she looked at him over the years had changed. A child's senses are like no other, and when my mother stopped looking at my father with love and started looking at him with contempt, the whole house suffered for it. I did not want my daughter to endure the same pain.

Gabriel was holding a book in one hand and hanging up the phone when I found him. "I want to go this week," I said.

He looked at me as if I'd spoken in one of the few languages he didn't understand. "Where?"

"Beit Chabab. I want you to take me up to the mountains this week." I crossed my arms. "I'm ready."

He almost laughed at my brazenness, but his anger got the best of him. "I said I would take you there when I'm ready. Don't test me."

"Don't hide things from me."

His face got bright red. "I don't take orders from you! Are you crazy?" He tossed the book at my head, and it grazed my left cheek as I flinched. My mouth went wide, and my hand flew to my ear.

Before I knew it, he was gripping my arm with his hand. "You will never go!" He let me go with a shove.

I slept on the couch that night with one eye open and woke to a hot August day. The balcony doors were wide-open, as they always were then, and the hum from our three ceiling fans had put me to sleep with Ann Marie on my chest. Our arguments were getting more and more frequent, but with added aggression and no make-up sex. Almost every one was a result of my asking to fly home and visit my family, or questioning his faithfulness. Had I been relentless, as he'd said? Maybe I was, but he'd treated me like a flight risk, a prisoner, and he was the one lying to me.

I placed my sleeping baby in her playpen, snuck two quick drags on a cigarette, and called Brigitte for some advice.

"Are you busy?" I asked when she answered.

"Until school starts again, I am always busy, but never for you."

"Can you come over?"

Brigitte sat with me on my balcony, and we drank white coffee from a tea set that had belonged to Gabriel's mother.

"You know how badly I want to go home and visit my family."

"Of course," she said.

"Do you think it's too much for me to ask?" There was more sarcasm than significance in my question.

"Is this about Gabriel?"

"Yes," I said. I hadn't confided in her about the lies he'd been telling and the secrets he was keeping from me. Or that he'd refused to take me to the mountains. She must have known, though, because it was such a common occurrence for so many of our neighbors. Yet we remained in the city every weekend.

She shrugged. "He's spent so much time in the States. I can't see why he's so opposed to the idea."

I nodded in agreement. "Me either. He says I'm being relentless and I will want to stay too long, and that he can't take the time from work and a bunch of other nonsense." My shoulders relaxed. "I'm heartbroken about it, and every time I mention it, we argue. Why should I walk on eggshells around here just because I want Ann Marie to meet her grandparents?"

"Where are these eggshells?"

I laughed. "It's an expression. It means I'm afraid to bring up the subject."

Her expression was still bewildered. "Are you happy here?"

She began speaking again before I answered. "Maybe he is worried that if you go home, you will come back sad and depressed about having left your family all over again."

The truth was that I loved my husband, but I wasn't happy in Beirut. "I'm not unhappy, but I miss my family. I need to know that I can see them and talk to them without restrictions. I've done nothing to deserve his distrust, and we have enough money to afford as many phone calls as I want. I never intended to abuse the phone bill. Even when I talk for five minutes with my sister, he scolds me like I've committed some crime and put us in the poorhouse. He's threatened to have the phone disconnected more times than he's told me he loves me in the past two months." I almost told her he threw a book at my face, but instead, I protected him.

She sighed. "I am sorry to hear that. You are a beautiful couple, and you have this beautiful little angel." She looked over at the playpen. "Do you want Sammy to talk to him?"

"No, absolutely not. I think it would only make matters worse for him to know we're talking behind his back."

"That is what friends do."

I smiled. "Yes. Thank you."

Brigitte crossed her arms. "You are a feisty girl. You know I tell you that. Men like Gabriel want to think they are the only thing that matters. He wants to believe that you are happy in his home country. That he can provide for you like your parents have, or better than they have. It's always about ego, my darling. If you make his ego strong, then he will give you the world. But if he thinks you are his challenger and not his champion, then he will never back down from the fight."

She was right. We'd been together for merely a year and gone through our share of chaos, both good and stressful. I wanted desperately for things to work between us, but I had my daughter to think about, and she deserved to have a relationship with her entire family. We both did.

"You are my wisest neighbor," I joked. "And I love you." She rolled her eyes. "I know you feel like a broken record."

Brigitte gave me the same confused glance she'd given me when I'd made the comment about walking on eggshells.

"You know, saying the same things over and over," I clarified. "But I think I finally understand what you're saying, and you're right. I don't want to fight with Gabriel."

But I wanted to get my way. Her advice finally gave me clarity, and I knew exactly what had to be done.

Brigitte left, and I fixed myself a bowl of yogurt with cherries for lunch, which I ate on the balcony. Just as I padded quietly back into the apartment to clean up, I heard the key in the front door. It was Gabriel.

"Hi," I said. "What are you doing home so early?" It was just after 1:00 p.m.

He looked around the apartment as if there were clues to a crime waiting to be found. There were none. His cologne wafted through the room as he walked past me and into the bedroom. I used to melt at the scent of it. "Honey . . ." I placed the dishes in the sink and followed him. "Can we talk about last night? What are you doing home in the middle of the day?"

I entered the bedroom to find him rummaging through the desk. He stuck something in his pocket and walked past me again. "Gabriel," I said in a low voice so as not to disturb Ann Marie. "What is going on? Would you stop walking past me?" I stomped my bare foot and chased him into the kitchen, where he opened a cabinet that housed a combination safe. He spun the dial, opened the door, took what he'd put in his pocket, and locked it away.

"What was that?" I asked.

"It's your passport." He turned his back on me. "I'm sorry, but you will never leave this country."

Chapter Eighteen

CATHERINE

Beirut, 1971

By the time Ann Marie was six months old, my desperation hit a new low. After Gabriel first took my passport, I lost it. My hands and limbs were trembling so much that I had to lie on the kitchen floor so I wouldn't pass out and hurt myself by tumbling onto the table and chairs. He'd come home that day like a flash of light and turned our relationship from partners and lovers to captor and hostage. As soon as I was able to stand and see straight, I rang Brigitte again. She had just left my apartment, leaving a trail of sage advice that was intended to bring me peace. No such luck.

"I can't understand you," she said. "Give me ten minutes."

She came back over and found me cradling my child, tears streaming down my face, lip quivering. "He locked up my passport!"

She covered her mouth.

"He wouldn't even speak to me. Came home seconds after you were gone. He left work to come here and put my passport in the safe."

"Do you know the combination?"

"No! Of course not."

Ann Marie began to wail.

Brigitte took the baby from me and bounced with her in her arms. "Did you yell at him?"

I shook my head and buried it in my hands. "I've done nothing but ask to see my family."

"Did you ask him again today when he came home?"

"No. He wouldn't even talk to me. I tried. All he said was that I was never going to leave this country." I looked up, furious now. "If he thinks for one second that he can lock me up and keep us from my family, he has another thing coming."

Brigitte bounced some more and cooed at Ann Marie, who was fussing. "May I fetch her a bottle?"

I nodded. "Thank you."

"Go on the terrace and try to find your breath. I will meet you out there."

I found my breath in a pack of cigarettes and a glass of vodka as my neighbor fed my child and placed her back into bed.

Brigitte took a seat next to me. "Let me help you."

"Escape?"

"No." She leaned forward. "The more you talk of going home, the less he is willing to allow it, yes?"

"Why do I need his permission to see my family?"

Her face hardened. "Your stubbornness has gotten you this far. I am trying to tell you that you are married to a proud Middle Eastern man." She clapped her hands in front of my face as if to wake me up. "And until you understand what that means for you and the baby, then his threats will be your reality."

"You keep asking me what I did wrong today, and I did nothing."

"I keep asking you so I can understand where we go from here. If you did not argue with him today, then let him come home from work this evening and pretend you are not upset with what he's done."

I laughed out loud. "So, he should get away with confiscating my passport?"

Brigitte sat back in her seat and crossed her legs. "Do you want to go home or not?"

Her message that day was not lost on me, and if I had to swallow my pride to see my family, then that's what I had to do. With every day that had passed since Ann Marie's birth, my relationship with Gabriel had become more and more strained, and his tolerance for my wants and needs became nonexistent. Back home, the feminist movement was plowing ahead with the force of a locomotive. But in Beirut, he wouldn't allow me to order off a menu for myself, meet a friend for lunch—not that I had many—and even asking a waiter for more ice in my water led him to publicly ostracize me. Anytime I went to leave the building during the day, Walid was there. Even walking down to the ocean with the baby turned into a day at the beach with Walid and Ann Marie.

And then something happened. I went to get the mail, and there was a letter for me from an address I didn't recognize. Inside was the article I'd written for the *Chicago Tribune* about my holiday lunch at Marshall Field's in the Walnut Room and a handwritten note on Abigail Rushton's personal stationery.

Dear CC,

My apologies for sending this so late, but it took me nearly as long to locate your address in Beirut from your cousin Henry. However, it was a wonderful reason to call him and catch up. But you can blame him for the tardiness of this letter! Anyway, I hope the copy of the article has made its way to you, and you should know it was quite well received. You are a talented writer. We had many inquiries from readers wanting to hear more about your other adventures and opinions. I told you,

*everyone loves a socialite. Hope you are well and settled
in Lebanon. I must say that is a place I have never been.
Do stay in touch.*

A.R.

Her letter lit the mass of smoldering kindle in my belly. It was a sign
that I should be writing more and not just in my journals, and it was a
sign that I should be living, not suffocating. Abigail's gesture made me
bound and determined to get home to my family. And if that meant
taking Brigitte's advice, then that was precisely what I would do.

That day, when Gabriel came home from work after locking up
my freedom, I never said one word about it. Never even mentioned the
Tribune article that I should've been clamoring to show him.

The new me.

I stopped using the phone, stopped talking about my family, and
focused solely on him and our home in Beirut. We began making love
again and talking about growing our family. Within three weeks, he was
a changed man. A man whose threats had been removed. A man who
was in control of his woman again. A man who was being hoodwinked.
A fool.

Early one Wednesday evening, I asked Walid to drive me to a market about ten miles away because I knew they had a bank of pay phones
in the back. Some of the students at AUB had mentioned that to me
as a great resource.

"Would you mind staying in the car with Ann Marie while I shop?"
She was asleep in her plastic infant seat.

His face lit up as if he'd been asked to represent his country in a
peace summit. "I would be honored! You do not have to worry for one
second, Miss. I am a father myself, as you know, and I will treat her as
if she were mine." He stood at attention.

I smiled and laughed a little too much on purpose. "Of course, you will. That's why I asked. You are truly the sweetest man I know." I placed a hand on his shoulder. "And I will only be about fifteen minutes."

"Yes, of course. We will be right here. You take your time, and do not be concerned for even a second."

I ran inside to the back of the store and placed a collect call to Laura. It had been months since we'd spoken, but I'd written to her that I would try and call on that very day. How did I pick that random Wednesday? Because that's how I did everything back then. All decisions were made to appear as arbitrary as possible.

"I need you to send me a ticket," I finally said after we'd quickly caught each other up. "I don't have much time to chat, but can you call a travel agent and have them arrange for me to come home next month?"

"Is everything OK?" she asked.

"Everything is fine, but I need your help with this."

"Sure, what date?"

"Maybe November 8 or any day that week, and then ask if she will mail the ticket to this address." I gave her Brigitte's apartment number.

"Maybe she can arrange for you to pick it up there at a local office in Beirut?" Laura suggested.

"Just have her send it. It will be much easier for me, and if I have to change the date, I will. Please pay for it, and I will pay you back."

"How exciting," Laura said.

"It is, but don't tell anyone. I mean it. I want to surprise my family." My heart was beating out of my chest. "I miss you all so much. You have no idea."

"I miss you, too, and can't wait to meet Ann Marie. I can't believe you have a daughter and I've never met her."

After hanging up, I grabbed a bunch of items off the shelves, paid for them, and returned to the car. Walid was so consumed with my sweet little girl that he never bothered to question why I'd chosen that market over any other.

The next week I began to rearrange the apartment. Items that Gabriel had locked up in a storage locker in the basement were brought to light. Mostly tchotchke-type things such as his fishing poles and some old framed photographs of him when he was a child.

"I want Ann Marie to see these things as she gets older and learn where she came from," I said to him when he came home, pleased with the changes I'd made, hoping he'd recognize the obvious absence of my own family photos. Our transfer to Beirut happened so quickly that I never had time to collect all the things I wanted from my home in Greenwich. Things like photo albums and quilts and all my seasonal clothes that were still packed in trucks in our basement when I first left for Chicago.

I began to misplace things like my winter coat and my favorite leather boots, and the wristwatch Laura had given me one year for my birthday, all on purpose and arbitrary, of course. Gabriel was willing to replace what I needed, and only once did I mention the personal belongings I'd left behind in the States.

"One of these years, I should have Laura fly them out to me, but they'll all be terribly out of fashion by then."

He laughed at my frivolous concerns.

Silly fool.

Whether he thought women like *the new me* actually existed or whether he presumed I was finally the girl he intended to marry didn't matter. I would see Brigitte, smiling proudly from her doorway, arms crossed, when she'd catch me kissing Gabriel goodbye each morning as he left for work.

The afternoon of Thursday, October 28, I saw Brigitte coming up the front walk from the butcher as I was drying some of Ann Marie's blankets on the terrace. A few minutes later, there was a knock on the door.

She examined me closely, frowning, with a plane ticket in her hand. "What is this?"

"It's exactly what you think it is." I went to reach for it, and she snapped it away from me. I dropped my arms to my sides. "You're going to keep it for yourself?" I asked.

"How could you put me in danger like this?"

"You always get the mail."

"What if I hadn't today? There are plenty of days that Sammy picks it up." Her hand was shaking. "Have you lived your entire life with no consequences?"

I almost lashed out at her, but I held my tongue. Before I'd met Gabriel, my life had been void of passion. Not opportunity and blessings, but true passion. Loving and marrying him forced me to abandon a writing career, abandon my home, my family, and now my self-worth. No, I had not lived my entire life without consequences.

But once again, I strained to bite my tongue. "I would have put you at more risk by telling you and then asking you to keep a secret for me."

"I'm not happy about this at all, Catherine."

"That I want to see my mother, or that I sent the ticket to your mailbox?"

Her expression softened. Ultimately, she felt sorry for me, and I knew that. "Of course, I want you to see your mother and father. I just wish you would not have involved me in a lie."

I extended my hand. "You know what Gabriel will do if he finds out."

We stared at each other, and then she handed me the ticket. She knew what he'd do.

"Thank you, and now there is nothing more to be said. This conversation never happened."

She blinked and placed a hand over her heart. "He will never forgive you if you plan to deceive him."

"He has already trapped me here and forbidden me from seeing my family. I can't think of much worse than that. It's me who's been deceived."

She patted her chest. "He does love you, you know."

I lowered my gaze and nodded. I loved him, too, despite everything, but it wasn't enough.

"How will you leave with no passport?"

"I'm working on that."

Chapter Nineteen

CATHERINE

Beirut, 1971

Back in the apartment with the ticket in my hand like a small grenade, I stood thinking of where to hide it. Under the mattress seemed too predictable. Anywhere in the kitchen too risky. Same with any of the dresser drawers. There was hardly a place that Gabriel would not accidentally rummage through. Suddenly, it occurred to me.

I walked into Ann Marie's room. It was a small space, painted a pale but cheerful shade of yellow with a crib, changing table, and matching chest of drawers. The three-piece set was a gift from Gabriel's sister, Serine, and her husband, Michael. In the closet were her clothes and linens and boxes of diapers. I reached inside one of the boxes, pulled out a diaper, and sat on the floor cross-legged. The ticket was almost the exact length of the tiny diaper and folded up perfectly inside it. He hadn't changed one diaper in six months, so there was little concern he'd start anytime soon. Especially with *the new me* being so accommodating and all.

Once I was through, I rang up my friend, Professor Randall Cunningham at AUB.

"How nice to hear from you, CC. Everything good with your daughter?"

"Yes, thank you. I'd like to bring her by campus one day."

"That would be great. Nothing brightens up a place like a baby."

The only time Walid was unavailable to me was Fridays from 11:00 a.m. to 3:00 p.m. "Would Friday be good?"

"I can't see why not. What time are you thinking?"

"One o'clock? That way I can stop in during lunch and not bother anyone." I didn't want to be too pushy, but the fact was that I couldn't have cared less if he made time to see Ann Marie or not, and he was likely just being kind; no one is ever terribly excited to see someone's baby. "Also, do you know if the embassy annex is open on Fridays?" I paused. "I seem to have misplaced my passport."

"As far as I know, they are open every day. Shall I check and call you back?"

"No, thank you. I will be there anyway. It's no trouble for me to stop in."

After hanging up the phone, I went to check on the money I'd been hiding in my lingerie drawer. All was well.

When Gabriel arrived home that evening, there were lamb chops, tabbouleh, and cabbage rolls with lemon. Even I was impressed. Gabriel came home happy and embraced me before kissing Ann Marie, who was in her bouncy seat atop the dining room table. After dinner, I changed the baby's diaper and sang her to sleep in her crib.

Once the kitchen was clean, I poured Gabriel a vodka and a glass of white wine for myself and joined him on the terrace, where he was reading the evening paper. It was a beautiful night, and almost all our neighbors were out on their respective balconies, shouting to each other in conversation.

"I finally got ahold of Professor Cunningham today. It's been weeks since he called asking to see the baby."

"How is he doing?"

"Good, good. I'm going to bring her by there tomorrow to see him and his staff. Remember that wonderful woman who works the front desk?" Distractions. "I think her name was Evelyn or something. Maybe the only woman in Beirut with a southern accent."

Gabriel peered over the top of the paper. "Tomorrow is Friday. Walid won't be able to take you."

I raised my eyebrows. "Oh, that's right." I conjured up a tiny yawn. "I used to walk there all the time, as you remember. It will be nice. I'll take Ann Marie in the carriage. It's only about a mile and a half."

He shrugged and went back to his paper, leaving me victorious.

Ann Marie and I spent about thirty minutes with Randall and his staff and then said our goodbyes. The US Embassy in Beirut had a small secondary office on campus to serve the needs of the many foreign students, and I hurried over there as soon as we left the professor.

I clumsily pushed the carriage through the door, causing a chime to ring as it opened. "I need a new passport," I said to the man behind the counter. He wore a mustard-colored, short-sleeve button-down shirt with a paisley tie, and his hair was parted way to the left side of his head and slicked down with an impressive amount of grease.

"Was yours stolen?" He spoke with a French accent.

"Yes," I answered without thinking.

"Then I will need a copy of the police report." He shuffled some papers he'd been writing on.

"I'm sorry, no, it wasn't stolen. I lost it."

He finally looked up from what he was doing and faced me, so I smiled at him as I rolled the carriage back and forth to keep the baby quiet. He craned his neck and glanced over at her for a moment.

He raised a brow. "You sure?"

"Yes, I misplaced it, and I have a ticket to go home and see my family in just over a week. It will be their first time meeting the baby." Charm, distract.

Uninterested, he reached for a form and handed it to me. "You will need to fill this out and bring a copy of your birth certificate along with forty dollars. If you come on a day when our secretary is working and she can get the camera to function properly, we can take your picture here." He placed the piece of paper on the countertop in front of me.

"I don't have a copy of my birth certificate," I said, crestfallen. "The original is back home in the States."

"I'm sorry, but we can't reissue a new one without it. Can someone send you a copy?"

"Not in time. Please, there must be something you can do. I used to work with Professor Randall Cunningham in the English department. He can vouch for me."

"You could vouch for yourself, if that were the case."

"You can call my family in Connecticut and have them verify any information."

He motioned to a large poster on the wall with the headline *Lost or Stolen Passports*. "I do not make the rules, Madame. Come back with a copy of your birth certificate, and I will be happy to get you a new passport."

Just then, I heard the door chime behind me.

"Miss Catherine!" Walid was out of breath. "I'm glad I found you here."

I gasped and thanked the Frenchman. "What are you doing here, Walid?"

A clever more cynical man would've questioned me, but Walid was just happy to find us. "Gabriel was worried about you having to walk both ways, and so he asked if I could pick you and Miss Ann Marie up at the professor's office. At first, I went to the wrong building, and when I found the right building, you had already left. Thankfully, they knew where I could find you."

I wanted to kill myself for telling them where I was headed. And Gabriel was worried about me, my ass.

Walid followed me out of the embassy office and outside into the courtyard. "I need a big favor from you," I said.

He was thrilled to accommodate.

"I'm doing something special for Gabriel, and I had to order it from the embassy office, so please, whatever you do, don't tell him where you found me, or it will ruin the surprise."

He did not hesitate. "I will not say a word. How exciting."

"Yes," I said and gave him a hug. "Thank you."

Walid put the carriage in the trunk, and I thanked him profusely for rescuing us from the walk home. "Maybe you can take us out to that market again in the next day or so? I know it's out of the way, but the lamb was superb."

He nodded from the front seat.

Back in the apartment, I fed Ann Marie her bottle and put her down for a nap. The day had not gone as planned, and I was sure Gabriel would be able to read the disappointment all over my face. I needed to get another call in to Laura to have her order a copy of my birth certificate and ask the travel agent to change the date of the ticket. Something I could possibly do on my own in Beirut, but at the risk of another surprise attack by Walid. *The new me* was not about to weep about it. The bump in the road home only made me more determined.

When Gabriel came home that evening, I didn't have anything planned for dinner, so I suggested the three of us take a walk to a local café and enjoy a meal under the stars. He agreed.

He ordered us a bottle of wine. "I was glad Walid was able to find you today."

My throat tightened. "Me too."

"How was everyone at the university?"

My mind was in overdrive trying to interpret his tone. "Good. It was nice to be back there. It's such a beautiful campus." I smiled, wary.

"I'm so glad to see you happy here." Gabriel reached for my hand. "Walid is always telling me what a lucky man I am and how much you are always thinking of me. He said you've asked him to drive out of the way for the best lamb at another market." He studied my face. "You're not hiding anything from me, are you?"

I shook my head. "Like what?" I blinked. "A secret lamb recipe?"

He kept his eyes on me and pulled the plane ticket out of his pocket. I thought my heart was going to stop beating at once. I glanced behind him, trying to judge how far we were from the front entrance, and how quickly I could grab the stroller and make my escape. But I could barely breathe, let alone strategize. I thought I might faint if I stood.

And then he reached for something else. My passport.

I tried to let out a nervous laugh, play it off as a silly mistake, but my chest became warm, and I began to perspire as I tried to come to grips with what I was seeing.

"I have something for you." He held them up and smiled. Upon closer examination, it was not the ticket from the diaper box.

"I don't need Walid to tell me how fortunate I am and how wonderful you have been. I've been thinking about how much your parents would love to meet their granddaughter and how you never had a real chance to say goodbye to everyone before Christmas last year. Serine is eager to meet her niece as well."

If I could have checked my pulse, I would have.

He continued. "I know you have more belongings you'd like to bring here, but most important are you and Ann Marie. And family."

My eyes were the only things I dared to move. He slid the ticket and the passport in front of me.

"Here you go. I want you to have a Merry Christmas this year."

I burst into tears. Every ounce of stress and fear and deception and regret came pouring out of me and onto my cheeks. I quickly reached for a napkin and wiped my face.

"My darling, I didn't think you would get so emotional," he said.

"Thank you, Gabriel. Thank you so much." I had to compose myself. "Wow!" I released a laugh and leaned across the table for a kiss.

Just then, the waiter brought the wine, and I lifted the ticket to read the details. Ann Marie and I would leave Beirut on December 22 and return to Beirut on January 3. Gabriel dismissed the waiter, poured the wine for us himself, and lifted his glass. "To a great trip."

We tapped our glasses. "Thank you," I said again. "Will you be coming with us?"

He shook his head no.

Chapter Twenty

Ann Marie

Chicago, 2008

"I knew something was wrong with you. Please tell me what's going on."

"I'm having a hard time getting my words out," Mom says, now back downstairs and sitting at the kitchen table with my cousin Rory and me. "I feel like it takes me forever to say what I'm thinking or answer a question." She pauses. "Bring me a piece of paper and a pen."

I open the junk drawer next to the fridge and come back with a lined yellow notepad and a ballpoint pen.

"Watch this." My mom takes the pen and begins to write a list of names. Mine, Rory's, her own, and my three boys, and then a few short phrases like *hello* and *how are you*. Her handwriting looks immediately skewed, with each word swinging upward at the end.

She looks up from the paper.

"I'm taking you to the doctor," I say without hesitation.

"We'll talk about it when you and Jen get back from your trip."

I shake my head. "I already told her we're not going."

She shudders. "When did you tell her that?"

"The minute you stepped out of that Town Car."

I'm expecting at least a short debate with her about how I should still go on my vacation, that she came all this way and made it this far, and don't be silly, I deserve a break. But instead, she just nods, and her eyes well up.

"I'm taking you to the ER to see a doctor, and whatever he or she says, no matter what, you're not leaving my side." I lean over and hug her. "I'm going to take care of you."

Her lips curl inward, and she nods again. Rory agrees to wait for the boys when they come home from school.

~

An attendee at the emergency room greets us. "Can I help you?"

"I think my mom had a stroke," I say.

She types something into the computer. "Can you give me her symptoms?" she asks me, even though Mom is standing next to me, looking more than capable of commanding a boardroom of people—dressed in full makeup, hair perfect, and not a pearl out of place. I turn and look at her. My mom is only fifty-seven years old, and she's too young for me to be using the word *stroke* when describing her. She's certainly too old for me to be speaking on her behalf, but I do anyway.

"She's having trouble forming thoughts and sentences, and her handwriting is all messed up."

The girl continues to type. "OK, have a seat and someone will call you."

We wait three hours, during which time we observe an elderly man who tripped on his front stoop and can't move his left foot, a three-year-old boy who cut his forehead open on the edge of a bookcase after chasing a balloon, a teenage girl whose eye was swollen shut after bumping into the back of her friend's head on a trampoline, a pregnant woman who can't stop vomiting, and a middle-aged woman with a troublesome rash on her neck.

"I should have called an ambulance. A gurney is the ticket to being seen immediately."

She smiles. "I'm fine. I feel terrible about your trip."

"I've already forgotten about it."

She scans my face in an affectionately judgmental way that only a mother can. "You should wear a little lip gloss when you go out," she says and mimics the act of applying it with her hand.

I cross my arms and blink. "All of a sudden, you have no problem coming up with your words?"

She dismisses my nonsense with a wave.

"I didn't have the right shade of red for this fluorescent ER lighting," I add.

Her shoulders limp forward. "I love you," Mom says. "You look beautiful with or without."

"OK, now you're really scaring me. Stick to the passive-aggressive insults if you want me to believe you're going to be just fine."

She laughs. "I should say that more often."

I tilt my head. "I know you love me."

"Catherine Clarke," a man calls from the hallway, and we rejoice with an incredible sense of victory. We both look in his direction, and I'm suddenly afflicted with my mother's case of cat's-got-your-tongue-itis. The voice calling her name is emanating from a well-dressed doctor who looks about my age. He's tall with dark wavy hair, sun-kissed cheeks, and blue eyes—a shade of aqua that is detectible all the way from where we're standing. He removes a pair of reading glasses from the pocket of his coat and looks around.

I wave, and we walk toward him.

"I'm Dr. Marcus," he says.

I grin, wishing I'd worn lip gloss, and extend my hand before he can say anything else. "Ann Marie Neelan." We shake. "And this is my mother, Catherine."

He shakes her hand. "I would not have guessed you were her mother."

"Thank you." Mom blushes. The handsome doctor's compliment has erased the three-hour wait it took to get it.

"Please follow me," he says.

Mom takes my hand and gives me that look as we follow behind him. That "Let's find out if he's available" look that mothers of daughters across the globe have perfected.

We enter the room behind him and close the door.

"Are you married, Dr. Marcus?" Mom asks.

"Wow," I mouth silently to her, and my eyes go wide.

His smile indicates how many times a week he's asked that question. "No, I'm not. You?" he asks my mom.

"No. We are not," she offers.

After many humiliating and humbling niceties come to an end, we get down to business and tell Dr. Marcus what's been going on. He listens and has her write some things down on paper so he can see how the letters are curling. She takes a pen and writes her full name, *Catherine Suzanne Clarke.* Then she writes her address and a couple of salutations such as *How are you? Have a nice day*, and so on.

Dr. Marcus stares intently and then blinks. "I think we'll do a CT scan today and see if we come up with anything." He looks at me, then at Mom. "Is that all right with you?"

Mom nods and folds her hands in her lap after placing the pen down.

"Thank you," I say as he stands.

"I'll be right back," he says and leaves the room.

I take a seat on the rolling stool that he'd been using. "Are you OK?" She nods.

"He thought we were sisters, so that's a bonus." I try and gauge her level of nervousness.

"At least we'll have some answers."

I nod. "Stay strong. We've been through much worse," I say. "Some old lady once told me that."

She laughs.

Every part of me believes we have a long journey ahead of us simply because there was something so inherently different about her from the moment she arrived. I choose to look at my canceled Mexico trip as a blessing and a long-overdue opportunity to be with my mom and spend time with her.

A nurse comes to take her away.

"Give me a hug. It's going to be fine," I say and watch her walk out.

The room becomes suddenly more miserable now that she's gone. The posters on the walls detail stupid signs of whooping cough and heart attacks. Who would need that information at this point? If I've come to the ER after collapsing from chest pains, why do I need a list of symptoms now? I glance at my cell phone, which has been in my hand since we arrived, and my first instinct is to call my mother. My second is to call Todd, and I hate myself for it. Instead, I call my neighbor Jen and let her know she's off the hook for carpool since I won't be going anywhere. She voices her concern and says she has tequila and salsa for me when I'm ready.

Mom returns a half hour later.

"How did it go?"

She shrugs. "As well as can be expected."

"Did you see Doctor Feel Good?"

Her eyes squint as she grins. "He escorted me out of the machine and said he'd be in to talk with us."

We sit in silence as I answer a couple of texts from Rory, who stayed back with Luke.

He doesn't want to play outside. How much TV is too much TV? she asks me.

I laugh out loud. Whatever makes him happy. I traded my Mom-of-the-Year trophy for a case of Chardonnay long ago.

There's Chardonnay?? she answers.

Another thirty or forty minutes pass. I lose count. Mom and I discuss what we should do for dinner, order in or cook. A topic we can easily debate for at least three more hours if necessary.

It's almost 4:00 p.m. when Dr. Marcus returns. "I apologize for the wait," he says and sits on the wheeled stool. "I have some results." He points to the images he's brought with him. "There is a dark spot here on the brain that I think you should have a look at."

Mom and I study the scan as if we can possibly make out the one dark spot he's referring to from any other random dark spot on the X-ray. "Is that from a stroke?" I ask.

"It's hard to say without further testing." He begins to write a name on a piece of paper. "Here." He reaches past Mom and hands it to me, unintentionally labeling her too feeble to look after herself, just like the attendee at the front desk did. "She's one of the best in the brain biz." He grins. "I would bring my own mother to her."

I look at the paper, which reads *Dr. Elena Crane*.

"She'll need to have a biopsy done as soon as possible. I will put a call in to Dr. Crane for you, as she can be booked for many months."

"That is very kind of you," Mom says.

"A biopsy? So, you think it's cancer?" I ask him.

"In this job, I try not to make a habit of guessing."

I see my mom squirm.

"Can we see her tomorrow? This Dr. Crane?"

"Call that number first thing in the morning, and they will do their best to get you in."

Mom gets to her feet. She's understandably had enough of this entire day. "Thank you so much." She extends her hand, and they shake.

I stand, too. "I'm more of a hugger," I say and give him a quick embrace. "Thank you so much."

"It's been a pleasure meeting you both. If it's all right with you, I'd like to follow up to see how everything goes." He looks at me.

"Of course, please, we'd really appreciate that," I say and don't dare look at my mother, who I know is smiling. "Let me write down my e-mail." He hands me a prescription pad and a pen.

Later that night when Mom is asleep, I tiptoe into her room and sniff the bottle of Chanel No 5 that she left on the dresser.

In the days that follow, her ability to speak deteriorates so quickly, there's no time to blink. A week after the biopsy, we get the news that she has brain cancer.

Chapter Twenty-One

CATHERINE

Beirut, 1971

There was little I could do to hide my excitement on December 21, the day before I was due to fly back to Connecticut. A place that I hadn't been in more than a year. A year in which I'd moved to Chicago, gotten pregnant, moved to Lebanon, given birth, and become terrified my husband would confine me again at a moment's notice. Brigitte brought me lunch that day, and her eldest daughter came over with Reema to watch Ann Marie for me.

There was laughter between us. Brigitte was once again preparing for Christmas dinner with family and neighbors—as she had been the year before when we'd first met—and she and I had spent the week wrapping presents and decorating the stairwell and our respective balconies with lights and wreaths. Walid had driven me and Gabriel and the baby to get a tree a couple of weeks ago, and it stood in our family room in a large corner between the couch and the balcony doors. There were gifts underneath for Ann Marie and myself and a new watch I'd bought for my husband. We agreed to open everything when I returned.

"I'm so happy for you, Catherine."

"Thank you. I really can't believe it," I said.

"And I'm very proud of Gabriel for what he's done."

I gave her a questioning look.

"Just that he came to this decision on his own. He knows how much this means to you."

I opened my mouth and was about to say that my daughter should've met her family long before then, that the only reason he'd done this was because I'd connived him and led him to believe I was content to be here for the rest of my life. But I simply nodded instead. "Yes." She knew the sacrifices I'd made to appease him.

"Are those all the bags you are taking?" she asked and pointed to the two small suitcases by the front door.

"There's one more duffel bag in the baby's room with her toys and diapers and a change of clothes for the plane. And then a larger suitcase on my bed, too. We Americans don't pack light." I winked at her. "I've also bought some gifts for my sisters and mom as well that are taking up most of one of the smaller ones. I didn't want to show up empty-handed after all this time."

There were still plenty of clothes hanging in my closet and folded up in my dresser. I'd packed almost all of Ann Marie's things, though, because she really didn't have very much other than little rompers and pajamas. Mother had sent a velvet holiday dress when she didn't know we'd be visiting, so I packed that as well, along with some little bootees and ruffled diaper covers.

Later that evening when Gabriel came home, there was a distance about him. He smiled and ate the dinner I made—lamb stew with fried eggplant—but he didn't have much to say. I'd prepared all sorts of answers to questions that he never asked of me: Who are you most excited to see? What will you do if the baby fusses on the plane? Who's picking you up at the airport? He'd shown very little interest in the trip. His body language seemed to scream regret over buying the ticket, but he wasn't interested in speaking with me, so I couldn't say for sure.

I thought he'd spend more time with Ann Marie or maybe want to put her to sleep that night, but it was very much business as usual, even a little cold. He and I shared a drink on the balcony after dinner, and then he made some phone calls and went to bed. He couldn't know how I was feeling about our relationship because he never asked and I never broached the subject. I began to understand my parents' relationship more once I had my own glimpse into marriage. Even after only one year, and what was still meant to be the honeymoon stage, I found myself coexisting with my husband, just as I'd seen my mother do over the years. I'd assumed it was because they'd been married for twenty-four years, but maybe all relationships were the same back then? You avoid saying things that you know will anger your spouse. You put on airs to let everyone around you think you're happy and that everything is perfect. I remember Brigitte's initial reaction to hearing about the discord between Gabriel and me and how she was almost shocked I was confiding in her. She'd overheard us arguing, but rather than ask what we'd been arguing about, she was more concerned with how I should avoid it happening again altogether. She'd coached me on how to be submissive, and while I'd mocked it at first, in the end her guidance might have just saved me.

The next morning Gabriel kissed the baby and me and left for work. Business as usual. He left the necessary paperwork needed for me to take Ann Marie out of Lebanon on my own and without him. She was a citizen of both America and Lebanon, but Lebanon had much stricter laws regarding having their young citizens removed without the father being present, or his written permission. I told him I'd call him on Christmas, and if he weren't home, I would try Brigitte and Sammy's number. Once he was gone, I made the bed and cleaned up the house and put a load of laundry in the dryer. I would be gone before it was done, so I left a note for him on the kitchen table.

Brigitte had to work that morning, so I left a holiday card and a box of pistachio cookies for the girls and a plastic tea set especially for my little Reema. Brigitte knew I had a special place in my heart for that girl. I used to say that her face was the first thing in that country to make me smile.

But what Brigitte didn't know—what no one knew—was that I had no intention of ever coming back.

~

I waved to Walid from my balcony, and he ran upstairs to help me with the bags. I thought about taking the rest of the items in my drawers, at least my favorite summer things like my white slacks and my yellow gingham bikini, but I didn't want Gabriel to have any suspicions before I arrived in Connecticut. Once all the bags were in the car, Walid took Ann Marie and got her settled.

"I'll be right down," I shouted to him, then went and grabbed the cash I'd kept hidden in my lingerie drawer.

In the baby's room, I reached into the box of diapers where I'd originally hid the plane ticket Laura had sent me. I folded it up and zipped it into my pocketbook so no one would ever find it. I didn't think Brigitte would ever mention it, for her own sake, but if she did . . . there would be no evidence.

Twelve hours later, we landed in Westchester.

Forty-eight hours after that, I sent Gabriel a telegram saying that I wanted a divorce.

Chapter Twenty-Two

CATHERINE

Greenwich, 1972

Even though I'd convinced myself that I never should have left home in the first place, I came to realize that everything happens for a reason, and that reason was Ann Marie.

She was the light of my life. In fact, I didn't even know my life was void of radiance until I had her back with me in the States. It was like my family—my parents and sisters—had been incomplete without her; she brought that much clarity and joy to each of us. Mom cleared out the two guest rooms in the back of the house so we'd have our own private area. I went to see Leonard Hannah, the editor of the *Greenwich Times*, and begged to have my job back, the one I'd never started. He gladly allowed me to work there and urged me to write about my time in Lebanon, so that's how I began my column. Paging through my journals and writing about the foods and the culture and the people of Beirut.

"I won't be able to write about Beirut forever," I told Leonard.

"Make it a series of articles comparing things over there with things over here. I think it could be interesting to those of us who've never taken a leap of faith to save our lives. Lord knows Greenwich has enough people who refuse to go as far as Stamford, let alone the Middle East."

Gabriel's initial reaction was to be expected. He was angry and upset with me. He reached out to my father to try and reason with him, but Dad told him that I was a grown woman who made her own decisions. He began calling the house repeatedly, with no concern for the bills anymore, but when he became hostile and threatening, I'd stop taking his calls unless he agreed to discuss our separation. Eventually, he had no choice but to do so.

Three weeks into my reentry—as my cousin Laura called it—Jessie came up to my room as I was getting dressed and brushing my hair. It was a weekday afternoon around 4:00 p.m., and Ann Marie had just woken up from her nap. She was on my bed, making noises and staring at the ceiling. Jessie knocked and entered without waiting for my response.

"What is it?" I asked when I saw the skeptical look on her face.

"There is someone here to see you."

"Who?"

She closed the door. "It's Serine Miller and her husband."

I placed the brush on my dressing table and went to sit on the bed. Belle Haven was a gated community, but Serine and her husband knew countless people who lived there, so there was no way to stop her from coming to the house. That much I'd known for sure. It was a visit I'd been dreading but expecting. Whether Gabriel had put his sister up to it or not, I would never know. She and I had met only once before, at the dinner party my parents had thrown for us after we'd eloped. Mother called it a wedding dinner and threw the affair just before we moved to Chicago in an effort to save face. About a hundred guests, including Serine and her husband, filled the dining hall at the Belle Haven Club and watched my parents pretend they were happy for us. Scotch and vodka work wonders when playing make-believe.

"Should I tell them you're busy?"

My mouth felt dry. "Is Mother home?"

Jessie shook her head. "At the club."

I took a deep breath and closed my eyes for a second. "No, I'll go down and see them." I stood. "I'm sure they're here to see their niece." I went to Ann Marie on the bed. She was about nine months old then, and the picture of health and perfection. Her thighs and cheeks were deliciously pudgy and soft, her dark hair had grown in enough to hold a tiny satin barrette, and she smelled of talcum powder and rose petals. I leaned in close to her on the bed and inhaled before scooping her up in my arms and walking downstairs.

Serine's face lit up when I walked into the foyer with the baby.

"Oh my, she is beautiful." Her eyes were teary.

"Thank you," I said.

Serine took a step closer. "How are you, CC?"

"I'm good. Glad to be home."

"I know Gabriel misses you both terribly."

I placed my lips on Ann Marie's head and said nothing.

"May I hold her?" she asked, and Jessie appeared out of nowhere.

"Please come sit in the den. Can I pour you a drink?" Jessie offered.

"That would be great," Michael said. "A seven and seven, please."

"Have a seat and I will bring it in." She gestured with her arm for us to leave the entryway.

Once we were seated in the den, I placed Ann Marie in Serine's lap. "She's a really good baby," I said.

Serine smiled and cooed, and I waited for her to say that the baby looked just like her father, but all she did was say how beautiful she was. "Thank you for letting us meet her. I'm sorry we didn't call ahead. Michael was in the neighborhood, and I thought you wouldn't mind if we stopped in. I've been waiting for some new pictures, and this is so much better." She looked at me. "Have you spoken to Gabriel?"

Serine and Gabriel hadn't communicated much over the past year. She'd phoned when the baby was born to congratulate us, and he'd called her a couple of months later on her birthday, and that was the extent of it. But it wasn't lost on me that she would've been one of the first people he would've contacted when he found out I wasn't coming back. I was only surprised it took this long for her to be "in the neighborhood."

"I have, yes." I sat on a chair opposite the couch where she and Michael sat. Jessie breezed in with his cocktail and placed it on the coffee table with a coaster underneath. She walked out, but I could sense she was lurking in the hallway.

Serine exchanged a glance with her husband. "We were sorry to hear that things didn't work out."

I winced a little. Probably every guest at our wedding dinner was whispering behind our backs and taking bets on how long an elopement like ours would last, having known each other for such a short time. Who were we kidding thinking love and passion could conquer all? I wasn't naive to people's comments and gossip, and I didn't believe that every cloud had a silver lining, but mine did. And Serine was holding her.

"I guess the cards were stacked against us. I still care about your brother," I said, tapping into the memories of my wedding that were at the top of my mind. "But we are just very different. We share this amazing little girl, though, and he will always be in our lives." I was disappointed by the sound of my own voice. It was meek and passive and not at all representative of how I felt about my husband, but it wasn't the right time to vent, and certainly not the right audience.

They stayed for about thirty minutes and were just about to leave when my mom walked in the room. She was still in her afternoon tennis outfit, and Jessie came in with a martini for her just as she took a seat. It was like a well-choreographed play.

Act One: Estranged family members enter the home uninvited. Tensions stir. Decisions are made. Escape plans thwarted. All parties gather and converse.

Act Two: The mistress of the house blows in after a long afternoon of physical exertion. Her housekeeper has her cocktail ready for her as she enters the room and is forced to confront the estranged family members.

Act Three: Tension ensues.

Michael stood and gave my mother a kiss on the cheek.

"How are you both?" Mom asked.

"Happy to meet our niece after all this time."

"As are we," Mother said, and I wanted to kiss her myself. Serine was likely oblivious to my mom's contempt for her brother, since Mother was a champ at masking her disdain. But where Serine was ignorant about my relationship with Gabriel and his attempts to ban me from leaving the country, Mother was not.

"Her father and I are thrilled to have them back," Mom said.

Serine forced a smile. "I'm sure you are. How lovely to have her named after you."

Mom smiled. "Will you be staying for dinner?" she asked in a tone that clearly implied the opposite.

Michael shook his head. "No, thank you. We've got to be heading back."

My sister Margaret walked in and waved to them. "Jessie said I should get the baby. She needs her bottle."

Serine handed Ann Marie off to her. "It must be wonderful to have all this help."

I nodded. "It is."

∼

Two months after Serine and Michael's visit, I got a telegram from Gabriel asking for permission to come see the baby and me, bring her a birthday present, and sign the divorce papers in person.

Chapter Twenty-Three

CATHERINE

Greenwich, 1972

My desk was littered with loose pages from my photo album and rolls of Kodak film waiting to be developed. I was trying to put together a book of pictures for Ann Marie's first birthday. A tin of hand cream sat next to a glass tumbler with flat Coca-Cola from three days ago. In the center of it all was Gabriel's Western Union telegram.

> I will arrive on Thursday, March 30, to prepare documents for divorce in America. Please allow me to see Ann Marie and say a proper goodbye.
>
> It is all I ask.

I lifted the thin piece of paper, read it again, and placed it facedown on my desk. He was arriving that day, and I needed to muster all the strength I had to be strong for my mother and my family and my little girl. I closed my eyes for a moment to calm my nerves. The day could not have ended fast enough.

"Jessie!" I called for her. "When you have a second, could you please bring Ann Marie up here?"

"Of course," I heard her say from the hall.

"Thank you."

I walked through my bathroom and took the back stairwell down to the kitchen. Our kitchen was quite spacious and equally quite yellow. Pineapples on the wallpaper, yellow appliances, and yellow gingham drapery adorned the windows above the sink that overlooked the yard. In the center of the room was a rectangular butcher-block table, and at the opposite end near the doorway leading to the butler's pantry was a large circular breakfast table with seating for ten and a brass chandelier that hung from above. Mother was seated in her usual spot, having coffee and reading the morning paper with rollers in her hair while a smoldering Virginia Slims teetered on the edge of an ashtray next to her.

"Good morning, darling."

"Morning, Mom." I reached up into the cupboard for a mug and poured myself a cup.

"The sugar is here on the table," she said. "Mary Grace was putting spoonfuls of it into her cornflakes."

"OK, thank you."

"How are you feeling?" She lowered the newspaper and looked over at me.

"Very nervous."

"Well, we all are. It's a full house today, what with your sisters off for spring break and your father home, too. He said he wouldn't head into the office until after Gabriel signed the papers and left."

I took a deep breath. "That's nice of him, but he doesn't need to stay here. It's going to be very brief, and I don't want to make a scene. I feel like Dad will only say something that will upset the situation."

"Well, it's a decision he's already made, so that's the end of it. Don't forget the Cunninghams are coming for dinner tonight, and I expect you to join us." She folded the paper in half and placed it on the table, as if the act of doing so was buying her some time to formulate her thoughts. My sister Patricia walked in and saved me from a lecture.

"Mary Grace has taken my racket and used it to swat flies, and now it's covered in dead flies. I'm never using it again because it is disgusting." She crossed her arms.

Mother ignored her.

"I'm not going to my lesson with that racket."

Mom stood and smoothed her housecoat. "For Pete's sake, leave us alone already. I'm talking with CC."

"You never do anything about Mary Grace!"

My mother turned to Patricia. "You may borrow mine if you'd like, or there are nearly a dozen other rackets in the shed. If you ask Jessie very kindly, I'm certain she will help you clean yours later. We are all very busy this morning, though. We have a visitor coming, and I don't want to hear another word from you or your sisters until he has gone."

She glanced at me leaning on the counter, sipping my coffee. "Who? Gabriel?" she asked.

"Ann Marie's father is coming here from another country today, and it may be a long time before he sees her again, so I need everyone to stay out of our way."

"Why can't he see her again?"

Mom turned back to the table and dismissed her. "That's enough. Now go." She rubbed her temples as if the questions had given her a headache. There was no pressing my mother for an explanation on anything.

Just as Mom was about to resurrect her conversation with me, my sisters Colleen and Margaret walked in and began rummaging for food, talking loudly about their plans for the day. Before Mom could shush them, I darted back up the stairs and into my room, where Jessie was waiting with Ann Marie.

"Little Miss is ready for you. I thought you might want to pick out her outfit."

Ann Marie was a week away from her first birthday and was crawling around like mad and pulling herself up on furniture. She darted toward me as soon as I stepped into the room.

"I was thinking the little blue dress with the whales on it." I lifted her off the floor and into my arms, breathing in her fresh powdery scent. "Oh, you smell so good, my little angel."

Jessie grabbed the dress from my breakfront and handed it to me. Downstairs, the house was in chaos. All four of my sisters were running in and out of the front and back doors with two of my cousins who'd come over to play tennis with them.

Father had his attorney drop off the paperwork the night before, so we were all ready with the formalities as they related to the divorce, at least. My stomach turned when the doorbell rang. I heard Margaret scream that she'd answer it, and then I could see the rest of my sisters rush out of the house into the backyard.

Jessie and I looked at each other in silence, and she made the sign of the cross over her heart. My father's voice carried up through the front stairwell.

"Welcome," we heard him say. "How was your trip?"

Gabriel's answer was muffled, and the sound of his voice sent chills down my spine. I strained to hear what he was saying and prayed to find a shred comfort in it, but it only unnerved me.

"Come," Jessie said and waved me toward her. "It's time. Let's get you down there and make this quick."

"He's an hour early," I protested.

"Just come."

I shook my head. "No. I'm not even dressed. The baby isn't ready." I handed Ann Marie to Jessie, along with the blue dress. She was still in her pajamas. "Dad will talk with him and have him sign some papers. He can wait."

"Shall I give her her breakfast?"

I shook my head. "I'll feed her as soon as I get out of the shower."

She scowled at me. "She's going to be fussy if she doesn't eat soon."

"Please just put her back in her crib. Tell him I'm in the shower and to wait in the living room and that we'll come down when I'm dressed."

I couldn't quite tell if Jessie disagreed with me or not, but she did what I asked, and I got in the shower. Maybe I should've run down to greet him at first, but he was early, and I chose to take my time because I needed my wits about me. Standing in the tub, I let the water hit my face and shoulders as the tiny room filled with steam. Five minutes later, I turned the spigot off and reached for a towel. As I was drying off, I heard Jessie yelling my name.

It all happened so fast, there was no time to blink before she was standing in front of me, hysterical.

"I knew he had a funny look on his face." She was wringing her hands, pacing in and out of the bathroom doorway.

"What are you talking about?" I took a step forward.

"Mr. Clarke got a phone call, and your mother refused to speak with Gabriel, who would not follow me into the living room. You know I was as polite as I would be with anyone, of course, and yet he insisted on waiting in the foyer . . . ," she rambled on.

"Where is he now?" I stopped her.

She pointed a finger behind her. "He had a funny look on his face!"

"Jessie, where is he?"

"He just walked out the front door with the baby."

"What?" I ran to the hallway and peered over the banister. "Gabriel!" I called out for him. "Mom?" I shouted.

In my room, Jessie was trying to get my attention, speaking a mile a minute.

The windows in my bedroom didn't overlook the driveway, and I was standing wrapped in my towel, dripping water on the carpet. "Can you please go and see that he brings her back inside immediately?" I asked emphatically. "Ann Marie is not even dressed, and it's cool outside."

Jessie didn't budge. "He's gone. He just took her out of the crib, put her in the car, and left."

Chapter Twenty-Four

ANN MARIE

Chicago, 2008

Mom is diagnosed with a malignant glioma. We got the results about three days ago, and today we're back at the hospital, waiting on Dr. Elena Crane, who will see Mom through the treatment process. Dr. Marcus and I have exchanged a few e-mails, and he said he'd stop in and see us if he was around. My mother has our china pattern picked out already.

"I'm sure the handsome doctor wants a still-married mom of three boys who now lives with her ailing mother." I wink.

Mom puts her hands in the prayer position, and we both laugh.

We're escorted to a patient room, where we wait for another twenty minutes, flipping through old copies of *Redbook*.

"I will never understand why doctors can't be on time," I say as the door opens.

"Hi, ladies. Good to see you both," Dr. Crane says. "How have you been feeling?" she asks my mom.

"I've been better."

The doctor smiles. "Of course. Well, we know that the tumor is inoperable, but we're going to do our best to treat it through targeted radiation and chemotherapy."

"Treat it?" I ask. "Like, make it go away?"

"More like tame it," she says, and we both look at my mother to see if she has anything to say.

"I don't want to be throwing up all day."

"In the thirty-two years I've practiced, I've never seen this particular treatment make a patient sick or nauseated, but it will make you very tired."

As we're walking out of the office, we find Dr. Marcus in the hall. "Hi, Doctor," I say with a wave.

"Please call me Scott." He has a stack of folders in his hand and a granola bar in the other. "I was just going to stop in and see you both. How did everything go?"

I look at my mom, and she excuses herself to go to the ladies' room.

We watch her turn the corner. "Thank you for stopping by, and for e-mailing me. I really appreciate it." I pause. "It's a lonely and scary process, as I'm sure you know."

"I do, and please don't hesitate to reach out or think you're pestering me whatsoever."

"OK." I nod. "Are you this attentive with all your non-patients?"

He laughs a little. "Well . . ."

"I'm sorry. That came out all wrong. I'm sure you are."

"I'm not." He looks at me.

I clear my throat and resist the urge to fall to my knees and break down in front of him. No one has any idea how frightened I am about possibly losing my mother. As a mother myself, I have no opportunity to crawl into a hole and stay there.

We stare at each other for a moment, and I'm comforted by the peace and understanding in his eyes. I can sense that he knows my heart is breaking. "I have three little boys," I blurt.

"I have a daughter." He smiles. "Looks like we have some things in common."

I nod and smile back. "I promise I'll keep in touch on how we're all doing."

"And I promise to reach out if I don't hear from you."

"Thank you."

Scott puts the granola bar in his front pocket and opens his arms. "You're a hugger, right?"

~

Once she began treatment, my mom never went home to Connecticut. I had her cousin Laura clean out her condo and ship her things to my house, which included her Rottweiler, Snoopy. Named for being meddlesome, not after the *Peanuts* character.

"The boys will be over the moon to have a dog, but a lot of people are scared of this breed. I'd better calm Jen Engel about it before she harps to the other neighbors."

"He's very sweet," Mom says.

"You know how people are."

"Just don't yell *spider*," she warns.

"Excuse me?"

"The only time he's been aggressive was once when I was in my kitchen and screamed because I saw an enormous black spider." She looks at me sheepishly.

I throw my arms up. "Great. Like I'm going to be able to make sure the boys never yell *spider* in the house. Do you have any idea how many bugs come through here each summer? It's like Grand Central for spiders and mosquitoes and silverfish."

She rolls her eyes at me. "Just don't yell about it."

There was no way Mom could manage all alone, and I didn't want to take any chances. She's with the boys and me now, where she belongs. She's happy, and the boys are happy to have a dog. According to Monica, my therapist, Mom and I desperately need each other, and I couldn't agree more.

The already chaotic world I'm living in has officially stopped moving forward and begun spinning in circles. Some mornings I sit on the edge of my bed, feeling like there's no floor beneath me. Like stepping off will send me plummeting into a black hole.

Adding to my baggage carousel is Todd, although I had some good news on a conference call with my attorneys the next morning. Todd's girlfriend is almost six months pregnant by now, and the great thing about that is she has zero interest in his current children.

"It's an unexpected blessing, if you can call it that," Stewart says. "If Todd's with her now and she doesn't want the boys living with them, then we'll certainly be filing for sole custody."

"Something Todd originally said he'd never allow," I add.

Amanda chimes in, "We also won a judgment against him that blocked him from laying any claim to the money in your trust or the boys'. I know you're happy to hear that."

"I am. Thank you," I say. But he's still acting like a prick and delaying signing documents and claiming he doesn't have any money, while simultaneously posting pictures of himself with his girlfriend at a spa in Scottsdale. "Were you able to do anything with the photos I sent?"

"Yes," Amanda says. "We were able to subpoena his credit card receipts. And since you're not divorced, he can't use marital funds to indulge himself or anyone else."

"You mean he can't say he has no money for child support and then treat his baby mama to a prenatal massage?"

I hear her chuckle on the line.

"All right," Stewart says. "Bottom line is that he has no reason not to sign the divorce papers, other than to be difficult at this point. So, I'll be more than happy to destroy him in court, if that's his wish. In fact, I'm going to set a trial date. That should be enough to scare him into acquiescing."

At least that will be settled soon.

I also make the grave mistake of Googling *glioblastoma* and haven't been able to sleep through the night ever since. Getting my bearings on a daily basis has become a challenge, and sadly, any social life I had has slipped through the cracks. I've been pushing people away, blaming my mother's illness for my indifference and impatience with everything. Monica says I'm scared to commit and have my heart broken again. She also thinks I have Daddy issues, only not the good kind.

"I'm paying you one hundred and ten dollars an hour to tell me what I could be reading in *Glamour* magazine," I say to her during one of our sessions.

She makes a face but maintains an air of composure. Monica Farlander is around my mother's age, in her late fifties. She has twin boys who are grown and married and live out of state. She has wiry gray hair and wears glasses with red fames. I'm guessing it's a look she's had since her thirties and that if she ever took off those red frames, she'd be unrecognizable. I'm very comfortable talking with her, but she rarely tells me what I want to hear. Maybe that's what a therapist is supposed to do. Make you look at things another way, especially yourself. I had been managing just fine without a therapist until my husband cheated on me. How is it that a well-adjusted, educated woman like myself with friends and children and organizational charts can be so easily uprooted? Todd is the one who tossed gasoline on our lives and lit a match, not me. So why am I the one sitting here with a therapist, trying to figure out what the hell happened? This wasn't my fault! I'd been doing everything right. If Monica can look me in the eyes and admit some men live solely for their penises and there's nothing I can do to change that, I'll pay triple her hourly fee.

I sigh. "I wish I knew why he did this to me."

She crosses her legs and arms. "Tell me why you married him."

My eyes wander to the corner of the room. "It's something I've been asking myself."

"I mean it. We both know what he's turned into, but you wouldn't have married the man he is now. What was it about him?"

"He was handsome and fun and charming. Oh, was he charming." I take a breath. "And I think he was impressed with my family. He always wanted to visit Greenwich and hang out with my mom. She loved him, too, my mother. He wasn't always the scumbag he is now, but he's always had a healthy ego and a sense of entitlement."

"How did you two meet?"

"Friend of a friend in college," I say. "I think he loved me once. At least, that's what I'd like to believe. When we moved into our first apartment together in Chicago, he used to cook dinner for me and pack my lunches for work. I had a job as a marketing assistant at an advertising agency, and he'd put little *Have a Great Day* notes in with my food. One time when I was sick with the flu, he took two 'L' trains to get to Manny's Deli in the South Loop because he insisted they had the best chicken noodle soup in the city." I smile for a second at the memory. "He certainly swept me off my feet and then just left me to fall on my ass."

"Do you wonder if your father may have been the same way?"

"I don't know much about him."

"Would you like to?"

I take a moment to answer. "Maybe."

"Maybe one of our goals can be for you to reach out to him," she suggests.

Her words halt the conversation, and I can feel myself getting uncomfortable. I reach inside my bag for a bottle of water and take a sip. Then I reach inside for something else and pull out my mom's journal.

"Funny you should bring him up," I say and place Mom's journal on the coffee table between us.

"What's that?"

"It's my mom's journal, one of many. She kept them for most of her life when she was a young woman and then a young bride and then a young single mother. I'm not quite sure yet when and if she's ever stopped writing in them."

"And she's given them to you?"

"She has." I pause. "At first, I wasn't sure why she was sending them, but now I worry she wants me to have them because she's . . . sick."

Monica stares at me for a moment. "Would you care to share with me what's inside?"

"I really would, although I've brought it here without her knowledge."

"If you're uncomfortable, then it's not necessary," she says.

"Something tells me Mom would agree it's necessary."

I lift the book off the table and open to the entry on Christmas Day, 1970.

Our first Christmas in Beirut. What a glorious morning I had. I'm feeling healthy and happy. I went to a lovely bakery this morning and bought some dessert to bring to Brigitte, but Gabriel has just told me that our plans have changed and that we're going to see some wealthy friend of his instead. I hated to cancel on Brigitte, but she didn't seem put out in the least. I guess I'm excited for a new holiday experience. It will be challenging for me to miss out on traditions and foods that I look forward to once a year, but I will just have to begin to build new traditions for my new family. Tonight should be fun and exciting, and I hope to make some new friends.

I close the journal before finishing the entry.

"Why are you crying?" Monica asks.

"Because she's young and hopeful and in love"—I dab my eyes—"and I don't know this person."

Monica nods and lets me catch my breath for a moment. "I want you to strongly consider reaching out to your father," she continues. "How do you feel about that?"

I nod my head. "I'm nervous about it."

She doesn't respond.

"I have nothing to say. It's been too long."

"Have you been writing in your gratitude notebook?" she asks.

"Yes."

"That's good."

"Until I threw it in the trash?"

She gives a little shrug. "There are no rules to break. It's whatever you are comfortable with."

"I hate when you're so accommodating. You should be mad that I didn't take your sage advice."

She lets out a small laugh. "Are you more comfortable when people are angry with you?"

I lean back into the couch. "I threw it away because I don't see the point of it, not because I wanted you to be mad at me. And no, I'm not remotely comfortable with anger. Just the opposite." I pause. "Also, I was focusing on the wrong things."

"Like what?"

"Like anger and revenge, I guess, when I really needed to focus on the boys and now my mom, and keeping the peace for everyone."

She smiles proudly. "So, maybe the pink notebook I gave you did precisely what it was supposed to do."

"Oh, and Todd knocked up his latest bitch. And I hate pink."

～

Mom is sitting at my kitchen table when I get home. She has her reading glasses on and is squinting at a laptop screen. Her pearls are draped around her neck, and she's dressed for the day with her hair washed and styled, but she looks tired. Behind her are two baskets of dirty laundry, and the dishes from breakfast are still where the boys left them on the island. I give her a kiss on the head and quickly clean up the mess.

It's been four weeks since the cancer cloud landed above our house, and Mom has just completed her second week of radiation and chemotherapy. The radiation and chemotherapy seem to have had an immediate effect on her in that she's dreadfully tired and appears disoriented throughout the day. But so far, the treatments have been gentle on her stomach, as Dr. Crane said they would be, and she continues to e-mail me with ways to make her more comfortable. Mom's a little angry about having to take so many pills, but at least her appetite is on fire, and she has no nausea.

The weather is starting to turn here in the Midwest, and soon she'll be confined to the house because of the snow and cold air. Her spirits seem to be good, but expressing any type of thought has become almost impossible and incredibly frustrating. It's agonizing to watch her try to communicate with the kids or the neighbors, especially when they don't quite understand.

"I have an idea," I say to her. "Let's get you one of those 'vow of silence' badges so when we're out and about, no one will say anything to you."

She laughs and nods with enthusiasm.

"It'll be fun to watch people's expressions when they look at you strangely."

She rolls her eyes.

Every day there are so many e-mails coming in from her friends and family back in Connecticut that I can't keep up. Everyone is eager to speak with her, but she can't stand talking on the telephone because it's too stressful. Which is ironic because while she refuses to talk on the phone, she still manages to sneak in late-night orders to QVC, as evidenced by the constant stream of jewelry showing up at my front door.

She looks at me, straining to say something. "I like you in yellow."

"Thanks, Mom. You look pretty, too. I like your earrings." I tap my ear. "Can I get you something to eat?"

She shakes her head and points to a banana peel in front of her.

"OK, good. You need to eat, even if you're not hungry." I walk over to her to see what she's doing on the computer. "Is that your e-mail?"

She nods.

"Who's Yasmine?" I ask. "Does this have anything to do with Beirut?"

Her face goes pale.

"I know I said I wouldn't read your journals without you, but I couldn't resist. I only read through the first few pages of one of them. It was Christmastime, and you were in Beirut. I hope you're not mad."

She shakes her head no, but seeing the slump of her shoulders and the dark circles under her eyes, I try to push my questions aside. "I'd really like to know more, but the last thing you need right now is anything that's going to upset you."

Mom turns slightly toward me. Her lips tighten, and her brow furrows as she struggles to communicate. She lifts a hand to steady herself and hold my attention. "It's time you know." Next, she grabs a journal that she had by her side and hands it to me.

She has a grocery coupon of mine holding the page.

I take the small book from her. It has a leather cover soft from years of wear. I open it. Mom gestures for me to read aloud.

> It's our one-year anniversary, and the tides have turned.
> I no longer feel loved and safe with him. I'm so ashamed
> to be writing this with our beautiful baby daughter next
> to me. I could just scream! Why is this happening? I'm
> grateful for the opportunity to write about things because

I have no one else I can confide in. Brigitte was kind and had some good advice, but I don't think I can stay in this marriage. And there's absolutely no talking to Gabriel! His tolerance for me has disappeared. The only thing that makes him happy is Ann Marie. He dotes on her like he used to dote on me. And that is not to sound jealous by any means, but he can't expect me to stay in this relationship if he continues to lie to me and ignore me and stop me from communicating with my family.

It was a stark contrast to the little I'd read about her first Christmas as a married woman. "Why didn't you ever tell me that you lived in Beirut? That I was born there?"

She grabs a notepad and writes. *Your father destroyed your birth certificate, and I wanted to erase that period from our lives. I should have told you.*

She starts to cough, and I stand to get her some water. I have a million questions, but I can't press her in her condition. She will tell me everything when she's better. But for now, we are two women who love each other and have a lot more in common than I thought.

Chapter Twenty-Five

CATHERINE

Greenwich, 1972

The air rushed out of my lungs, and despite the pandemonium in my childhood home, time stood still for me.

Colleen and Margaret were standing nearby, catching their breath. "We ran all up and down the streets and then to the gate, but there was no sign of him," I heard Colleen say quietly to my father. "The guard said he saw him drive out." Belle Haven required that guests check in, but the exit gate opened for anyone to leave.

Talcum powder still tickled my nostrils, and the tiny blue dress with embroidered whales was balled up in my lap. It was a gift from Laura, and I'd chosen it especially for today because blue was Gabriel's favorite color. The glass of ice water Jessie had brought to me after I'd collapsed was still beside the couch, untouched and sweating all over Mother's antique end table. I remember thinking she'd be angry I hadn't used a coaster. Father was on the phone with Serine. I heard him say he'd phoned the police.

If there was a single word to describe myself in that moment, it would've been *denial*. My mind went to better times. Our honeymoon in Rome where we ate gelato for breakfast and talked about making love on the Spanish Steps at midnight. Holding hands and traipsing through the ruins of the Coliseum while counting stray cats and listening to Gabriel serenade me with Frank Sinatra tunes. Anything to comfort myself. To reassure me that Ann Marie was with a kind, loving man who would never harm her. A father who was gentle and devoted and who just wanted some time alone with his daughter before heading back to Beirut.

My body rocked as Jessie stroked my back. "It's fine," I whispered. "He'll bring her back. He was probably overwhelmed with the number of people here this morning. I told Mother he wouldn't feel comfortable with all these eyes on him." Her hand stopped at the nape of my neck.

"It's going to be fine," Jessie mumbled.

My sisters were all outside. Once Mother realized they were doing nothing but staring at me and hurling insults at Gabriel and his family, she forbade them from entering the house. My aunt Hazel arrived and said something to me, but I don't recall what it was. Something about involving her brother's friend Joe Lombardi, who was a police officer.

My dad approached me, and Jessie walked off. "Did you hear her?" I looked up at him.

"Hazel's sent Officer Lombardi over to Gabriel's sister's house."

"I thought she said Gabriel wasn't at her house," I said.

"We want to be sure."

"Do you think Serine is lying?"

"We just want to talk to her. She obviously must know where he is."

I placed the dress on the couch next to me and tightened the ties on my robe. I hadn't had a chance to get dressed or dry my hair. I hadn't had a chance to say hello to him, something I'd rehearsed in my head for days. I hadn't had a chance to talk with him, to change my baby's diaper, to feed her . . .

"Oh my God!" I blurted. It had been almost an hour of dead calm, and then my whole body crumbled and convulsed again. I could barely catch my breath. Jessie rushed back to my side, and I met her eyes. We shared the same look of pain and loss and fear. "Her breakfast, Jess, she never even had her breakfast. She must be starving." I sobbed. "He won't know that. He won't know what to feed her. He won't know why she's crying. All of her food is here, and she's not even out of her pajamas."

Jessie knelt, shushing me in a gentle embrace. My words came fast and furious still, everything on my mind hurling out of my mouth with great fervor until I was too exhausted to say another word. My eyes were swollen and glossy. I forced myself to remember the good times again. Any memory I could muster that would reassure me he'd never hurt her. He loved her as much as I did. He would bring her back to me. He would never hurt her.

I lost count of the number of people who showed up at the house that morning. My aunt and uncle, their friends on the police force, my cousins, our next-door neighbors, and eventually Serine. The sight of her was the most troubling because we all assumed Gabriel had been at her house, but he never went back there.

She approached me with trepidation. "We will find him."

I nodded. "Of course. I'm sure he felt a bit surprised to see so many people here this morning. I tried to tell my mother that he'd want some time alone with her, but he arrived so early that we didn't have time to properly receive him," I babbled. "And, oh! Ann Marie hasn't eaten today. Please, when you see him . . ." I clutched her hand. "Please, Serine, she hasn't had her breakfast today. She must be so fussy and hungry by now. I can't even think what he would have for her to eat."

She sniffed. "I will tell him." Serine nodded, one mother to another.

I mustered a smile and then locked eyes with Jessie, who was standing behind Serine, scowling. "Can you give Serine a jar of peaches and some oatmeal to take back with her? Maybe the mashed carrots, too, since it's almost lunchtime."

Jessie didn't budge.

"Please?" I begged. "She hasn't eaten." I raised my voice, and the tone startled everyone. All eyes were on me when I finally stood. My legs were wobbly, but I barreled past the crowd, holding my robe, and went to fetch some jarred food for Ann Marie. Jessie quickly came up behind me with a brown paper bag and Ann Marie's favorite pink rubber spoon. She did not say a word, just took the jars from the cupboard in front of me and put them in the sack. When I looked down, the sundress was in my left hand.

I sat in the kitchen where Mom had been a couple of hours earlier, enjoying her coffee and morning paper. The dress was on the table in front of me. I willed myself to think only positive thoughts. I closed my eyes and thought of the day she was born, almost exactly one year to the day, evoking memories of Gabriel and me in the hospital. I was so scared of childbirth and wished my mother had been with me in Beirut. She said she would try and make it, but they had a wedding on the Cape, mother's college roommate's daughter, and I understood. She never approved of me living in Lebanon, anyway, let alone having my child there. But Gabriel had been there, and he was terrific at that moment. I'd never seen anyone as happy as he was when the nurse handed him his baby girl. That is how he would always look at her. He would never harm her, and he would bring her back to me. I knew it, and I told myself that over and over as the hours passed.

But I was wrong.

Chapter Twenty-Six

CATHERINE

Greenwich, 1972

My father was never without a drink and a cigarette that day. Lunch passed without any mention. My sisters were in and out of the pantry, whining softly to Jessie about their hunger pangs when she wasn't by my side. Mother eventually sent them all to the club. I remember looking down at my watch, praying the hands would stop and the day would not end until Ann Marie was back in my arms.

"How cruel of him to behave in this way," I heard my mother say to her sister. My aunt Hazel followed with some nasty words about Gabriel.

"I'm going to go looking for them." I stood. It was nearly 6:00 p.m., and I'd had enough of my parents' insistence that I stay at the house and remain calm.

Mother walked toward Jessie and me. "The Cunninghams will be here in an hour for dinner," she said to Jessie.

Jessie's mouth dropped open. "Are we still entertaining tonight, ma'am?" Jessie asked.

Mother looked incredulous. "Well, of course, we are. I've not called and canceled. I have no doubt the baby will be home soon."

Looking back, the absurdity of hosting a dinner party in the midst of what was going on in my home and my head and my heart was insane, and yet exemplified my mother to a tee. But at the time, I didn't question it. Mother would have considered it rude to disinvite the Cunninghams simply on account of an abduction. How embarrassing to explain. Why should the neighbors be inconvenienced and miss out on a pitcher of dry martinis because Mrs. Ann Marie Clarke's only granddaughter and namesake had gone missing?

I flew through the living room, up the back stairs, and into my room, where I changed into jeans and a T-shirt. Throwing my hair into a ponytail, I grabbed the car keys off my nightstand and ran back down and out the front door, ignoring my mother's insistent hollering from behind.

When I arrived at Serine's house, it, too, was filled with people who all fell silent when I walked into the kitchen. Her husband, Michael, greeted me with a hug.

"Have you heard from him?" I asked.

Michael shook his head.

"I know he has another local friend. Someone who he met here one summer and whose parents know my parents from the club," I said.

"Tom Sheppard?"

"Shep, yes! I think he lives on Doubling Street. Maybe he's reached out to him?"

Serine came toward me, took my hand, and led me out the back door to her terrace. She was a few years older than Gabriel, so almost fifteen years my senior. Her eight-year-old son, Gerard, followed us.

"Please come sit. Get some fresh air. Can I get you something to eat?"

I said nothing.

"Gerard," she said to him, "please fetch a glass of lemonade and a sandwich for Catherine."

Gerard ran off, and we sat facing each other on opposite lawn chairs.

"He hasn't contacted you at all since he was at my house this morning?" I asked.

She shook her head.

"I thought he was staying here."

She was wringing her hands. "He arrived late last night and stayed here with us, yes. I'm expecting him to spend at least another night or two." She forced a pitiful smile. "I'm certain he will be back tonight. He must have let the day get away from him. He was so excited to see her."

I sat forward. "What did he say about her? Did he say anything about taking her somewhere or wanting to be alone with her? Please, Serine, he must have said something. Did he mention me at all? Do you have a phone number for his friend Tom?"

She furrowed her brow and slightly shook her head. "We will try and get his number." The look in her eyes was worrisome.

I continued with my questions. "Do you know that he didn't even say hello to me? He was early, and I was in the shower. He just walked into her room, took her from her crib, and left. He didn't even change her, Serine. She's still in her pajamas." I searched her eyes. "He must've said something to you!"

Serine remained calm, her voice almost a whisper. "We spoke of his flight and his fatigue. Yes, of course he mentioned he was very excited to see the baby, but he did not give me any details of his plans. I had no idea he'd even gone over to your house today until your mother called me this morning, asking if he was here."

"But what did he say to you when he woke up this morning? When he walked out of the house?" I pleaded. "He wouldn't just leave without discussing his plans." All of this mysterious behavior was inconceivable.

"He said nothing to me. I was just getting Gerard up and dressed, and he and Michael had coffee. Michael said he made no mention of heading to your house when he left. Just that he had to run some errands."

"Did he borrow your car?"

Her lip trembled as she spoke. "Oh, Catherine. I just feel terrible for this scare he has given you and your family. This is the most selfish thing . . ."

"Serine, please." My breath came rapidly in little spurts. "Please focus and help me find Ann Marie. Whose car is he driving?"

"A rental car. He insisted that we not bother picking him up at Westchester so late in the evening. Officer Lombardi was asking us about the car, too, but it was dark when he pulled up, and all Michael and I could remember was that it was a dark color, maybe brown or black." She reached for my hand, but I moved it away. "He loves that little girl, and I don't know if he is trying to hurt you on purpose or what his intentions are. I'm sure you know he was very upset when you left and said you were never coming back, but that is no reason to put Ann Marie in the middle like this. I know he will not harm her. He will bring her back, and he will apologize. I know my brother."

But I knew him, too, and she was right. He was trying to hurt me like I'd hurt him. To prove to me once again exactly who was in control.

Serine began to cry.

"Shh, please don't cry. I know he loves her and would never put her in harm's way, but this is unacceptable." I reached for her hand. "You're probably right. He's probably trying to teach me a lesson, but using our daughter like this is cruel. Not only to me, but also to Ann Marie, and you, and my whole family. He has us all sick with worry."

Serine was about to speak when Michael yelled from the screen door. "CC, your mom is on the phone!"

I ran inside.

The receiver was dangling on the kitchen wall. "Mom?" I grabbed it and said.

"The police have found Tom Sheppard. He has some information, and I think you'd better come home. He's coming over to speak with us."

My eyes widened. "Yes, OK. I'm leaving now."

When I returned home, my parents, Aunt Hazel, three policemen, my four siblings, Jessie, and a man named Tom Sheppard were all in the family room. Among them was a very tall man I recognized immediately, and from the look on his face, he remembered me, too.

"I'm Officer Joe Lombardi." He extended his hand and was exactly as I remembered, with bright orange hair, towering above everyone else in the room.

"I'm CC." We shook hands and then he patted me on the shoulder, letting his palm rest there for an extra second or two.

"Do you have any news?" I asked.

He shook his head.

"I want to press charges," I said. "Have we done that yet?" I looked over at my father and then back at Joe. "We need to put a warrant out for his arrest."

"We can't quite arrest a man for spending time with his daughter, but we're doing everything we can to find them. We were able to get some information on the vehicle from Serine and Michael, and I have two guys driving around trying to locate it."

He had about as much hope in his eyes as I did.

Joe turned to Tom Sheppard and waved him over. "Tom, why don't you fill CC in on what you told me? About when Mr. Haddad arrived here in Greenwich."

My attention went to Tom. "Serine told me he arrived last night," I said.

Tom shook his head and glanced at Joe before speaking. Mother and Dad came closer to the three of us.

"What do you mean?" my father questioned him. "Serine said he arrived at her house late yesterday evening."

"He must've told her that," Tom began. "But he was at my house two days ago and then left last night to stay with Serine."

"She lied to us?" I asked.

"I don't think so, no. Gabriel lied to her, I believe."

"That's why he didn't want a ride from the airport," I said. "But why?"

Tom just shrugged. He was the least concerned of anyone in the room, and acting a little too inconvenienced for my taste.

"Did you know he was coming here today?" I pressed. "Did you have any idea that he planned to do this to us? To upset my family in this way? If he harms her, then you're also responsible!"

Officer Lombardi loosely wrapped his long arm around my shoulders and ushered me into the library as I broke down again. Jessie followed, and I sobbed into my palms, choking on my own breath. My sister Colleen came and closed the door.

The sun set around 8:45 p.m., right about the time the house phone rang. Most of the guests were still in the dining room, but I'd been sitting on the front porch steps since Tom and Officer Lombardi left.

I ran inside to answer it. "Hello?"

"CC?"

"Yes, this is she."

"It's Tom Sheppard. We met today at your home."

"Yes, yes, what's going on? Have you seen Gabriel?" I asked, clutching the receiver as if I could squeeze the information out of him.

"I'm so sorry about everything . . ." His voice was kinder than before.

I took a deep breath and interrupted him. "It's me who should apologize for yelling at you. It's not your fault. You couldn't have known he would pull something like this—"

"CC, listen to me." His words were rushed now. "I am so sorry, but he's gone."

"Gone where? Please tell me."

"He's gone back to Beirut."

A wave of relief came over me. My free hand felt for the armchair behind me, and I lowered myself onto the edge of the seat cushion. My sister Margaret had walked in when she'd heard the phone. I pressed the receiver to my ear and swore I could hear my heart beating through it.

My mouth opened, but the words were slow to come. "I see. So did he leave Ann Marie with you? Do you have her? Is she OK?"

"No, CC . . ."

"She must be with Serine, then. I'm on my way now. Please call her for me and ask that she stay put."

There was a moment of silence followed by five words that shattered my existence. "He's taken her with him."

Chapter Twenty-Seven

Ann Marie

Chicago, 2008

Christmas is a week away, and it's evident that my mother feels like she's dying. She's asked me to grab the boxes of journals from my garage and is insisting we go through them.

"You refused to discuss my father and my past for decades, and now I'm supposed to sit and reminisce? You realize the doctor hasn't started your countdown clock," I remind her and remain hopeful. So desperately hopeful.

She swallows. Her throat is always dry. "You're going to argue with your mother who has cancer?" The words come slowly.

I smile. "Please stop. I don't care about any of it. I love you and just want to focus on you. You can barely talk as it is. Let's not waste your breath on this right now," I say, yet I'm eager for more clarity. There is a part of me that feels I deserve to know everything, and part of me that is scared of the discovery. But after reading about their time as newlyweds, I've been able to find comfort in the fact that my parents were in love once. I hope my kids will one day feel the same.

I've been trying to keep things light and humorous as she would want her life to be, but the truth is that I simply want to do anything to help my mom. She's all I have besides my boys, and the thought of losing her has prohibited me from focusing on anything else. My attorneys got Todd's attorneys to agree to let me take the house off the market for four months while I concentrate on Mom, but soon it will have to be sold, and according to Todd, "Buyers aren't going to want to see a cancer patient on her deathbed in what could be their child's bedroom." Prince Charming has nothing on him.

She doesn't want anyone's pity; she's never been that person. She dresses every morning as she always has, which makes it that much more difficult. To look at her, she's not a sick woman, and she doesn't deserve any of this. She deserves to travel, to experience being a grandmother and watch me eventually grow up and find happiness. To see a man look at me with love in his eyes again. She deserves affection and hugs and tennis games and happy hours and many more years on this earth. I can't even fathom not being able to pick up the phone and hear her voice whenever I need to and just know that she's listening on the other end. No one will ever listen to me like she will. No one will ever love me like she does, and I can't bear the thought of that loss.

I try not to burden too many people with how I'm feeling, because it is a burden. People don't mean for it to be, but it's an uncomfortable topic. You can see the resistance in their faces and body language. Nobody has the perfect thing to say, and that's OK. I've learned in a very short time that those perfect words simply don't exist. I've taken to reading cancer blogs online and finding solace in similar experiences of strangers courageous enough to write about it. Misery loves company.

She waves to me to come to the couch where she's sitting in our family room. Snoopy is at her feet and never more than an arm's reach from her. He's very sweet, but we're still getting to know each other, Snoopy and me. Last week he ate three Baby Einstein DVDs and two pairs of Luke's shoes, targeting the weakest in the house. There are over-turned boxes of LEGO bricks—always so many—and Disney figurines all over the floor. On the table in front of her is a cardboard box filled with more journals and newspaper clippings, articles from her days as a writer for the *Greenwich Times*. Snoopy follows me with his eyes as I approach and scoot by him.

Mom taps the box.

"Are you sure?"

She rolls her eyes at me, and I think the minute she stops doing that, we're in real trouble.

"I'm feeling good today, and I want to tell you more things about your father and what happened when you were little. You deserve to know." She takes a breath. "It may help you understand what you're going through with Todd."

I kiss her cheek. "My father was a son of a bitch who left you when you were twenty-five and didn't pay child support. Grandma told me years ago in her bedroom with a pitcher of martinis on her dressing table."

She slaps my leg.

"I'm kidding. I know it will help me. Thank you for doing this."

"He was a son of a bitch, but he also loved me once, very much," she says. "This is important. If I leave this world before my time, I will regret not being here to answer these questions for you." She looks at me and then turns away. I notice the nervous way she rubs her hands together.

"I love you, and I'll do anything you want," I say.

"I would like you to call him and tell him I'm sick."

So many years have passed since the last time I spoke with my father that I've lost count. Fifteen? Eighteen? It was in high school. My history class was studying ancestry, and I was hit with a pang of persistence. I remember coming home—Mom and I lived in Greenwich at the time—and telling her that I wanted to speak to him. She'd laughed and brushed it off as she had over the years, but I was relentless—angry, even—at both my parents. How dare they have this history between them in which I was at the core, and not allow me to know about it? When I saw the conversation was upsetting her, I'd backed off for a day or two, but I didn't give up until she agreed to help me get ahold of him with the help of his sister, my aunt Serine. My parents never spoke to each other. Serine and a team of attorneys were their only source of communication.

"Hello?" His voice had been deep and gruff.

"Hi, it's Ann Marie," I'd said. The connection had been a little crackly. He had moved from Beirut to Rome, and Mom heard a rumor that he'd remarried. We didn't know if he had any other children at the time, but I learned later that he did.

"How are you?" he'd said after a pause.

"I'm good."

I remember he'd asked what grade I was in and where we were living, but Mom forbade me to tell him or disclose our phone number, even though Serine knew how to find us. And then he asked me a question that I didn't know how to process.

"Do you miss me?"

I'd had to think about it for a moment, which made me feel bad because I should've missed him, but how can you miss someone you don't know? "I'm not sure," I'd responded.

"I miss you very much. I mean that, Ann Marie. More than you will ever know." He took a breath. "Thank you for calling. I have to go now."

I'd had high hopes for that call. Even canceled an ice-skating lesson because I assumed I'd be on the phone for hours. "OK," I'd said and looked at my mom, who had been reading a magazine at our kitchen table, doing a horrible job at pretending she wasn't listening. We'd exchanged a look. "Well, I'll talk to you another time. Bye."

Mom had placed the magazine on the table and held her arms out for an embrace, but I'd walked right past her and slammed my bedroom door. That was the last time I'd talked to him.

I let out a sigh. "Why do you want him to know you're sick?"

She crosses her legs at her ankles and scratches Snoopy's head. "I just want him to know. I've been going through these books, and I would want to know if Gabriel were dying."

My heart hurts. "Please stop saying that."

She reaches for my hand. "Please stop denying it."

~

That night when Mom and the boys are in bed, I yearn to be with her at happier times again and grab the journal I had read to Monica and pick up where I left off.

> *December 25, 1970*
> *I was able to talk to Margaret this morning and made sure they were still doing the jelly-bean trail in my absence. I know how much Mother loves that tradition. We all do. No better way to find our Christmas stockings than at the end of a jelly-bean trail! I wish I could be there with them, chasing each other and kicking candy all over the floor for poor Jessie to clean up. I miss everyone terribly.*

I feel a little sad as I turn the page.

> *I'm exhausted. The party was a lovely affair, and they had all of my favorite foods, which was a great treat. My feet were sore from dancing, and Gabriel rubbed them in the car on the ride home. He looked so handsome in a sport coat and tie, and I had to wear a frumpy long blouse*

because I can't button my dress pants anymore. Time for some maternity clothes. Almost forgot! He bought me the most stunning emerald necklace. I nearly fell over backward when I opened it. It's a piece I will treasure forever, and so many people complimented me on it this evening.

Lastly, I just met the most awful woman on the planet named Yasmine.

I shut the book and smile, craving jelly beans.

Chapter Twenty-Eight

CATHERINE

Greenwich, 1972

In the two days that followed Ann Marie's abduction, I was never left alone, not for five minutes. After my initial breakdown, Mother and Jessie had someone scheduled to be by my side at all times and had my sisters sleeping on my bedroom floor at night. Sometimes in the middle of the night, I'd sneak out of bed and into Ann Marie's room. I'd take her crib mattress and curl up on it, and Jessie would have to tear me out of there in the morning. Every day there were lawyers and family friends and members of the club coming by the house. Everyone with a new connection, a new source for us to try, and all of whom seemed to move at a snail's pace.

But hope and headway were rare commodities. My husband had boarded a plane with our daughter and flown home, essentially to a country where my family's substantial influence had little bearing. Even my uncle Fitz, the senator from Connecticut who was being primed to run as a Democratic presidential nominee in the next few years, was struggling with how to handle the situation. There was little our family could not achieve within the United States, but Beirut was proving to be another story. The only saving grace was that my father had gotten

Gabriel to sign the divorce papers as soon as he'd walked in our house, but they did not hold the same weight overseas.

"As an American, Catherine has no rights or jurisdiction in Lebanon," I overheard as I walked into my father's office with my sister Patricia trailing behind me. The man who was speaking stood when he noticed me.

Father tapped a cigarette out in an ashtray on his desk. "This is Charley Stillwater, your uncle Fitz's right-hand man. Charley, this is my eldest daughter, CC."

The man nodded. "Pleasure to meet you. I'm sorry it's under these circumstances," he said politely and with a thick British accent.

It'd been days since I'd looked in the mirror, but his expression told me all I needed to know about my appearance. His lips curled inward with regret, and his eyes filled with pity.

I crossed my arms over my chest. There was no comfortable physical position for my body to maintain, sitting or standing. My limbs ached, my head was constantly pounding, my face and feet were swollen, my throat was sore, my breaths hurried. I was in a state of controlled, perpetual panic, and outbursts were not tolerated. "Nothing can be accomplished with chaos," Mother would say, and then I would repeat those words to myself as I attempted to fall asleep. A chore that would've been impossible without weed and pills.

"I didn't mean to disrupt," I said. "You were saying . . . about my rights?"

He glanced at my father, who spoke. "Your uncle Fitz and his staff are doing everything they can. I want you to know that." He took a breath and began to pace. "It's a little difficult, but we will fight this every step of the way."

Charley spoke. "We are just trying to line up the right people in Beirut to get ahold of Gabriel—and the baby—and first see that—"

"Her name is Ann Marie," I said.

"Yes, of course," he added.

"Don't interrupt the man!" my father snapped and choked on his Scotch. "Go on, Charley."

"Locating them and making certain that Ann Marie is safe is our first priority. Getting her back to you is our immediate second."

He was a nice-looking man. Young, maybe thirty years old, blond thinning hair kept very short, blue eyes, and a very smart linen suit worn with loafers and no socks. Just as my uncle Fitz did.

"I want to leave for Beirut as soon as possible," I declared. "Why am I even still here?" I looked at my father, but he didn't meet my gaze. "If he jumped on a plane with her, then I'll do the same." I looked to Charley for support.

"It isn't going to be that easy," he said.

"It was easy for Gabriel," I shouted, and Patricia led me to one of the leather chairs against the wall. "Dad, please. I know you can get us on a plane."

My father lit a cigarette and filled the air with smoke before starting. "We can assume that he's not going to allow you access to Ann Marie without a fight, and we are not going over there without all of our ammunition. I'm not going to have you put in harm's way with no rights, no citizenship, and no family. They will jail you for much less than trying to kidnap your own child."

I burst into tears. Everyone in the house was so used to my breaking down by then that there was little attempt to console me anymore. Charley and my father walked out, and Patricia went to fetch Jessie, who brought me a Coke and sat with me. Once I calmed down, she walked me upstairs to my room and encouraged me to shower. It was the last place I'd been when Ann Marie was taken.

"Go on now. I'll wait out here for you." She sat at my dressing table.

I walked over to give her a hug and glanced at the telegram from last week.

Please allow me to see Ann Marie and say a proper goodbye.

"How could he have done this to me? To our baby?" My heart grew heavy and my head light. "How?" I stumbled backward. "Does he hate me that much?"

Jessie shook her head. Everyone was out of words.

"I know he loves her, but this is about me," I continued. "This is about me." I pounded my chest with the palm of my hand. My thoughts were spinning, thinking of the telegram and trying to replay the scene in my head. Many people in my family assumed he'd seen his daughter and had a burst of great courage. A father under fire who'd rather die than allow a woman to control his destiny. A man sick at the thought of leaving his only child behind for who knew how long. But I knew better. I knew he'd planned the whole thing. He was way too polite. Much too understanding and cooperative. When had he ever asked my permission for anything? *A proper goodbye. It is all I ask.* I should have known.

I clawed at my skin in the shower. A bar of Ivory soap was no match for the amount of self-hatred I needed to rinse off me.

The next morning I walked down the back stairs and found my mother exactly where she always was when the sun came up. Sitting in her chair in full makeup, hair in rollers pulled up in a turban, cigarette resting in her bright yellow ashtray with the newspaper and a black coffee in front of her.

"Morning, darling. How did you sleep?"

I shrugged. "I didn't."

"Your father is waiting for you in his office."

The clock read 9:00 a.m. "He hasn't left for work yet?"

She shook her head and took a drag.

After pouring myself a glass of orange juice, I walked into my father's study and found him packing up his briefcase for the day.

"Jason is here," I said as I looked out the window that overlooked our driveway. His driver was leaning against the car, smoking.

"This came for you yesterday." He held out a piece of paper, and my heart skipped a beat. One glance at the telegram, and I knew who it was from.

"What does it say?" I froze.

He didn't answer.

"Is she all right?"

He waved the paper at me, and I snatched it from him.

Sorry you chose not to join us. We miss you. Please come home.

Chapter Twenty-Nine

CATHERINE

Greenwich, 1972

I ran into the kitchen. "I need to use the phone," I said to Colleen, who was sitting on the stool, leaning against the wall with the cord wrapped around her ankle.

"I'm on it," she mouthed.

I took my index finger and pressed down on the switch hook. "This is important."

Colleen screamed at me and then stormed out. Jessie walked in when she heard the commotion. "What's she fussing about?"

"Never mind her. I need you to do me a favor."

"Of course."

"I have to run up to my room, but I need to make a very important phone call, so please sit here for a minute and don't let anyone pick up the line. It's really important." I nearly squealed with excitement. "I can't believe I didn't think of this earlier. I've been in a complete fog."

"Think of what?" Jessie asked.

"Just wait here. Please."

I flew up the stairs two at a time and reached for the stack of journals I'd had during my year in Beirut. In the first one on the inside of the cover were some phone numbers I'd written down soon after we'd arrived. There were only three: Walid, the local butcher, and Brigitte. Jessie was waiting for me when I got back to the kitchen.

"What has you like this?" She waved her hand, alluding to my enthusiasm. "What are you up to?"

"Do you remember me telling you about my neighbor and friend over there, Brigitte?"

Jessie nodded. "You have her phone number?"

"Yes, of course I do! I just can't believe I didn't call her immediately."

Jessie got up off the stool, and I placed the receiver between my ear and shoulder and dialed the international number, fingers trembling. It would be dinnertime over there; she would have to be home. My breath caught in my throat when I heard the sound of her voice. I wanted to reach through the phone and embrace her. I could barely speak without crying.

"Brigitte, it's Catherine," I said, sniffing and smiling through my tears. My precious baby was feet away, within arm's reach of this woman. I would have done anything to be her in that moment.

There was silence on the other end. I wiped my nose and eyes. "Brigitte?"

I could hear her breathing.

"Brigitte, it's Catherine. Can you hear me?" Jessie gave me a concerned look as if it were a poor connection.

And then after a moment passed, she spoke. "I can hear you," she said, her tone faint and aloof.

"Oh, thank God. You are not going to believe what happened, what Gabriel has done," I started. If there was anyone on the globe who could truly understand and appreciate everything he'd put me through, it was her. "He has kidnapped Ann Marie. He came to my home and snatched her out of her crib and ran. Fled the country." I sniffed again. "Have you seen them? Please tell me she is all right and safe. Please tell me you've seen her?"

There was more silence. Jessie was pacing and adding to my anxiety. She kept giving me gestures and wanting to know what was going on.

But I knew exactly what had happened. Brigitte had turned on me.

I cupped the receiver and slid to the floor. "Please do not hang up on me. I know you're still there. You are a mother, Brigitte, and I thank God you don't know what I am going through. Please, Brigitte, please tell me she's all right."

"How could you do that to Gabriel . . . to all of us here who cared for you and loved you? You have some nerve calling me after the risks you put me through. You have not called me once since you left Beirut, and now I am your friend again?"

"You were always my friend." I began to shake. "If you hate me, I will have to live with that. I love you and the girls, but my husband has taken my baby."

"You took her first." Her words cut me like a blade, slicing through every section of my heart, piece by piece.

I cried and cried into the phone, and she stayed on the line. My breaths came in gasps. "Is she all right?" I managed to whisper. "Please tell me if she is safe."

"She is doing just fine," Brigitte said and hung up.

Chapter Thirty

Ann Marie

Chicago, 2008

I've read a few pages in Mom's journals about the first couple of months she spent living in Lebanon, and some about less favorable times. It's time I confront her for more details. She's been on a string of good days where her speech is concerned, and last night she was able to read a book to the boys.

"Is Nana going to be OK?" Ryan asks me as I'm scrambling eggs for everyone the next morning, and his words land like a punch to the gut.

"Oh, honey, of course she is," I answer without hesitation.

"Because she said she doesn't know how much longer she'll be around to read to us."

I close my eyes for a long pause, and then open them and resume scrambling. "She probably said that because she's losing her voice."

"I'm sorry that she is sick and losing her voice."

"Me too, sweetie."

"I'd be really sad if that happened to you."

I place the whisk down on the countertop next to the stove and open my arms. "Come here and give me a big hug." Ryan walks over and leans his body into mine. "Don't you worry about me, all right? I'm going to be just fine and healthy and love you forever and ever. I plan on being around for lots of years, telling you to brush your teeth and tie your shoes until I'm an old lady." I kiss the top of his head, and he smiles at me.

As I'm driving home from dropping the kids off at school, I see Todd's car in my driveway. I throw the car in park and race inside to find him with my mother in the family room. Snoopy is in the yard.

"Get out," I say.

"Hi to you, too, Ann Marie."

"Get out," I repeat, and my mother gives me a look as if I'm being overly dramatic.

Todd lifts his hands in defense. "Calm down, for fuck's sake. I actually knocked this time. Your mom let me in."

I look over at her, and she nods. "What are you doing here?" I ask him.

Todd lowers his hands and gestures to Mom. "I heard that your mom was in town and that she wasn't feeling well. I knew she was staying here, and I just wanted to stop in and say hello and wish her well."

I let out a massive laugh.

"I mean it," he says.

"You should've called me, and I could've saved you the trip. She has no interest in seeing you."

Mom takes the remote and shuts off the TV hanging above the fireplace. Then she stands and glares at me for being rude.

"Thank you, Todd," she says, holding her right hand to her neck. "That was nice of you to look in on me." Her voice is a scratchy whisper but intelligible.

I take a breath and relax my shoulders, but I'm still pissed.

"I hope you make a full recovery," he says and walks toward the door, so I follow him out. He stops and turns to face me on the driveway. "Before you say another thing, I'm very sorry to see her this way. Forget what's going on between us for a minute. I really am sorry. I hope you know that."

If I allow myself to be vulnerable, I will embrace him and have a breakdown right here in front of the house and beg him to not make me go through this alone. I want so badly to share this nightmare with someone who cares about Mom and me. I take a deep breath. "Thank you," I say as sincerely as I can muster. "I mean it. And I apologize for being so rude."

Once he's gone, my mom sits back down on the couch.

"Sorry about that," I say.

She waves her hand. "It's nothing, and you don't have to be impolite."

I roll my eyes. "I actually apologized to him. It was very nice of him to stop by. But now that he's gone, I would like to talk to you about what I've read, if you don't mind."

She leans back into the sectional and pats the cushion near her.

"Do you feel like talking?" I ask.

"I talked to that asshole. I can talk to you." We both have a good laugh.

"It's ironic that he was here when I got home because I was thinking a lot about Todd last night when I was reading about when you first moved to Beirut. It was kind of nice to read about the good times you shared with my father and how much you loved him. I can't help but think that I would've liked to know those things as I was growing up."

She nods. "I made some poor choices."

"Please don't feel bad; that's not my intention. And now that I'm going through a divorce of my own, I completely get how the hatred takes over even when I try to be the bigger, more rational person."

"It's not just that our marriage didn't survive," she says. "There is so much that happened. We divorced, yes, but that was nothing compared to the suffering I endured. There was so much pain where you were concerned. I was never sure I'd be able to speak to you about it." She begins to cough. "I forbade my family from talking about him for fear that you would find out and never forgive me."

"Find out what?"

Chapter Thirty-One

CATHERINE

January 1973

Charley Stillwater and I sat on the runway at Logan International Airport in Boston for an hour while they deiced the plane. We'd had two cigarettes each before the flight even took off. Roughly ten months after I'd lost my daughter, I was finally on my way to getting her back.

We landed in Beirut at midnight. Pain blossomed in my chest as I stepped out of the airport, remembering the only other time I'd arrived there. There were no words to describe how chillingly familiar the place felt. A car drove us to the InterContinental Phoenicia hotel, past Rue Clémenceau, where our . . . Gabriel's apartment was. I pleaded with Charley to stop there.

"We can't go like thieves in the night," he said. "I know you don't think I understand your urgency, but I do. And I can assure you that we'll make things worse for ourselves and your daughter if we don't follow the law to the letter."

"I still have a key. I know almost every family in that building. Please promise me we can be there at the crack of dawn." Finally just being in the same country as my daughter had brought me the first real sense of peace that I could recall. The lack of hope and optimism up until then had been debilitating. I'd lost twelve pounds off my already slim frame. Handfuls of hair that initially had fallen out had only just started growing back, forcing me to wear a short bob.

"You know that's not going to happen," Charley said. "We cannot step foot in that building uninvited. Would you want to risk being put in a Lebanese prison?"

I slumped back in the seat of the car and watched as we drove through my past life to the hotel overlooking the beach and the marina. A place I'd been countless times before, sometimes happy, sometimes miserable.

The next morning, I met Charley for breakfast in the lobby restaurant. "As you know, you won't be in the hotel except for one more night, and I'll be leaving early next week. In the meantime, Fitz has arranged for you to stay with a friend who is an influential businessman here with strong political ties. He'll be working closely with me and your father and uncle and another man in Fitz's office, a lawyer named Stewart Fishman, who is working on expediting things with a team of Lebanese attorneys. It will be his job to make sure you don't have to stay here longer than necessary. This host family will be a critical part of your success, if you are to have any."

I shot him a wounded look.

"I didn't mean it like that, CC. I'm sorry."

"It's fine. You've been amazing. Truly. Thank you for everything you've done. I just want to hold her and wake up from this nightmare." I'd aged a decade in months.

"I'm going to call for the car, and then we'll head over there," he said and signed the bill to the room.

We met at the front of the hotel and got in the back seat of a limousine. About fifteen minutes later, we pulled up in front of a familiar house with its wine-colored exterior and trio of archways.

My stomach turned, and I said nothing as I got out of the car, wrapped a scarf around my head, and followed Charley through the foyer to the back of the house, where we were greeted by a man who introduced himself as Wassef. He asked us to sit and wait for a moment and then he left the room.

I quickly removed my scarf. "These people are not going to help us," I said to Charley.

"Of course they are." He patted my knee. "Just relax. I know it's a lot to take in in twenty-four hours' time."

"Charley, listen to me. I've been to this house before. The owner's name is Danny, right?"

He nodded and stared at me, curious.

"They are friends with Gabriel. If this is the best we've got, I may as well get back on the plane." I had to fight back tears of defeat and frustration. God forbid my father and uncle had included me in any of their planning. I begged Father to let me work with them to help devise a strategy, but no one was interested in the opinion of a naive young woman who'd landed herself in a situation made up entirely of bad decisions.

"He knows your name and your family and your situation. They know everything about you. There's nothing to worry about."

My chest was warm. I removed my coat. "If that's the case, then Gabriel knows I'm here as well."

As I was whispering to Charley, Wassef walked back into the room with Danny Khalid. His charming wife, Yasmine, was two steps behind.

Charley stood, and so did I. "Danny, good to see you. I'm Charley Stillwater, an attorney for the Downing family." He turned to me. "And I've only just found out that you and Catherine here are already acquainted."

I tucked my short hair behind my ear and forced a smile. "Lovely to see you again."

"Cheesecake!" Danny yelled, throwing his arms in the air and then coming over to me for an embrace. He pulled away with his hands resting on my shoulders, arms straight. "We are here to help. I am sorry for what happened to your daughter. I will get you some New York cheesecake to make you feel at home."

"Thank you," I said quietly, trying to look anywhere but at the wretched woman behind him. She hadn't even said hello to Charley, who eventually stepped forward.

"Mrs. Khalid, I presume?" he said with a nod, sensing she wasn't going to shake his hand so he may as well not offer it.

"Yasmine, please," Danny insisted with a wave of his hand as he'd done at his Christmas party another lifetime ago.

Yasmine came closer to us but remained silent.

"Thank you for opening your home to CC. This is very generous of you."

She raised her brows. "I was unaware she would be staying with us until this morning. I might have suggested somewhere else that would be better for her."

"I'm sure that can be arranged if need be, right, Charley?" I couldn't help but respond quickly.

"No, actually—" Charley began.

"It's settled," Danny interrupted him. "Come." He ushered us to the dining room where there was coffee—both black and white—and tea. Wassef followed; Yasmine did not. He looked a little surprised to see me follow along. "Catherine, you can go with Yasmine while we discuss things in here."

I glanced at Charley. "I'd really like to sit in, if you wouldn't mind."

Danny grinned, his arms and hands animated. "Don't worry. Wait for us and relax."

Sitting in a room by myself in a home where I was unwelcome was the last thing I wanted to do. There wasn't one man involved who thought I had anything to add. The whole debacle made me think I'd have to devise a plan of my own. I wasn't prepared to wait another ten months.

"Can I get you anything?" asked a maid standing in the doorway.

"Just some water, please. Thank you." I walked through a pair of glass French doors onto a large outdoor terrace that overlooked the sea in the distance. I leaned over the edge and let out a long breath. When I turned to come inside, I saw Yasmine staring at me from the window with her arms crossed. She turned her back and walked away, so I followed her.

"I don't want to be here any more than you want me here," I said from behind her. "I know you have no intention of helping me, and I'll find somewhere else to stay."

She turned around and snickered. "You know nothing about my intentions."

"I know you weren't friendly to me the first time I was in your home, and I know you weren't friendly this time." I swallowed.

"You're a foolish young woman."

"I would respond with exactly what I think of you, but I was raised better than that."

Yasmine crossed her arms. "Ah, yes, you Americans are the epitome of class."

"All I know is you would never be treated poorly as a guest in my home." I shrugged. "Even someone as miserable as you." The sight of her made me sick to my stomach, so I walked back out on the terrace, where there was water and hot tea waiting for me.

"If I have to call my uncle myself, I will. I'm not staying there," I said to Charley in the car on the way back to the hotel. "She's a horrible person. She called me a fool to my face. Those are not the words of a woman who is going to help me get my daughter back. It's too much stress in an already bad situation."

Charley sighed. "Danny is a powerful man and a good friend to Fitz. Not only is he our number-one ally here, he really is the best man for the job. Let me talk to him."

"Please do. He must have someone else I can stay with."

"I'll try, but for the time being, you'll need to stay there. Just try and stay out of her way."

Chapter Thirty-Two

CATHERINE

Beirut, 1973

Desperation will cause people to take risks they would never take under normal circumstances, and that is exactly what happened after my first week in the Khalids' home. I grew tired of waiting, tired of avoiding Yasmine, tired of her condescending looks and comments, tired of being told to be patient and do the right thing when my child needed me.

When I had been in Greenwich, I would lie awake at night feeling helpless, wishing I had the power to do something.

Now that I was back in Beirut, I did. At 1:00 a.m., I dressed in dark clothing and walked out the front door. Ras Beirut was an upscale part of the city on the edge of the waterfront. The area consisted mostly of residential apartment buildings with a few impressive old homes like the Khalids', called *qasr's*, nestled in the middle of the city for those who could afford them. There was a tall gated fence around the perimeter, and I was relieved to find it unlocked. The streets were lit, and there was some activity, not as much as during the day but enough that I felt I could blend in without being too conspicuous. If I ran, I figured it would take me about thirty minutes to get back to Gabriel's apartment, but if I jumped in a cab or service car, it would be much quicker. At the last minute, I decided to take the walkway down by the water. It might cost me some extra time, but I thought it would be the safest and draw the least amount of attention.

Once I got to AUB, I cut through the campus and walked briskly up a few streets to Rue Clémenceau, where our building stood. I paused to catch my breath, but there was no taming my adrenaline. I reached in my front pocket to feel the keys, making sure they were real. From the street, there were no lights on in the apartment, but from the outside it looked the same as it had the last time I'd stood there a little over one year ago.

I was a woman with a goal but without a plan. Looking back, it was a perilous idea, but I was fueled by my despair and concern for my daughter's well-being. I really can't think of another mother who wouldn't have done the same thing.

Two men ambled behind me on the sidewalk, speaking in Arabic and smoking cigarettes. They passed by without a glance. I walked hastily to the front door and opened it with the first of my two keys. I paused to take a breath at the bottom of the stairwell. Whatever consequences came of it, I would have my daughter and be back en route to the Khalids' home to deal with them later.

I tiptoed up the stairs, praying that I wouldn't run into anyone. By the time I reached the top, I had to pause to suppress my fear and summon my courage. I took the second key out of my pocket, gently placed it in the lock, and turned. Nothing.

I slid it out and double-checked that I hadn't put the wrong one in and tried again. Nothing. My forehead was damp with perspiration. *He must have changed the locks,* I thought to myself. Back and forth I tried with a little more force, but it wouldn't open. As I was taking the key out a second time, the door opened.

A man I didn't recognize started screaming at me in Arabic. I took a step back and almost fell over. I raised my hands, trying to quiet him, which worked to some degree when he assumed I'd made a mistake.

Glancing behind him, I could see there was different furniture in the apartment. Gabriel hadn't changed the locks. He'd moved where I wouldn't be able to find them.

I apologized profusely in English and Arabic and raced out of the building before someone alerted the authorities.

There was no wind left in my sails by the time I got to the curb. It was the middle of the night, and I was back at square one. I walked back down toward the waterfront, where some fishermen were perched under streetlamps, the scent of their fresh catch wafting through the air as the occasional car whizzed by behind them. A few blocks up, I walked into the lobby of the InterContinental Phoenicia and ordered a cup of coffee, wishing I still had a room there and a chance to be alone.

After I'd finished, I trudged back to the Khalids' home with tears in my eyes and anguish in my heart. I didn't come down for breakfast the next morning.

"Miss?" One of the staff knocked on my door. "Would you like something to eat?"

"No, thank you."

"Mr. Khalid has asked that you come down and meet him in his study at eleven thirty."

"Thank you. I will be there."

Yasmine was seated in the room with him when I entered.

"Catherine! Please have a seat. I've arranged for the two of you to have lunch today," he said.

"What?" Yasmine scowled. "I have other plans."

"You will cancel them for today and have lunch with Catherine. She is a very important guest, and you will do as I say."

Neither she nor I was happy with the idea.

"I have a car coming at noon to take you both out of the house," he said and began to walk out. "Do not let me find out that either of you canceled on the lunch."

We rode in silence to a French bistro near the university campus. There was a large bar on one wall of the restaurant covered in gold leaf, and black crystal chandeliers hanging from the ceiling. We were seated out back in a covered porch that had Plexiglas walls, both of us with our arms and legs crossed until the wine came.

"This may be the only way I will get through the meal," she said as the waiter filled our glasses.

I refused to play an insulting game of tête-à-tête, choosing to sip in silence, but I was worried that our continued dislike for each other would upset Danny, and worse, get in the way of finding Ann Marie.

After my second glass, I had the courage to engage her in conversation and was willing to do whatever I needed to do to keep the peace if the Khalids' were my best shot. "It's nice of your husband to send us here today. I only want to find my daughter, as you know. I don't want to be trouble."

Yasmine was on her second glass as well. "We somehow got off on the wrong foot."

"Yes." I uncrossed my legs and sat at the edge of my chair. "And if it was something I did, then I apologize, although I have to be honest. I just thought you disliked me from the moment you met me. No matter what I could have done."

She tilted her glass up and drained the last drop. The waiter brought us another bottle.

Yasmine studied my face. "Did you know Gabriel was engaged to be married before he met you?"

My eyes went wide, and by the look on my face, she knew I did not. "It's true," she said. "To my sister."

My hand went to my forehead. "I had no idea."

The waiter draped a white linen napkin over his forearm and poured some more wine.

"Thank you," she said to him and took a sip. "Yes. It was about a year before he went to the States. He proposed to my sister, Rynne, and then broke it off over the phone when he was in America. A few months later, we found out that he had married someone else." She looked away and then back at me. "My Christmas party was the first time I had seen him since."

"I'm surprised you and Danny were so polite to either of us."

She took a deep breath. "It's a complicated web of relationships, but Danny is not a fan of Gabriel's, either."

I was glad to hear that.

"But he is a gracious host and insists I am the same."

"Gabriel never told me that he was engaged before. I'm very sorry about your sister." I lifted my glass and took a drink. "But she may have been better without him, if you ask me." I placed my glass back on the table. "I don't know if we were doomed from the start, but I try not to look at it that way. When we first moved away from Greenwich, Connecticut—where I grew up—to Chicago, he encouraged me to get a job and said that we would be there for a while. Then he moved me away after only a few months. I was newly pregnant and missing my family, and I trusted him to look after me here, but he was gone for many hours each day and left me with a driver who felt more like a spy. Then, as soon as I had Ann Marie, he forbade me from using the phone and speaking with my family." I paused and shook my head, remembering. "I caught him in so many lies, and I know he was cheating on me with a woman in the mountains. And then when he locked up my passport, I knew I had to save myself."

She made a tsk sound. "That's terrible. I believe that you didn't know about my sister. I would like to apologize for blaming you and taking it out on you. That was wrong of me."

"I'm sure you couldn't help yourself."

She smiled.

"Is that why you called me a fool? Because I didn't know what I was getting into?"

She shook her head, her expression softer. "I don't know why I said that. If I'm honest with you, I think you are the opposite. I think you are brave for coming here, and Danny and I both can't imagine how hard this must be for you."

No one knew what I was going through. Despite the people lined up to help, I felt truly alone when it came to fighting for my daughter, whom I feared wouldn't even remember me.

"I feel helpless, not brave. I'm scared that she won't want to come home. That she won't recognize me. That he's going to fight me to the bitter end, and that I'll never see her again." I dabbed under my eye with a napkin. "I can hardly sleep at night. Days and weeks and months have passed, and yes, I'm finally back here, and I know everyone is doing what they can, but sometimes it feels like it's no one's priority but mine. I imagine she has a cold or an ear infection. I'm sure she's already speaking and maybe walking. I will never hear her say *Mama* for the first time, if she's even said it at all. He's robbed me of so much more than my heart and my happiness. He's taken memories away from me."

Yasmine sighed. "It's so very grave what he's done." She took another sip of wine. "Danny and I have tried to have a child for many years. I have an older brother, and he is the only one on my side who has been blessed with children. I have two nieces and a nephew who I adore, and about two years ago, I got pregnant." She smiled at the thought. "I called my mother and father immediately, and we were all so happy. Danny cried, he was so overjoyed . . . but then three months later, I lost the baby." She shrugged. "No one knows why. The doctor insisted that it was nothing I had done and that miscarriages happen all too often, but to be glad I was able to at least get pregnant, and it would happen again for us." She paused. "It has not happened again. I do not pretend to know what it's like to lose a daughter in the way that you have, but I have lost a child, and I have felt helpless in that regard."

"I'm very sorry."

She shook her head. "I have many blessings of my own. I'm only thirty-two years old, and I won't give up trying for our baby."

"I will pray for you."

"And I will pray for you." She raised her glass. "To wine and women and new friends."

Yasmine and I decided to walk home that day instead of taking the car. We strolled arm in arm along the waterfront and up through the side streets of Ras Beirut, laughing and crying and thanking God and wine—the great equalizer—for finally bringing us together. I had a friend again, and I was going to need one.

Chapter Thirty-Three

ANN MARIE

Chicago, 2008

Just as my mom is at a place in her life where she's ready to reveal something, she loses her voice. The deterioration has been mind-blowingly rapid, like water flooding a broken dam.

She's now seated at my kitchen island after having a horrible coughing spell. I make her some herbal tea, and she's resting and checking her e-mails. She closes the laptop and mimes a square shape with her hands.

"You want me to get the box?"

She nods.

I sigh. "Mom, I really don't think that's a good idea. First, because you're in no condition to be reminiscing or explaining anything to me, and second, I think we have enough drama going on here. Maybe it should wait. I don't want you to get upset."

She shakes her head.

"Should I be scared?" I ask.

She places her hand on her heart and then makes the box shape again.

I retrieve the cardboard box filled with her journals, along with the one from my nightstand, and bring them all to the family room. She joins me in there and sits on the floor in front of the box and starts to rummage through them. Her face is anxious, like she's just sat down to take an exam she hasn't studied for, and her inner struggle is surfacing. Through her eyes, I can see that her brain is working so hard to fight the tumor on this one. She takes a few journals out of the box and flips through them, looking for something at the top of each page. She tosses a couple on the floor next to her. The whole scene is painful to watch. Her eyesight is suffering, and her brain isn't processing her thoughts into actions. I'm afraid to step in and upset her, so I sit and sweat for about fifteen minutes until she finds what she's looking for. When she turns to face me, her expression is filled with relief.

Mom gives me the journal and asks me to turn the pages by mimicking the act with her hand. I scoot closer to her and take a long breath. All I can think about is Stewart Fishman's expression the first time we met, and how shocked he was to discover who I was. He knew more about me than I did.

Slowly, I flip through the pages, trying not to focus on the words. Mom squints as I'm doing so and then stops my hand, pointing to the page header and tapping it repeatedly so I will read it aloud.

"February 2, 1972."

She grimaces and takes a moment to rub her temples. I know she'll get mad if I suggest putting this off, so I sit quietly as she grapples with her memory.

I start flipping again, and her breathing intensifies. It's exhausting what she's trying to accomplish, but I continue to do as she asks.

"March 21, 1972."

She waves her hand slowly, as if I'm getting close. "This one just says April."

She nods and points to a page, placing her whole palm on it this time.

"April 1972?"

She nods and closes her eyes for a second.

"Should I read this page?" I swallow the lump in my throat.

Mom looks at me and then gets up off the floor and sits on the couch. She pats the cushion next to her. We both sit, and I place the journal in my lap, reading aloud.

April 1972
I don't know how long it's been since Ann Marie was
taken.

I read the words over and then glance at the header again. I would've been a year old. "Ann Marie was taken," I repeat, and my mom looks at me and then at the book, willing me to continue.

I haven't been able to write for obvious reasons, but
Mother is encouraging me to do so. I cry every minute.
I can't eat because I keep thinking my baby is hungry. I
can't sleep because I think she's uncomfortable. And I can
hardly breathe because she's not with me. I don't want
to live without my daughter. Everyone says I need to be
strong, but I failed her when she needed me the most, and
now I may never see her again.

"Who took me from you?"

She taps the book.

I place the journal on the couch. "I can't do this." I stand and cross the room. My heart is racing. I can't believe what I just read. My hands go to my face, and I press my fingertips into my eyes, rubbing. When I look back at her, she's just sitting there with the same neutral expression and inability to explain anything.

"Why are you doing this?" I ask. I pace the room as she watches me. "Maybe I don't want to know what's in there," I say and stop moving.

"I just need you to get better." My eyes sting. "I'm not going to lose my husband and my mother in the same year."

She holds up her hand, and I wait. "Please," she says.

"Ann Marie was taken?" I throw my arms in the air, and her gaze goes to the floor. "Why are you doing this to me? I don't need any more anxiety right now." I shake my head.

"Please," she manages again.

My tears are flowing now, and I sit back down next to her. "No, you please. Please get better. I need you to fight for me."

She struggles to say a few quiet words. "I always have." Then she hands me the journal, and I relent.

> *Everyone believes Gabriel won't harm her except for me. I want to believe it, and I pray for her safety every day, but how can I trust him? He's trying to get back at me, and he's done it. He knows the one thing that would destroy me would be to separate me from my daughter. Please, God, keep her safe. I'm coming for her.*

"Gabriel? My father took me from you?"

She looks at me.

"Is this what Stewart was talking about?"

She nods.

"Oh, Mom. I'm so sorry." I place my hand on the page. "I can't even imagine what you went through. How long were we apart?"

She begins to cry as I rapidly turn the pages, scanning the dates at the top and the handwritten words beneath them until I can find something—anything—that mentions a reunion between us.

"Oh my God," I whisper to myself.

Chapter Thirty-Four

Ann Marie

Chicago, 2008

I stay awake until midnight so I can reach my father first thing in the morning in Rome, where he now lives. My stomach is in knots. It's a phone call that I've dreaded and anticipated for so many reasons, and now with what I know, I can barely dial the phone.

For years, I'd beg my mom to allow me to reach out to him, only to have her shoot down the idea. Eventually, it just became easier to appease her, and ultimately, my memory of him faded with time, along with the will to have him in my life. There were many times that I felt guilty about my part in the lack of a relationship. I felt like I should've done more, should've invited him to my wedding, should've sent him photos of his grandchildren, but he'd never reached out to me, either, and once I had kids of my own, it was more difficult for me to forgive his indifference.

But now that I was privy to the truth—or at least some of it—how could I not confront him? He might be the only person capable of providing me with any answers.

"Hello?" he answers quickly.

"It's Ann Marie," I say.

There is a pause. "How are you?"

"I'm OK, thanks. How are you and your family?" I ask. He remarried when I was in my twenties and has two children with his current wife. The few details I know about him read like a résumé.

"Good, good. I heard you are going through a divorce. I'm very worried about you."

I clear my throat. "Who told you?"

"Serine."

We both hang on the line for an awkward moment. There is so much to say, but I'm really only calling for one reason. Can I be selfish and ask the things I want to ask, even if they involve only him and me? I seem to have this opportunity only every other decade or so.

"I want to help you. I e-mailed your mother a few months ago when I first heard, but she did not get back to me."

"You did? She never mentioned that."

"Yes, yes, I did."

I rub my forehead and lean back on my headboard. "Thank you, but there's not much anyone can do except for the attorneys."

"Is this why you're calling?"

"No, actually, I'm calling about Mom."

"Is she all right?"

I take a second, as the words are always hard to get out. "She has brain cancer." I hear him draw a breath. "And she wanted you to know," I say.

"How long?"

"How long have we known?"

"How long does she have?"

I pull a pillow onto my lap. "We don't know for sure, but it's not looking good." My words catch in my throat.

"Please, Ann Marie, can I speak with her?"

"It's late here, after midnight, and she's asleep now, but she can't talk very well anyway. She has a tumor that is pressing on her brain. It's very hard for her to speak."

He is silent.

"It's so awful," I add. "She's going through treatment and trying to stay positive. We all are. I hope you don't mind me calling you, especially right before Christmas and—"

"I want to see her."

I sit up. "What?"

"I want to come and see her. I will book a flight today, and I want to be there for her. For both of you."

"Umm . . ."

"Please send me an e-mail with your address. I will fly into Chicago next week after the New Year and find my own way to your house. I will stay in a hotel. You don't need to bother."

"Maybe I should ask her . . . ," I start.

"I will call you tomorrow with my dates. Thank you for calling me, Ann Marie. I can't tell you how I would feel if something had happened to her and no one had informed me."

She said the same thing about him, I think to myself.

"Wait!" I say before he ends the call. "There's something else."

"What is it?"

I clear my throat. "She told me, well, I know what happened. When I was young. When I was a baby." I'm stammering. "That you abducted me."

I can hear him release a breath into the phone. "She must be worse than you are telling me."

My throat chokes up, and I begin to get teary eyed. "Why did you do that to her? And why has no one told me?" I sniff. "I deserve to know."

"Did she tell you that she took you first?"

"She didn't tell me anything because she can't speak!" I say in a loud whisper so as to not wake the house. My hands are shaking. "She's been asking me to read her journals, so I'm uncovering all these secrets with no one to explain them." I lift my head and reach for a tissue. "I e-mailed her cousin Laura, but I haven't heard back from her."

"Her family will only tell you one side. They will vilify me."

"They already have. I just never knew why."

Since I have no idea what he looks like today, my image of him as a young man is frozen in time from the few photographs I've seen. There was a small photo album in my grandparents' house, and I remember sitting with my grandmother, going through them when I was about nine years old.

"That is your father," was all she would say as we turned the sticky photo pages covered with a loose cellophane protector.

I can only imagine the questions I must've had but was too afraid to ask. My heart aches for that confused little nine-year-old girl.

"It was an incredibly painful time for everyone, and your mother and I both made selfish choices," he says, and I cringe at him insulting her in any manner. "That is all in the past now. I will come to see you, and you can ask me anything you'd like, in person, as it should be discussed. Not over the phone."

We hang up the phone, and I cry myself to sleep, trying to imagine why she would burden me with this now. Why, when my marriage is crumbling and my mother is sick, do I need to know these things now?

~

The next morning is Christmas Eve, and I find my mom and Snoopy in the kitchen. He raises a brow when I enter the room but doesn't do much else. His ears perk up when she tries to speak and actually gets the words to come out. "Morning," Mom says. I think Snoopy misses the sound of her voice, too. It's been a little more than a month since her diagnosis.

I take a seat at the breakfast table, where she's sitting. "Well, hey there. A good morning to you as well." I smile. "So, I have some news that I hope you're going to be OK with." I scan her face. "We have a visitor coming."

She can't quite form an expression, but I'm getting more and more accustomed to reading her eyes. "I called my father last night." I smile and give her two thumbs up.

She stares at me.

"He's coming next week, after the holiday, to see you in person."

She turns her head to the side, looking out the glass doors onto our snow-covered patio. Ryan and Jimmy come in, arguing about a deflated soccer ball, and Snoopy runs to them, wagging his short nub of a tail.

"Guys, please," I say. "I'm trying to talk to Nana."

"I'm starving," Jimmy informs me.

"There's no air in this ball," Ryan says. "Dad's the only one who knows how to use the air pump."

They both start to sit at the table, scraping the chair legs on the hardwood floor as they pull their seats out. Mom turns her head back to the commotion and smiles.

"Hi, Nana," Ryan says. Jimmy is busy petting the dog.

She lifts a hand to hold his attention. It's her only move to indicate she's going to try and say something. Ryan and I stare at her. "Tonight," she starts. "Who comes tonight?"

Ryan answers. "Santa," he says and gives me a great idea.

She nods and releases a breathy cough.

"Why don't you guys go in the family room and I'll bring some bowls of cereal in there?" I shoo them back out. Snoopy looks conflicted and almost follows the boys but returns to Mom's side instead. "And, by the way, I know how to use the air pump!" I shout after them.

"Back to my father. He didn't give me much of a choice," I add. "I hope you're not upset."

Mom shook her head. "I'm not."

She looks frail sitting next to me. Wearing a forest-green long-sleeve sweater and khaki pants with her hair in a chignon and her nails buffed and filed. There's a sad look in her eyes that I understand. She's dressed for the day but won't be going anywhere. I find it hard to say the right things around her.

I reach for her hand. "Is it what you were hoping for?" I wonder. "That he would come here?" My expression is incredulous.

She looks at me and shrugs.

"You're not sure if you were hoping to see him again?"

She inhales through her nose. "I would like that, yes."

I avert my eyes for a moment. "I told him what I know. Which is not much."

She raises a brow.

"He said if you're revealing things to me, then you really must be sick," I say and then stand and kiss her on the head, inhaling her perfume. "I have a surprise for you later tonight."

She lifts her hand, and I wait. "I hate surprises."

"Me too!" I can't help but laugh. "But you're going to like this one."

～

Thank God for Christmas Eve, the one night a year my sons go to bed without an argument. At 9:00 p.m., I knock on Mom's bedroom door. Snoopy is alert with his eyes fixated on me when I enter, and I see that she's fallen asleep with a book on her chest. "Hi, Snoop dog," I say with a giggle. He lays his head back down on the comforter since I lost the "no dogs on the bed" battle.

"Mom." I gently shake her shoulder. "Mom."

She opens her eyes.

"Do you think you can come downstairs with me?"

She gets a frightened look on her face.

"Everything is fine," I assure her. "I just want your help with something."

She sits up, and Snoopy jumps to the floor, ready for action. I help her with her robe and lead her into the living room, where I have the boys' stockings laid out on the coffee table along with three jumbo bags of jelly beans.

"We're going to make jelly-bean trails for them," I say, smiling and bouncing on my toes. Mom is staring at the table when I look over at her. "Oh, Mom, please don't cry." I run to her side, and we embrace.

"Thank you," she whispers.

Chapter Thirty-Five

CATHERINE

Beirut, 1973

"You've been granted visitation," Charley Stillwater said to me. It had been four months since I'd arrived back in Beirut. "As you know, we filed papers seeking divorce on the grounds of mental cruelty and asked for full custody of the child. The case is still pending here, even though he signed papers in Connecticut, but the courts are taking that into consideration, and we've been granted a temporary win. We've spoken with Gabriel's attorney, and he's being served with papers today. Gabriel is now legally bound to comply with our demands, and he must let you know Ann Marie's whereabouts within twenty-four hours. You have been granted visitation," he repeated.

I stood holding the phone in one hand and squeezing Yasmine's arm with the other, as both our ears rested on the handset. It wasn't exactly what I'd hoped for, but it was a small victory. She pulled away and clapped.

"What does that mean, exactly?" I ask him.

"That you'll be allowed to see her and spend time with her."

"How often?"

"We're still trying to determine that, but at least we'll know where she is and have some answers on her condition."

"That's great news, thank you. How will I get ahold of Gabriel?"

"I have a number here for you to call. Do you have something to write with?"

Yasmine pulled open the desk drawer and got a pen and paper.

"Yes, go ahead," I said.

"If you have any trouble, let me know. He's changed his phone number many times over the past few months, but his lawyer assured us this is current."

When I hung up the phone, I ran my hands through my hair. I was wearing a white cotton sundress with an eyelet pattern on the bodice and sandals that day.

"I'm going to call Gabriel now," I said.

Yasmine nodded. "You should. It's been a long-enough wait."

She and I both pressed our ears to the phone again and nearly fell off the couch when he answered. Yasmine pulled away and let me have my moment.

"It's me," I said. "I know you know I'm here, and I'm calling to see Ann Marie." My legs began to shake. I could've sworn I heard him laugh.

"You and your stupid attorneys," he said.

"Just tell me where I can find her."

"You will never find her," he said and hung up.

"Gabriel?" I shouted. "Gabriel?"

Yasmine grabbed the phone. "Hello? Gabriel?" she said, but he was gone.

I grabbed the phone back from her and redialed over and over again, but there was never another answer. The conversation happened so fast and then vanished like a dream.

She knelt in front of me. "Don't lose yourself." Yasmine placed her hands on my cheeks. "I will not let you collapse. He has a court order, and he will have to comply."

I looked into her eyes. "Please hand me the phone. I'm calling Charley back."

After telling him what occurred, he offered to get Ann Marie's location from the attorney but said it might take a day to reach him, given the time difference.

When I woke up the next morning, one of the maids handed me a note from Danny.

She's in the mountains. That's all we know.

I could barely get myself out of bed. With the note in my lap and my hands in my hair, I couldn't take another setback. I thought I was strong, but he was stronger. We may have had the law on our side, but what good did it do? I couldn't go storming into a police station and complain about my husband. I'd be laughed out onto the street and likely arrested. Gabriel had fought me every step of the way when I asked to visit his home in the mountains. He'd always refused to take me there. It was the perfect hiding place. "I'm so sorry," I whispered aloud, wishing my baby could hear me. Curled up, clutching the piece of paper, I repeated the sentiment in my head until I had an idea and a prayer.

I jolted upright, pulled open the drawer of my nightstand, and grabbed an old journal. Written on the inside flap was the number I was looking for. Once downstairs, I picked up the phone and dialed an old friend.

Chapter Thirty-Six

CATHERINE

Beirut, 1973

Yasmine and I stood outside in front of her house the next morning, waiting for him. He was twenty minutes late. When I'd called him the day before, there was something so gentle and familiar about his tone. Once again, I felt like there might be some hope. I couldn't help but think how differently his reception had been from Brigitte's, and I had no other choice but to trust him, if he would let me.

"Stop pacing," Yasmine said.

"I'm not pacing; I just want to get on the road already." Just then a car pulled up, a Volkswagen Beetle, and out came Walid. I rejoiced at the sight of him. He ran over and gave me a hug. "Miss Catherine! It is very good to be seeing you again."

"You have no idea how nice it is to see a friendly face. I've missed you."

He blushed. "I have missed you, too."

I took a deep breath. "This is Yasmine Khalid."

Walid bent forward. "A pleasure."

"Catherine has told me such wonderful things about you," she said. "Do you mind if I ask you a question?"

"No, Miss."

"Does Gabriel know you're here?"

I'd asked Walid about Gabriel when we'd spoken on the phone. He said he hadn't worked for him in many months, that Gabriel had moved and cut ties with many people after I'd left, and even more so once my family started looking for him. However, he did say that if Gabriel reached out to him and asked, that he would not be able to lie. Another risk I was going to have to take.

"No, Miss. He does not." He glanced at me. "But if he is there, at his home, I will have to respect his wishes, whatever they may be."

"Thank you," I said. "Can we get going? I know it's a long ride."

The three of us drove just over two hours up winding roads, through lush hillside trees and overgrown landscapes. Once in the town of Beit Chabab, we passed monasteries and churches and cement stairwells veering off the roads leading to private residences. There were not many tall structures, and almost all the homes required taking a secluded road that led through more and more trees at every stretch and turn. The streets were paved but bumpy and strewn with loose rocks that crunched under his tires as we sped through. The air was warm, and Walid's car had no air-conditioning, so we all had to tolerate each other's body odor for most of the day. Walid stopped for a woman on her bike to pass in front of us, and then he pulled onto a narrow brick drive with an open gate at the end. Once through, he stopped the car and turned around, his arm hanging on the headrest behind him.

"We're here," he said, and I immediately felt nauseated.

"She's in there," I whispered to Yasmine. "I know it."

The square-shaped house was made of white brick and covered almost entirely in ivy. The windows had light-blue shutters and were very symmetrical with the first level, having the same number as the second floor. The color of the front door matched the shutters, and there were three chimneys atop a slanted gray roof.

There was no containing me in that car. I flew to the front door of the home and knocked with my fist. After a moment and no immediate answer, I kept knocking until my knuckles bled. Neither Yasmine nor Walid dared to stop me. I was just about to switch hands when a small hinged window on the door opened.

"Can I help you?" a woman asked in French.

"I'm here for Ann Marie, my daughter."

The woman peered through the thin iron bars that covered the square opening and looked past me to where Yasmine was standing over my shoulder.

"There is a court order. Now please open the door," Yasmine added from behind.

"I don't know anything about that, but I do know this is private property, and I will have to call the police if you don't leave immediately."

"This is the girl's mother," Yasmine said.

The woman met my eyes and then looked me over.

"Please," I begged. It was hard for me to see the woman's face clearly, but she looked to be in her early fifties. *She must've been somebody's mother,* I thought to myself, *and if not, she surely had a mother of her own.* I'd come across very few people who did not at least try to understand my pain and suffering. I took a step back so she had a better view of my face and placed my hands on my chest. "My baby is in there. Please."

"She is asleep. You will have to come back another time." And with that, the window closed.

I threw my body at the door and pounded with every limb. Walid and Yasmine pulled me away. "Miss Catherine, you don't want to get the police involved," he said over my pleas. "I cannot stress how tight this community is. They will never turn on one another. If the police turn up, you may never see your daughter again. We will come back tomorrow."

And so we did. And the next day, and the next day, and the next after that. Each time with the same result.

Walid drove me to the mountains every day for two weeks, and every time we were told that the baby was sleeping and we'd have to try again. The police were never called, and Walid never allowed me to push those people, insisting that I had to be strong for Ann Marie. Her second birthday came and went during those weeks, and I left a stuffed penguin that Reema had given me and a set of alphabet blocks in front of the door that would never open.

We assumed Ann Marie was there, in Gabriel's mountain home, but Yasmine suggested we take her picture, which was at least a year old, to the local monasteries, some of which had orphanages and schools. Trying to imagine her asking for her mother, or a glass of milk or a hug, were thoughts I struggled to suppress on an hourly basis. Each day after we were turned away at Gabriel's home, we'd visit the monastery schools. Walid would speak for me, holding a picture of this missing little girl with big brown eyes and sweeping curls, and I would just watch as people shook their heads.

I'd lost more weight and more faith, but I never gave up. It was difficult for me to eat, not knowing if my child was hungry or not. At night, Yasmine would sit with me, and we'd listen to Frank Sinatra records while she helped me continue to learn French and Arabic. I had daily phone calls with Charley Stillwater and his team of attorneys, who worked tirelessly on my case.

And then one morning, six months into my stay in Beirut, I got word that my uncle Fitz had announced he'd be running for president as the Democratic nominee. A week later, Charley called the Khalids' house at 7:00 a.m. to tell me that we'd won our custody battle in Lebanon.

"Gabriel has been ordered to deliver the baby to the police station by noon today."

I could barely organize my thoughts. "Oh my God." I was sitting at a desk in the Khalids' library, rubbing my eyes.

"I spoke to Danny yesterday and let him know there was a very strong possibility of this happening, so he will be able to advise you on what to do."

"Gabriel has been ordered to comply before and failed," I reminded him.

"It's different this time."

"How?" I asked.

"The local authorities are involved now. The judge was not pleased to hear that Gabriel ignored his initial ruling, and he will be arrested if he does not show up with Ann Marie today."

"What if he hides her again and risks arrest? I'm not putting anything past him at this point."

"His attorneys are working with us, and they're under major diplomatic pressure to get this done quickly and peacefully."

Yasmine came into the room in her robe just as I hung up the phone. "Danny told me." She was smiling. "I believe you will have your baby back today." She placed a hand on her heart. "I can feel it."

I pushed back from the desk and faced her. "I'm so scared."

She pulled a chair up next to me. "Of what?"

"She's two and a half years old now. Gabriel took her when she was eleven months." I sighed. "She's not going to know who I am. What if she's frightened by me?"

Yasmine stood in a single motion and walked to the window, her back straight. Even in a robe, she exuded elegance. She crossed her arms. "A child knows her mother, just as a mother knows her child." She turned back to face me. "She is young still, and even if her reaction is not initially what you hope for, she will know you."

I moved through my room upstairs, turning on lights and straightening things up. I had a large four-poster bed, with red silk fabric hanging from above like a tent. The floor was made of marble, and there were two matching marble pillars at the end of the room near the window. A dresser and two red velvet chairs sat opposite the bed. We didn't have a crib, but the Khalids had purchased a tiny toddler bed for Ann Marie soon after I had arrived. It had been sitting empty for almost a year near the window, with just a fitted sheet and nothing more. I pulled off the sheet, put a fresh on one, and made the rest of the bed with clean linens and blankets. When I was through, I dressed in a pair of bell-bottom jeans, a purple blouse, and a pair of suede pumps with a low heel. Yasmine sent one of the maids to the store to pick up some extra fruit and milk and cookies, but the truth was, I had no idea what my daughter liked to eat. I no longer knew anything about her.

"Catherine!" Danny's voice boomed from the foyer below. "It's time to go!"

I grabbed my purse and ran down the stairs.

"I will call your father when we return, since it's so early in the morning there right now."

"Thank you."

He placed a hand on my shoulder. "We will get her back today. Don't be nervous."

"I'm trying. I really am."

I didn't say a word during the car ride to the station. Danny and Wassef were in the front seat, and Yasmine was in the back with me, holding my hand as I stared out the window on the verge of an emotional breakdown.

"She will be there," Yasmine whispered and squeezed my hand.

Noon came and went, while the four of us sat in a waiting room at the local police station with Styrofoam coffee cups on the table in front of us. I could barely speak.

At 1:30 p.m., we got news that they were on their way. The officers assisting us that afternoon confirmed that Ann Marie was with Gabriel's attorney and a nanny, and they would arrive in the next half hour.

In my hands were a stuffed bear she'd had when she was a baby and a photograph of the two of us. Just after 2:00 p.m., there was some commotion at the front desk. I could see through a doorway that a woman had walked into the station with a child and two other men. I placed the items I was holding on the table and sprang to my feet. Yasmine followed me. We both stopped in our tracks when we saw her.

Yasmine grabbed my arm. "Oh my God, look at her. The whole time we were looking for a little girl," she whispered.

Ann Marie was very thin, wearing pajamas that hung off her shoulders, and her hair had been cut short like a boy. It was dark brown and thick and would've been wavy and lush had it not been so shorn. I made eye contact with the woman holding her hand. She was dressed in a white uniform, like that of a nurse or housemaid, and my daughter was clinging to her side. I dropped to my knees so that she and I could be eye level. The nurse lady took a step forward, and Ann Marie hid behind her leg, but she looked at me. There were more than half a dozen people in the room, but she looked right at me.

I placed my hands on my knees. I did not want to cry in front of that scared little girl. I wanted to show her only love and happiness in that moment. "Hi," I said and lowered my chin. You could've heard a pin drop.

She looked at her nanny, who said something in French.

"She only speaks French and Arabic," the woman said.

"*Salut,*" I said, and she waved at me and then retreated back behind her nanny after looking around the room filled with strangers.

"This is overwhelming for her. Can we please have some privacy?" I asked. Everyone cleared out except for the nanny, Yasmine, and myself.

"Can you bring me the bear?" I said to Yasmine, and she did.

"*Pour toi,*" I said and held out the teddy bear. She looked at the woman she was holding on to before taking it from me.

I got to my feet. "Have you told her who I am?" I asked the woman.

"She has been told that I am her mama and you are her nanny."

It was a blow to the gut, but I brushed it off. "Please let go of her hand," I said, and the woman did as I asked. I knelt again and held my arms wide. "Can I have a hug?" I asked in French. The little girl before me released her grip on the nanny's hand and stepped into my embrace. She studied my face when we were through.

"*Je t'aime*. I love you," I said.

She stared at me with no trepidation whatsoever.

"I think it's time we go," I said to Yasmine but kept my eyes on Ann Marie. Yasmine waved at the men, and the nanny was quickly escorted away. Ann Marie began to cry as the chaos ensued.

"Wait! Please wait!" I scooped her up into my arms and found the nanny and Gabriel's attorney in the next room. The woman was visibly shaken, but I knew she could understand me. "Thank you," I began. "Thank you for caring for her and loving her and whatever you have done to keep my daughter healthy and safe."

There were tears in her eyes. She leaned close to kiss my daughter on the forehead. Ann Marie reached out to the nanny with both arms as I held her in mine, and the woman spoke to her in Arabic. Ann Marie clung to me once she understood.

Back at the Khalids, we had a bit of a rough start. There were times she was smiling and diverted with ice cream and toys, but in between she would have moments of crying and confusion. There was little I could do to help other than hold her when she would allow it. Occasionally when she was playing, she would ask for Mama, and I would just point to myself, hoping she would eventually associate me with the word, and she did.

I stayed calm and remained steadfast, and the only times I became unnerved was when she would ask for her dada. She would look at me, and I would just smile and say, "Mama loves you." I gave her some of the presents that were still unopened from her first birthday. A tea set, a colorful xylophone, and a See 'N Say with farm animals. Children are resilient, yes, but mostly when they are loved and safe and confident of those two things. Once she was back in my arms, I knew she felt uprooted and some initial uncertainty, but I could sense that she knew me. A mother knows, and I was certain of it.

I finally had my baby back, and nothing else mattered.

Once Ann Marie was with me, Charley called to check in and make sure everything went as planned.

"If I live to be one hundred, I will never find the words to thank you for what you've done for me," I said to him.

"It's been my pleasure, and I can promise you I did not work alone. I can't tell you how relieved we all are to hear that mother and daughter have been reunited."

"Thank you again."

He took a deep breath. "Your journey is not over, I'm afraid."

Chapter Thirty-Seven

ANN MARIE

Chicago, January 2009

We had a scare yesterday on New Year's Eve, causing Mom to spend two nights in the hospital because she was having difficulty breathing, but the doctor called this morning to say she responded well to treatment and is able to come home. I spent the morning cleaning her sheets, doing laundry, prioritizing which bills to pay, vacuuming dog hair, and taking care of a myriad of other tasks I've been neglecting. I walk by the Christmas tree and laugh. Praise Jesus if I get that thing taken down by Easter.

I sit down with my laptop and a Lean Cuisine and see an e-mail from Dr. Marcus. I can hardly contain my smile.

> Hi, Ann Marie. I wanted to check in and see how you and your mom are doing. Please let me know.
>
> —Scott

I reply:

Hi, Dr. Scott. It's so great to hear from you. Thank you for reaching out. I wish I had better news, but Mom landed herself in the hospital for a couple of days. I'm picking her up this afternoon, though, so we're hoping she'll be comfortable. Besides that, everything is crazy as always.

Again, thank you for asking. It really means a lot to both of us.

—AM

The next e-mail is from Amanda at Stewart Fishman's office and has some encouraging news.

Todd has agreed to a property settlement in lieu of alimony, so he will waive his interest in the house, but he'll still be responsible for child support. You will obtain full title to the property, which of course means you'll be solely responsible for taxes, insurance, mortgage, et cetera. Our next step is to schedule what's called a prove-up date, where both sides have to prove that our settlement is agreeable to the court. Once we do that, and the court finds that the agreement is not unconscionable, we'll be finished. Usually takes a week or two. Since you are not the one who filed for divorce, you have the option to be present or not. Todd will be required to be there, since he's the filer, but if all goes well, you should be divorced that day.

—Amanda

I reply that I have no interest in attending the hearing, and to let me know when I can get on with my life as an unmarried woman. Taking on the house myself is a daunting task, but I'm thrilled that Mom and I and the boys will have this home for the foreseeable future.

Snoopy is moping around and running to the front hall whenever he hears a car drive by. I walk over and give him a pat on the head. "She's coming home today, bud. Now go and sit with the boys. They go back to school in a week."

He wags his tail and jogs off to be with the kids in the family room, as if he understands me. Then, just as I get back to the kitchen, I hear a key in the front door, which sends the dog back up the hall like a boomerang.

"Shh, quiet!" I say to halt his barking, but he won't stop, and I find Todd is cowering in the doorway after letting himself inside.

"What the fuck, Ann Marie? Get this thing out of my face!"

I cross my arms, and Snoopy continues to bark. "I thought you agreed to knocking first?"

"Get this dog away from me!"

"Shh," I say, trying to quiet Snoopy and grab hold of his collar. "Sit, sit, shh. Good boy." Snoopy stares at Todd as if he were a wounded squirrel perched on a low-hanging branch. "He's a good judge of character. What can I say?"

"I don't want this dog around the boys."

"Too bad. It's my mom's dog, and he's not going anywhere." I'm done appeasing him. "Do you need something?"

Todd regains his composure and reaches for something in his pocket. "I have a check for you." He hands it to me.

"What's this?" I ask after unfolding it and seeing the amount.

"It's the child support."

"It's *half* the child support."

Todd rolls his neck. "It's all I have this month."

The thought of having to call my attorney, file a complaint, and let him know that Todd is not complying with the judgment makes me sick to my stomach. Dealing with chasing this money around and around and adding more attorney fees to try and get it is the absolute very last thing I need to deal with right now, and Todd knows that. My head is throbbing with rage as he continues to do whatever the hell he pleases with zero regard for the law and his boys.

"I'll be sure and tell the judge that," I say.

He takes his middle finger and thrusts it in the air, and for a moment I actually feel sorry for the other woman who's walking the earth carrying his child. Before I can say anything else, he turns and starts to walk away.

I let go of Snoopy's collar and yell, "SPIDER!"

∼

"It wasn't nearly as gory as I'd hoped." I recount the scene for my mom when I get to the hospital later that day. "I think Snoopy actually wanted to love on Todd, but Todd didn't stick around long enough to find out."

Mom smiles and gives me a thumbs-up.

"He came to drop off half the child support." I roll my eyes. "Maybe he thinks I should tell the boys they each get half a chicken nugget for dinner."

Mom looks distressed now.

"I'm kidding! It's fine. We'll be just fine." The words come quickly, if only I believed them myself. "Please don't worry about us. Everything will work out."

She holds a hand up, trying to form a response. So I give her a pad of paper and a pen. "Do you want to try writing?"

She nods, and I sit waiting for her to put her words on paper, something she's able to do about an eighth of the time. She holds up the pad when she's through. *Have you read any more?*

I look at her. "The journals?"

She nods.

"I want to go through them with you. And I've just been so busy back at home. I managed to clean and organize and get a lot done while you were in here on vacation." I wink.

She places her hands over her heart, pleading with me.

"I promise you, we'll read them together. Every single word. Just give it some time." I pause. "I know you've opened the floodgates, and you're worried I will have questions, but all I need right now is for you to get better. Please respect that."

She nods.

"Dr. Marcus asked about you."

She looks at me wide-eyed.

"I got an e-mail from him today, and yes, I responded, and yes, he's madly in love with me."

She twitches, which is now her version of laughing.

A nurse walks in with her discharge papers and a few more vials of pills. My kitchen counter already looks like the back room of a pharmacy, so these will fit right in. I sign the paperwork and roll Mom out to the parking garage in a wheelchair, making her look even worse than she probably feels, but the truth is that I don't know exactly how she feels. We're each trying to hide things from each other. She's trying to hide her pain and suffering and self-pity, and I'm trying to hide my fear and devastation, but I have a terrible poker face. We're really two people just trying to love and protect each other. Three, if you count the dog.

When we get home, Snoopy runs to her, and I have to hold his collar to keep all four paws on the ground. All she has to do is lift her arm in one sweeping move, and he goes down. In only a very short time, he's learned to respond to her silent commands, sitting and lying down with just a wave of her hand.

I get her settled on the couch in the family room. "I wish you wouldn't insist on wearing heels," I say as I place a blanket over her lap. "They're not very safe, and they're certainly not necessary in the house."

She brushes me off with a wave and then holds three fingers in the air, her sign for the boys.

"Luke and Jimmy are over at Edith Stern's house, and Ryan is at the Engels'. I thought you might want to come home to some peace and quiet."

She shakes her head.

"They'll be home soon enough. Don't you worry."

She points to her purse, and I bring it to her. "I'm going to let Snoopy out since we've been gone most of the day. Come on, bud!" I say, and he follows me to the patio doors and then bounds through the snow, sniffing out the perfect spot to urinate.

I wait for him and wipe off his paws with a dish towel when he comes back inside. I check my laptop, and there are seven new e-mails from my attorney in the past two hours, but I've had enough for today so I shut my computer. I open the fridge and stare at the contents, waiting for a genie to pop out and tell me what to make for dinner. "Our dinner choices are spaghetti with peas, grilled cheese, or breakfast," I yell to her and then shut the door. She's waving me over when I look across the island, and there is a piece of paper in her hand.

"What's up?" I search her eyes for an answer. There's something to be said for the intimacy of communicating without words.

She hands me a check for $2,000, rendering me speechless, too.

She pushes my hand.

"What on earth is this for?"

Mom smiles and places her purse on the coffee table.

"Mom, you're going to need this money. *We* are going to need this money for your hospital bills and medication. Have you seen how many vials of pills are over there? We still have a long road ahead of us."

She purses her lips and pushes my hand again, forcing the money on me, and then she grabs a pad of paper. It takes her about ten minutes to write four words. *For more chicken nuggets,* it says.

I smile and burst into tears. Not because I need the money—which I desperately do—but because I take it as a sign that she's giving up. I need her to be strong and believe in her own recovery, not start giving her money away.

"Thank you." We embrace. "I certainly hope QVC doesn't have to suffer for this."

She shakes her head no.

I let out a small laugh and wipe my cheeks. "No, I don't suppose they will."

That night before bed, I refresh my e-mail for the thousandth time and bask in the glow of the screen as a response from Dr. Scott appears.

Hello again,

I wish you would've e-mailed me when she was first admitted. I could have checked in on her for you, but I'm glad to hear she's back in your care. Send me an e-mail in the morning with an update. In the meantime, I hope you know that I meant what I said. I'm here for you, so please don't hesitate to reach out. And I know what you're thinking, so I'm going to go ahead and answer it . . . No, I don't say that to everyone. Have a good night.

—Scott

Chapter Thirty-Eight

CATHERINE

Beirut, 1974

Ann Marie and I moved out of the Khalids' house after the Christmas holiday and into our own apartment. It was near the grounds of the university campus and only blocks from where Gabriel and I used to live. I was still legally forbidden from leaving with my daughter because, as an American citizen, I didn't have the right to take a Lebanese child out of the country. My Lebanese attorney, working with Fitz and Charley and Stewart Fishman—who was personally working on getting me a new passport—had managed to ban Gabriel from having any access to her because of his past behavior and his refusal to obey the initial court order. We'd heard he fled to Cyprus or Cairo but didn't know for sure.

Our new home was a tiny, furnished one-bedroom apartment with a butcher-type retail shop on the first floor that served food to go and had a few convenience items. Not a full grocery but things like milk, candy, cigarettes, and such. I would take Ann Marie down there once in a while and walk through the store, pointing out items and trying to teach her how to say them in English. The man behind the counter was a lovely man named George, maybe in his early sixties. He would smile and wave to her when we'd stop in, but I was told to keep my distance from people, so I never really stopped to chat. He probably thought I was horribly unfriendly.

Ann Marie and I shared a full-size bed and slept together each night curled up like puppies. The walls of the apartment were bare but clean. The windows had been washed and the curtains pressed before we'd moved in, and there was a balcony where she and I would sit and get some fresh air while eating our breakfast. Under normal circumstances, the place was perfectly livable. Under my circumstances, it felt like a house of cards, ready to collapse along with my nerves at any moment. All I knew was that we'd be living there for an infinite amount of time until everything was ready and in place for our escape. I was told to wait for a call—could be days, could be months—but once it came, I'd better be ready.

One morning we were in our little kitchenette and I was singing Frank Sinatra tunes to her while making breakfast. She was perched on the counter next to me as I crooned a cappella when I suddenly cut my finger slicing a block of cheese. Ann Marie panicked, screaming with tears running down her puffy cheeks at the sight of blood, so I remained calm.

"It's OK," I said and ran my hand under the water. She watched intently as she caught her breath and saw the blood wash off my skin.

"*Non!*" she yelled.

"It's OK, my sweet girl. Watch." I pointed to her eyes. "I'm going to make it better. I will show you."

Step by step, I cleaned the wound, dried the cut with a clean towel, and wrapped a bandage on my finger. "All better." I kissed my own hand and then placed it in front of her lips for her to do the same. She softly kissed the bandage and looked at me.

I grinned. "All better," I repeated with a nod, asking her to say it, too, if she could.

She smiled. "All better."

After breakfast, we walked downstairs to the shop. It was an unsettling time to be in Beirut, as there was civil and political unrest among the Christians and Shiites and Palestinians. In the paper, I would read about incidents that had begun to happen all over the city, like kidnappings and murders in otherwise upscale, peaceful communities. There were prominent leaders being targeted and people coming into their homes without provocation and being murdered in front of their families. And then the streets would be closed down, sometimes for weeks, and there would be sand piles and Jeeps and tanks blocking the flow of traffic. One evening, I heard a bunch of commotion in the street, and I ran to the window. Outside were four to five cars stopped in the middle of the road. Then a bunch of men got out and ran through the building across from mine, looking for someone. Neighbors flocked to their balconies to see what was going on, just praying the target wasn't someone in their households.

About two weeks after we moved in, Yasmine and Danny came by to visit with us. They had been inviting us over, but I'd become so paranoid during that time and wasn't comfortable straying far from the apartment. Even a trip to the beach held too many dangers, as far as I was concerned, and I didn't want to miss the call.

"We're going to get you out, but it's going to be very last-minute, so make sure you always have everything ready," Danny said.

"If I never see any of these possessions again, it will be too soon."

"Well, you can't board a plane with no luggage. It will seem suspect," he said. "We are working on getting you new passports. And for your protection, we'll be issuing you both false identities. You will have little time to memorize everything about them, yours and Ann Marie's, but make sure you know exactly what they say about who you are and where you're from."

I nodded. "I understand, and we're ready." I glanced over at Ann Marie sitting in Yasmine's lap, paging through a Dr. Seuss book. "I keep a carry-on bag packed at all times, and we just keep wearing the same few outfits over and over. There is not much else here that belongs to us, other than the toys and baby stuff." I cast my eyes across the room. The walls were beige and bare, save for the front windows with their green-and-blue-striped curtains. A large rust-colored couch sat against the wall with a rectangular wood coffee table in front of that, and a small table with four chairs where we ate. Across from the couch was a little bookshelf where we kept Ann Marie's toys and books. "Everything is replaceable if we ever get home."

He took a breath and patted me on the knee. "You will get home."

"What if I mess up at the airport? What if I'm questioned?"

He shook his head. "You will have all the papers you need, and there will be no reason for that to happen. If it does, Wassef will be there with you, as another passenger, and he will step in if needed, but he will not be boarding the plane."

"What about Ann Marie? The first time we left here, she needed documentation and permission from her father."

"She'll be an American citizen who is traveling abroad this time. You both will." He paused. "I can assure you there will be no details left undiscovered. We are working to make certain you won't have any problems. Now, are you sure you won't join us for dinner?"

I stood and gave him a hug. "No, thank you for everything, though. We're going to stay here."

And stay we did. Another three months passed with little news and even less contact from Charley or my father. It became a full-on waiting game, and there were days I thought she and I would never leave. I'd stare at the blank walls and the dust-covered windows, wondering when I should just throw in the towel and find a proper home that didn't smell like raw meat and exhaust fumes. I did my best to teach her English and speak to her in French as well. We didn't venture out very much other than the grocery down the block and the butcher below, and even then I made it a point to keep to myself.

One morning Ann Marie woke me very early, babbling in two languages, and she seemed a little stir-crazy. We both were. The streets were quieter than normal at that hour, so I thought I'd put her in the stroller and get some fresh air. We bundled up and walked a few blocks to a neighborhood bakery that opened when the sun rose. My daughter delighted at the scent of fresh bread and pastry, and we sat in the shop's front window and shared a *Manakeesh* with lemon and olive oil as I sipped a mug of Turkish coffee.

Just as I was cleaning up our table, three policemen stormed through the front door and walked to the back of the bakery. I dropped what was in my hand, ran back to our table, grabbed Ann Marie's arm with one hand and the stroller with the other, and hurried out the front door as a large military tank pulled up. I could see people looking down on us from balconies wearing robes and pajamas. Some were screaming in Arabic, others were silent, and some were yelling at the driver of the tank. I dragged my daughter by the hand and led her clumsily down the sidewalk. After a few feet, she tripped over herself and fell to the pavement. I scooped her up into my arms, held her against my hip, and ran, leaving the stroller behind until we reached our building.

The butcher, George, was just opening his doors as we arrived.

"Is everything all right?" he asked, reading my face.

"No, no, it isn't!" I took a deep breath, and he ushered us inside with great care, lifting Ann Marie off her feet and into a chair.

It took a moment for my heart rate to normalize. "I'm fine," I assured him. "Thank you. We just had a scare at the bakery down the street."

He glanced out the door but couldn't see from where we were standing. "What happened?"

I shook my head. "I really don't know. Some police came in and went to the back, and I just got out as quickly as I could." I paused to catch my breath. "It very well could've been nothing, but I just can't take any chances these days." I made eye contact with him. "I mean . . . no one can."

"Everyone is on edge." He placed a hand on my shoulder. "I'm sure you did the right thing." He glanced down at Ann Marie's hand, which was covered in blood.

"Oh my!" I said when I followed his gaze. "Honey, you scraped your knee right through your pant leg. Let's go get you cleaned up."

"Let me help," George said, and Ann Marie began to cry when she realized there was blood involved. She and I stood in his store as I tried to calm her, and he went to fetch a napkin behind the meat counter, ducking to avoid three spiral strips of bright yellow tape covered in dead flies.

"It's not even that bad, honey. We're going to make it all better, remember?" I assured her.

Her bottom lip jutted out, and she continued to cry until he picked her up and placed her on the front counter.

"How about some gum?" He pulled a pack of Trident off the rack.

"Oh, she's not allowed to have chewing gum yet," I began. "But thank . . ."

Ann Marie leaned forward and snagged the pack from his grasp. "All better," she said.

George and I both laughed, but as soon as he began to get chummy with me, I was eager to leave. "Don't make too many friends," Danny had warned me, in case people started to get curious about an American woman with a daughter who didn't speak her language. I wasn't allowed to contact Walid or any of my past acquaintances, and Brigitte had proved she wanted nothing to do with us. There was a constant worry that Gabriel was still plotting something, and no one would've put anything past him.

"Make sure we are the only people who know where you are," Danny had said. "You don't need to be telling strangers your address anyway."

"So, is everything else all right for you both?" George asked inno- cently enough. It was obvious I wasn't a student, and the number of single American women that would choose to live in Beirut—at a time when you could smell war in the air and even many Lebanese citizens were fleeing—was minimal at best. I may have been the only one.

"Yes, I . . . I mean we are just fine. My husband is away very often on business. He's a research assistant at AUB." I lifted my daughter off the counter. "Do you have the time?"

He checked his watch. "Just after seven thirty."

"Thank you so much for your help," I said and walked out to the back stairwell that led to our second-floor apartment.

I untied the scarf from Ann Marie's head and helped her out of her jacket. "I think that's enough excitement for one week," I said to her. "How about a nice glass of warm milk?"

She heard me but just continued to marvel at the gum.

The phone rang as I was turning the burner on. I hadn't even taken my own coat off. "Hello?" I said.

There was a short moment of silence before I heard Danny's voice. "It's time."

Chapter Thirty-Nine

CATHERINE

Beirut, 1974

I stretched the phone cord over to the stove and turned off the flame under the pot of milk as my heart began to whirl. Ann Marie was sitting on the floor in front of the couch, ripping tiny pieces of foil off the chewing gum. "Just tell me what I need to do," I said.

"In thirty minutes, there will be a knock at your door. Ask who it is before opening it, and if she says it's a floral delivery, open the door."

I swallowed.

"Take the envelope and flowers from her, and close your door," he continued. "Inside the package, you'll find your new passport. You are to memorize whatever it says. I have not seen it, so I can't give you any help at this time. Make sure you know your name, your child's name, both of your birthdays, the date the passport was issued, and of course, your country of origin." He cleared his throat. "There should be a section for your spouse, if you have one, and I don't know what it will say, but it's optional, so I'm hoping there are just three *X*s in that space."

"What if someone asks me if I'm married?"

"You say, 'Of course, and he's in Boston on business.' You are on your way to be reunited with him."

"What if they ask why I'm here in Beirut?"

"You were here on vacation and visiting a friend who attends the university."

"What is that friend's name?"

"They won't have time to check."

I rub my neck and pace as I listen to him.

"There will be a stamped date of entry as well, when you first arrived here, and it should be only a couple of weeks ago. Make sure you know that date as well."

"OK, thank you. I will be ready."

"Once you're in possession of the passport, you'll have two hours to get to the airport. You will have to get yourself there in a taxi or service car. No one you've had any contact with in Beirut can drive you there. Not even Yasmine or myself. Especially not Yasmine or myself."

The reason we left the Khalids' home to begin with was because Fitz and my father were worried that it would be a target for Gabriel once he knew we were staying there. That Gabriel might try to harm all three of us and report Danny to the authorities on false charges. No one wanted any unnecessary attention during that time.

"Thank you, Danny."

"You are most welcome, my darling. Now get on that plane, and introduce your daughter to some good ol' American cheesecake. I hear they even serve it at the airports there!"

I let out a nervous laugh. "That and a slice of apple pie."

"Be very careful today, but be confident. You don't want to grab anyone's attention by being jumpy. They are trained to look for uneasiness. Be confident," he repeated.

We ended the call, and I got the packed carry-on bag out of our only closet. I rinsed a couple of dishes and placed them back on the shelves, and then I waited for the mystery woman to arrive. I'd chewed off almost all the fingernails on my right hand when there was a knock at the door, thirty-two minutes after Danny had called.

Ann Marie looked at me when she heard it.

"It's OK," I whispered and stood. "Who is it?" I asked discreetly, not wanting the upstairs neighbor to hear if he were home, and reached for the knob.

"Afternoon, Miss, I have flowers for you." It was a man's voice.

For a moment, my breathing stopped completely. My hand trembled as I retracted it from the knob, and then I nearly fainted when the phone rang behind me. I stepped backward, away from the door, as if it might explode.

"Mama," Ann Marie said, sensing my uneasiness.

"J-just a minute," I said aloud and answered the phone. "Yes?" My eyes remained fixated on the door.

"It's Danny—" he began to say when I interrupted.

"There's a man at the door!" I whispered loudly into the mouthpiece. "You said a woman was going to come here and deliver flowers."

"Yes, that is why I'm calling. I was given some incorrect information. Place the phone down, go to the door, and ask him who the flowers are for. If he says Donna, then open the door. I will hold."

"And what if he doesn't say Donna?" I looked over at Ann Marie and felt like we were two helpless kittens with a coyote on the other side of the door. There was nothing I could've done to protect her if that man wanted to harm us.

"You need to trust me."

"If he does not say Donna, I'm going to have a heart attack at the ripe age of twenty-five." I placed the phone on the counter and did as I was told.

I cleared my throat. "Who are the flowers for?"

"Donna," the man said.

I made the sign of the cross and opened the door. I nearly fell backward when I saw George, the butcher, holding a bouquet of flowers.

The shock nearly winded me. "George? What are you doing here?" It was impossible to know what was going on, but there was little time to waste.

He held out the flowers and an envelope. "These are for you."

"Can you wait here a moment?" I left the door open and went to the phone. I caught Ann Marie waving at him as I walked by her. "It's the butcher from downstairs, and he said Donna."

"Good, then get to work." Danny hung up.

I hurried back to George and took the things from him. Seeing him standing there filled me with unbelievable confusion. I shook my head. "Have you been involved the whole time?"

He nodded. "I have."

"I don't know exactly what you've done for us, but thank you."

"It's no trouble at all," he said, then disappeared down the steps.

Once he was gone, I closed the door and looked at the passport.

- Donna Carlyle
- Born: March 10, 1949
- Birthplace: Boston, Massachusetts
- Minors: Mary Carlyle
- Born: June 6, 1971
- Birthplace: Boston, Massachusetts
- Country of Origin: United States
- Issue Date: October 21, 1970
- Expiration Date: October 21, 1980
- Spouse: X X X
- Date of Entry: April 22, 1974

Not wanting to waste one more minute in that apartment, I grabbed my purse, the carry-on, a small duffel bag with some of Ann Marie's toys—making sure we had nothing to declare—and headed out the door.

We stood on the street corner for only about five minutes before a taxi pulled up. The driver got out to help me, placing our things in the trunk, and after I buckled Ann Marie into the back seat, I turned to see George watching us from the front window of his shop. I paused and lifted my hand. "Thank you," I mouthed.

He nodded and gave me a thumbs-up.

Roughly eleven months later was the start of the Lebanese Civil War. It ended fifteen years later in 1990, resulting in an estimated 120,000 fatalities and an exodus of almost one million people from Lebanon.

Chapter Forty

ANN MARIE

Chicago, 2009

I want to be able to say my mom isn't going down without a fight, but that's not quite the case. I'm finding her chemo pills all over the house, which I've chastised her about constantly, but she claims she doesn't want any more poison in her body. She continues to order spirituality books on Amazon and jewelry on QVC, but she refuses to take her medication. Every time I look at her sitting on my couch in her heels and baubles, I liken it to the scene in *Titanic* where the aristocrats were sipping brandy and refusing to wear their life vests as the ship went down.

The hardest part about my journey with her is that she can't tell me how she's feeling. Her tumor has cut the current that sends the thoughts in her head out through her mouth, and it's incredibly frustrating for both of us. Her sisters and cousins are e-mailing me and calling daily, begging to come see her, but she keeps refusing company. Finally, my aunts Margaret and Colleen booked tickets once they heard my father had been allowed to come, and they're due to arrive in a few weeks. Once I told her they were coming hell or high water, Mom's been working on forcing out a few words. Ironically, the only one she can easily say is *great*. It's become her mantra and a testament to her unflappable spirit.

How are you, Mom? *Great!*

How about a glass of water? *Great!*

Would you like to watch a *SpongeBob* marathon with Jimmy? *Great!*

Is it OK if Snoopy poops in your tub? *Great!*

Between the boys and me, it's our new favorite pastime, trying to come up with the most outrageous questions for her to answer: *Great!*

"After I drop the boys at school and Luke at Mrs. Stern's, I have to head downtown to see Stewart Fishman and the gang. Despite evidence to the contrary, it looks as though pigs can fly, and I might actually get some closure on the divorce today," I tell her. "Fingers crossed. He says he has some papers for me to sign before he heads to court."

Mom places her hands in the prayer position. "Great." She nods.

"I would love for you come with me. Stewart promised me a free hour if I show up with you in person."

She shakes her head.

"Come on, he knows you can't talk. It will be fun. You're dressed and ready to go. Let's put these home-shopping purchases to good use."

My mom is a proud woman and forces an awkward smile, something else the tumor is sabotaging.

"I'll tell him you send your love."

~

"Traffic was miserable, and now I have only an hour before I have to get back on the highway and head home," I say to Stewart as he walks into the conference room.

He takes a seat at the head of the table and sets down a mug of coffee. "I was very sorry to get the e-mail about your mom."

I fold my hands in my lap. "I was sorry to have to send it."

"How's she doing?"

"Great!" I say, and he looks at me like I'm nuts. "I'm kidding." I rub my eyes. "It's literally the only word she can say, and I couldn't help myself."

"What's the only word?"

"'Great.' Her brain won't allow anything else to pass through her vocal cords."

He shakes his head and makes that face that people make. Especially those who knew her in her prime. Furrowed brow, pursed lips, and sad eyes.

"She sends her love," I add. "And I've learned a little bit about what happened to me when I was young. I didn't know when we first met . . . which I think was obvious."

He nods. "Yes."

"Thank you for lying and trying to make it seem like you'd made a mistake, but you're a horrible actor, and I knew there was more to the story."

"I was surprised you didn't know anything, but it wasn't my story to tell. Also, there's a little thing called attorney-client privilege barring me from discussing details of her case with you or anyone else." He takes a deep breath, and his expression goes from sad to serious. "You and I were brought together for a reason."

"I see that now."

"I wasn't able to help your mother as quickly and effectively as I wanted to, and now I can make it up to her by helping you."

I smile. "Let's see that redemption reflected in the bill."

Thomas is spraying Windex on his computer screen when I walk out of the conference room and into the reception area. "You're looking at a free woman," I say.

He stops what he's doing to applaud me.

"Thank you."

"It's about time," he says. "I'm going to miss you around here."

"I bet you say that to all the girls."

"Only the ones who bring me coffee."

For months, I've imagined walking out of the attorney's office a free woman, and I expected to feel more elated than deflated. I take my phone out of my purse and stare at it for a good long minute before texting Todd.

> I've anticipated this day for a long time and debated what to say to you. I'm sorry we had to end up like this, and I'm sorry for my part. I hope our mutual love for the boys will allow us to be civil to each other from here on out.

Thanks to the godsend that is my neighbor Jen Engel, all my boys are home from their after-school activities, and Luke from Mrs. Stern's, with bags of McDonald's in front of them. Mom is sitting on the couch, fully dressed, just as she's been since the morning, with Snoopy at her feet. I kiss the top of her head.

"I'm divorced," I whisper in her ear so the boys don't hear.

She looks up at me with a goofy excuse for a grin.

"Stewart Fishman wants you to know that he took good care of me because of his admiration for you."

She raises her brows.

"It's true," I say.

Once the sun sets and the kids are bathed and brushed, I find Mom and Snoopy in front of the small kitchen TV. "The boys are in bed, so I'm going to go up and read in my room."

She turns her neck a little and nods.

"You OK?" I ask.

"Great!"

"Love you," I say and head to my room. "Can you close the front door before you come up?" We have a Plexiglas storm door that's always closed, but I like to leave the main wooden door open throughout the day to let the light in.

She nods.

About forty minutes later, I hear a loud *clunk, clunk, clunk* on the stairs, followed by Snoopy barking.

"Mom!" I jump out of bed, run through the hall, and find her crumpled up at the bottom of the staircase with the dog pacing by her side. "Oh my God!" I race to her, hands trembling, not wanting to move her until I know she's all right. "Please, Mom, look at me. Are you OK?"

Mom looks into my eyes, and I can tell she's severely humbled by what just happened. She gets herself to an upright position, but she's defeated.

"It's those damn shoes!" I point at her feet. Camel-colored suede pumps with a wedge heel. "Starting today, there is a strict no-shoes-in-the-house policy."

She rubs her lower back.

"Can I take a look?"

She shakes her head.

"Please don't be stubborn." We look into each other's eyes, and I see she's crying. "I need to know if you are hurt," I say. "Touch the spot on your body if there's any pain."

She shakes her head again and lifts her hand to point out the storm door.

I turn my head and look outside. "It's a full moon," I say quietly.

We both have a good cry as my foyer glows from the moonlight. "I think that means your daughter knows best."

She wipes her cheek.

"No more goddamned heels in the house."

Once she's in bed, I go to my room and e-mail Dr. Scott.

> Hi, Scott,
>
> Hope all is well with you and your daughter. My
> mom fell tonight on the stairs. She seems to be
> OK. I had her move her arms and legs and fingers,
> and she said there was no pain. She'll probably just
> wake up with a nasty bruise, but it was really scary.
> Mostly because I saw her get emotional for the first
> time. Up until now, she's been trying to stay posi-
> tive and keep her chin up for the boys and me, but
> tonight I saw her inner struggle, and it killed me.
>
> Sorry to unload on you at such a late hour! But
> when I got in bed just now, you were the only per-
> son I wanted to talk to. Good thing for you I only
> have your e-mail and not your phone number.
>
> Take care,
>
> —AM

A minute later, he e-mails me back.

> Now you have both. 312-555-5668. Call me.

He picks up on the first ring. "Hi." His voice is tired but polite.
"It's your very favorite non-patient."
"How are you?"
"Grateful that you don't sleep at night, either."
"So, your mom had a fall?"

"She insists on wearing heels wherever she goes, which isn't very far. So she wears them all day around the house and to walk the dog and whatnot." I pause. "I thought I was going to find her dead body when I heard her tumbling down the stairs."

He makes a breathy noise. "Most people don't die from falling down a few stairs. Especially cancer patients."

I laugh, but I want to sob. "I don't know how you do it."

"Do what?"

"Deal with injuries and illness and cancer patients all day long. I can barely get through a phone call when one of her family members asks for an update."

Scott clears his throat. "I lost my mom to cancer when I was in college. I switched from prelaw to premed after she passed during my sophomore year."

"I'm so sorry."

"Thank you. I like to think I have some insight into what you and other people are going through."

My eyes tear up, but I don't want him to know I'm crying. "Can I ask about your ex-wife?" Curiosity gets the best of me.

"She and I split up about three years ago. I got a call in the middle of the night from a woman who said her husband was sleeping with my wife."

"Holy shit," I say.

"Yeah."

"I'd tell you about my marriage, but I'm actually feeling relaxed at the moment and don't want to get all riled up."

"I can appreciate that. Another time, maybe."

I roll onto my side and pull the covers up, wishing I didn't feel better listening to other people's problems. "Thanks for taking my call and for opening up to me. Maybe one day we can get together and lighten the conversation," I offer.

"I would like that."

We say our goodbyes, and I hang up with a smile on my face. I place my cell phone on my nightstand and pick up one of Mom's journals that I'd put there last night.

One day I'll go through them in order, but for now I like to surprise myself with little nuggets of her story. Our story. I turn to the middle of the book.

> *May 4, 1974*
> *To think George has been in on this all along! My hand is shaking. I prayed and prayed for this day to come, and now that it's finally here, I'm more frightened than ever. I need to get out of this apartment and don't have time to write, but I wanted to jot something down quickly.*
>
> *I pray this is not my last journal entry, but if it is, I want my daughter to know that I'm a fighter and I fought for her and loved her more than I have ever loved anyone or anything in my life. I thank God for her every day. Please keep us safe on the remainder of this journey. I hope one day she can forgive me for this.*

I close the book and hug it tightly against my chest. She is a fighter, and she always has been, and in my mind, there was nothing to forgive.

Chapter Forty-One

CATHERINE

Beirut, 1974

We arrive at Beirut International Airport about an hour after George delivered my new passport. Our flight wasn't for four more hours, but I was eager to get out of that apartment and through customs. The line was moderate; there were mostly families and some businessmen. It was rare to see a woman and child alone, but I was relieved to see at least one other pair headed for Boston. It's a funny thing, suspicion. Being the guilty party, I was desperate to glide through the airport unnoticed. It was a seemingly simple task that offered numerous opportunities to fail when trying to accomplish it with a small child.

We got in line and stood there about ten minutes before Ann Marie decided she needed to use the bathroom. Having just completed her potty training about two months prior, I wasn't in a position to push my luck, but I just wanted to get through the line. She began to grab her dress and pull on my leg, and I could feel my chest start to sweat from the anxiety. If I tried to speak to her in three different languages to get my message across, it could've been disastrous. Instead, I gathered our things and left our place in line. That move turned a few heads, but mostly from people who just seemed pleased to be traveling without children.

By the time we got back in line and close to the customs officer, I thought my head was going to explode. I focused heavily on breathing through my nostrils—in through the nose and out through the mouth—and kept repeating simple directives to myself. Smile but don't grin. Answer questions in a friendly tone, but don't give more information than necessary. Breathe. I handed my passport to the officer and held Ann Marie's hand. She was speaking to me about her chewing gum when he said something.

"Chin up, please."

I looked him in the eyes as he held the passport up and compared my face with the photo.

"Anything to declare?" he asked.

"No, sir."

"Place your bags on the table."

I released Ann Marie's hand and did as he asked, unzipping each one so he could easily rummage through them. There was purposely nothing in them but clothes and toys; I hadn't even packed a tube of toothpaste, something I realized only when he began to pull things out. Ann Marie was antsy after waiting so long, and she had little interest in standing still while the man went through our things.

"May I?" I grabbed a book off the table as he was emptying the duffel.

He nodded, and I handed her the book. The one good thing about fussy children is that people often have little tolerance for them and are encouraged to move them along. She sat on the ground with her book, and I kept gesturing for her to stand up. When she began to speak Arabic, the man stopped what he was doing and looked at her.

"Yes." I jumped right in without missing a beat. "Up, *fawq*." I began flailing my arms up and down. "*Fawq*, up. *Asfal*, down."

Ann Marie began to stand up and plop back down as if it were a game.

"We've been learning the language during our stay," I said to him.

He just watched as my daughter stood up and down with my instruction.

"OK," I said to her. "All done. No more." I patted my leg, instructing her to stand by my side. "Today we're going home."

She picked up her book from the floor and understood.

My skin was burning up. When the officer looked at me, I thought I was going to burst into flames. "Very nice," he said and zipped up our bags. "Next!" He waved to the man behind me.

I gave Ann Marie a little push with my hands and quickly grabbed our things off the table. She waved to the officer and said goodbye in French.

There wasn't a moment that day when I wasn't looking over my shoulder. I nearly had whiplash by the time we checked our bags and got to the gate. I found two chairs in a corner with our backs to the window so I could have a clear view of the airport and everyone's comings and goings. I stayed seated while Ann Marie wandered around from row to row, engaging strangers with her smile. Every once in a while, she'd walk a little too far and look back at me, testing her boundaries. I would shake my head no and wave her back. In a short time, she'd come to trust me. She was calling me Mama by then, but she'd been calling the woman who dropped her at the police station the same thing. What did the word even mean to her? She was heading *home* with her *mother*, and yet with so little understanding of either of those two words. My heart ached at the idea that she didn't have a home. That she'd lived in God only knew how many places.

"Children are resilient," Mother would tell me before my daughter and I were reunited. "And she will always know her mother."

I came to believe the second part, but I worried about my absence in those first critical years of her life. Would she be able to love if she wasn't loved herself? Would she have a fear of abandonment her whole life? Now that she was three years old, would I be able to reshape whatever damage had been done? She was a skinny little girl when she came back to me. Was that genetics, or had she been underfed and hungry? These were questions to which I would never have answers. They were months and memories that she and I were both robbed of, and I thought about them often. How would the residual effects of the trauma play out in her adult life, and how would I ever forgive myself? How could she ever forgive me for allowing this to happen to her? It was important to me that she never learn the truth, but I knew that might be too much to ask.

I reached into my purse and pulled out my journal and a pen. It was difficult to wake up in the morning, let alone keep up with my writing after Ann Marie had been taken from me, but I knew one day she'd have questions. I felt a great responsibility to give her as many answers as I could, even if I didn't have all of them myself.

My hand was jittery from the stress and excitement of the day, but I wanted to write down a few last-minute thoughts.

Once I was through, we boarded the flight that afternoon, and I held my breath until we landed in Boston.

Chapter Forty-Two

CATHERINE

Connecticut, 1974

Because of the time difference, we landed around 2:00 p.m., essentially more than twenty-four hours from when our journey began, and still had a three-hour car ride ahead of us. Laura and her brother, Henry, were at the gate waiting to greet us. We burst into tears at the sight of one another. My hair had grown past my shoulders at that point, and I was looking more like my old self again.

Laura came close and gave me a kiss on the cheek. There was a kind man who'd offered to take my things off the plane because Ann Marie was asleep, slumped over my shoulder like a sack of flour.

"Let me carry her for you," Henry offered.

I stroked her back and shook my head. "I would hate for her to wake up and see your face before mine."

He acted snubbed. "Many woman actually fight for that privilege," he joked and grabbed my bags from the other passenger.

Laura wiped her eyes. "We're just so relieved. I called your mom early this morning, and she'd only just been told you were on the plane. I guess with the time difference, your dad and whoever was helping you in Beirut were unable to reach each other. I can't tell you what it's been like for everyone here. We've been so worried."

I went to answer her, but I could barely contain my emotions. I just smiled and shook my head in disbelief. I felt like I'd been walking a tightrope for eighteen months with nowhere to step off and ground my feet, unable to live my life or even plan an afternoon. Just barely hanging on hour by hour, day by day, praying and begging to get to this point. We walked through the airport, and my head felt clearer. Maybe there was now space for some much-needed optimism.

Ann Marie awoke in the back seat of Henry's car, screaming and inconsolable about an hour into the ride. I'd been asleep myself and nearly had a heart attack when I heard her. She was scared and tired and dripping with sweat. The look of fear on her face was like a knife in my heart. Henry had to pull over so that I could take the time to introduce them to her and she could feel safe in the car again. Once we were back on the road, I held her in my lap while Laura and I sang songs and played patty-cake until she nodded off again.

When we were about twenty minutes from Belle Haven, I woke her up so she wouldn't feel blindsided being carried into a house full of people.

"Remember what Mommy has been saying, OK? Today we're going *home*."

She looked into my eyes.

"Does she understand you?" Laura asked.

"Somewhat. She's learned a few key words, but I'm trying to use the other languages as little as possible so she has no choice but to relearn everything. *Maison*," I said in French. "Home."

She looked out the window and placed her hand on the glass but didn't speak.

When Henry pulled through the front gate and up the winding driveway, I whispered it again in her ear. "Home."

As soon as the car came to a stop, the front door opened, and much to my daughter's delight, the dogs came flying out to greet us. She clapped and giggled and begged to be let out of the car.

Mother was standing in the doorway, watching the scene with her arms held out. "Welcome home!" she said and called for my sisters.

I took Ann Marie's hand and led her inside. There was a mass of people at the front door, smiling and clapping and pinching her cheeks. After about a minute of that, she'd had enough and retreated to my side. I waved for everyone to step back, and they did, but all eyes were on her, and I was so grateful to finally be the one she would cling to. I knelt down and leaned into her ear to teach her a new word.

"Family," I whispered and pointed to everyone.

Chapter Forty-Three

CATHERINE AND ANN MARIE

Chicago, 2009

It's been a rough week for Mom, but today is the big reunion, and I can see that it's ignited a spark in her eyes. She lost another few pounds, and she's finding it harder and harder to focus on simple conversations. Her speech is gone almost entirely. I've learned how to manage her with questions that require only a nod or a headshake. Anything above and beyond a yes-or-no answer is deemed inconsequential. As for me, I'm a wreck. Monica says I'm in denial, and Scott says I have to come to terms with the disease, but neither of those two options can prepare me for losing my mom. The boys and I pray for her every night, but I know I need to let go and prove to her that we're going to be fine, and I can be strong for her like she was for me. I think about the years she spent without me and how much her death parallels my abduction as a child. It's clear why she needed me to know what happened. To show me if she could pull through the worst life has to offer, then so can I.

The boys are with their dad today. I made sure they wouldn't be home, even though they were curious about meeting my father. It's an odd thing to discover your mom has a parent you've never met, but it was too much to have a house full of people. Especially when I'm not sure how this encounter is going to go down. But this is important to my mom, and whether or not she can articulate why, I know she needs this day to happen.

"I picked up some mini turkey and Brie sandwiches from Foodstuffs, and some of their roasted red-pepper dip. Do you think he'll want a beer or anything?"

Mom shrugs.

I open the fridge. There's soda, beer, wine, orange juice, and bottles of water. "He won't go thirsty," I say and close the door. She's sitting on the couch in the family room with Snoopy on the cushion next to her and a fleece blanket over her legs. About an hour ago, I helped blow-dry her hair and apply some makeup, taking careful effort not to clump her mascara.

"Would you like to wear your emerald pendant?"

She looks at me, and I go get it from her jewelry case.

Mom looks good, but she looks sick. The TV is turned to CNN, and the dismal housing market is the topic.

Snoopy's head jolts up off his resting paws when the doorbell rings.

"Should I lock him in the mudroom?" I point to the dog.

She hesitates and then nods.

"Come on, Snoop." He lays his head back down and won't budge.

Mom shrugs.

"I'll get the door."

I nip at my fingernail and then open the front door.

"Hello, my dear girl." His hand goes to his heart.

My father and I embrace, only he isn't the father I remember from the few photographs I have of him. His hair is gray, and there are lines on his face. Quite the contrast from the handsome young stranger standing in Saint Mark's Square with pigeons on his arms. He's tall and still has a commanding presence and voice, one of the few memories I have of him. Buried deep in the back of my mind are little scenes where he used to grab onto my hands and spin me around until my feet lifted off the ground.

"First the wind up!" he'd shout. And then he'd lie on his back with my stomach resting on the soles of his feet, and I would fly through the air like Superman with him screaming for me to watch out for buildings and airplanes and seagulls. I never knew details about that time until now, and I shudder to think what my mother was going through as he was spinning me around and around.

It's so easy to dislike someone you never have to see, but having him in front of me—grinning with pride—makes it all that more difficult. I can imagine he'd like for us to move forward and not relive the past, but I'm just not sure that's going to be possible in this moment.

"Hi. Please come inside," I say. From what little I know, he's a man of great pride and stubbornness, but age humbles even the most obstinate people.

He's holding a bouquet of yellow tulips. "How sweet, thank you. Are these for Mom?"

He nods. "I know you must have questions for me."

"Yes and no," I say. "I don't know all the details about what happened to me, and I don't know why it was kept a secret, but I do know why she told me."

"She and I both made mistakes and poor choices."

"I won't speak ill of her today or ever, but when I learn the truth, all of it, I will do so with an open mind."

"Thank you." His eyes wander behind me, inside the house.

I step aside and close the door. "She's back here."

My father follows me to the family room, where Snoopy is now off the couch, seated in front of the coffee table with his ears on high alert. "He's mostly friendly," I start. "I know some people are scared of Rottweilers, but this one is actually . . ." I look up at my father and stop speaking when I realize he's crying.

I drag Snoopy by the collar and lock him up and then walk back to the kitchen where I can see through to the family room. My father is kneeling in front of her with Mom's hand in his. He lowers his forehead onto her lap. She looks up at me, and I expect her to roll her eyes, but she does not.

After a moment that will forever be frozen in my mind, he lifts his head and takes a seat where Snoopy was. I look around not knowing what to do but wanting them to have some time alone. She and I had not discussed or imagined he would react like this. They were staring into each other's eyes, and my father was trying to speak to her.

"Just stick to the basics. Yes-and-no questions only," I say.

"I want her to know how sorry I am to see her this way," he says to me but keeps his gaze on her.

"She can understand you."

Mom nods, and he whispers something in her ear. She makes her awkward smile and nods again.

I bring some food to the coffee table in front of them. "I'm going to let Snoopy out. I'll be back in a few minutes."

They are still in the same spot when I return twenty minutes later. My father has a small plate in front of him with some crumbs on it, and Mom is drinking some water. He stands when he sees me.

"I think I will leave you both now." He gives my mom a very long hug and then wipes his eyes.

Mom looks up at him and nods. She is longing to say something, and my heart aches for her as she struggles but can't find her voice.

"I . . . I know this means a lot to her." I look at her and then back at my father. "When you said you were coming all the way here to visit us, she was really touched."

Mom nods again.

"I wish I hadn't waited so long," he says, and by his expression, I can't help but think he's not referring to her illness whatsoever.

I walk him to the foyer, and he takes a deep breath. "I didn't think I would be so emotional," he says.

I cross my arms. "It's hard, seeing her this way."

"It is heartbreaking. I'm so very sorry." He shakes his head. "I'm worried about you."

"I'll be fine. I'm really only concerned with Mom right now."

"Please keep in touch with me every step of the way, and let me know how she's doing."

He places a warm, comforting hand on my cheek and gives me a glimpse into what I've missed over the years. The strength and confidence that comes from the love between a father and a daughter. I can see the hopeless look in his eyes. It's one I recognize in myself lately, and now I know why he came. For the same reason she wanted me to call him. It was because of love. They loved each other once, madly and deeply, and despite all the ugliness from their past, maybe she thought I would need him now more than ever.

"I've been a disappointment to you and your mother, but now I would like to be here for you both, if I can." He pulled back his hand. "I know you're doing this for her, and I don't know if you are very angry with me, but I can admit when I've been wrong, and I can also say I'm sorry for the things I did and failed to do. I've not been the father to you that I wanted to be. If you can forgive me, I promise I will never let you down again."

I draw in a sharp breath. It's all too much for me to take, standing in the front hallway of my home with my mother dying in one room and my father coming to life in another. He's an older man now, a grandfather, and I can't help but think of Todd and my own boys when I look at him. I want my boys to have a loving relationship with their dad. I don't want them to be burdened with my animosity and pain. If there's a part of me that's willing to forgive Todd, there must be a part of me that's willing to forgive my father. I don't want to hate him, too. And maybe I don't know enough yet, and maybe I never will, but I do know that if my mother is able to find love in her heart after everything she went through, then maybe, one day, I can, too.

I stand facing him with my arms planted firmly at my sides. "I promise to try," I say, and then open the door for him to leave.

~

Mom is bedridden a few days later. The boys eat their dinner in her room and read books to her while we play her favorite songs on a CD player. We have a nurse who comes every day, and Dr. Scott has started stopping by as often as possible. If his presence in my life is the one blessing that results from her brain cancer, it's entirely because my mother has willed it to happen.

~

Four months after she arrived in my driveway on a cool November evening, my mom took her last breath. She died in my home with me, my boys, Snoopy, and Frank Sinatra by her side.

Except for going to the bathroom, Snoopy didn't leave her room for two weeks after her body was removed. The boys set up his food and water bowls in there, and Ryan slept on the floor in a sleeping bag curled up next to him.

One morning, I wake up before sunrise and am surprised to find Mom's box of journals overturned in the family room with Snoopy lying beside them. I haven't approached the box in the weeks since she passed. He lifts his head when I enter and wags his tiny excuse for a tail. "Fancy meeting you here," I say.

I walk over to the mess he's made and scratch his chin. "Did you do this?"

He wags some more.

I place my coffee mug on the table and go to pick them up when I notice my mom's pearls dangling from the edge of one like a bookmark. "What has she done?"

Snoopy tilts his head.

I take a seat on the floor, and Snoopy rests his chin on my leg. I gently open the journal to the page she marked for me and cradle her necklace in my lap.

> *May 4, 1974*
> *We are at the airport on our way home together.*
>
> *There were many, many days and nights that I thought we would never get to this place. One where I have you back in my life and safe, and on our way home. I worry that you don't understand what home means, and some days I think I don't know the meaning myself. It's been an astonishing few years, with very little happiness in my life until now. I've lived so many places and have been uprooted more times than I care to think about. I don't have the mental strength to write very much, and you're spinning around the airport about to collapse from dizziness, but I have a few important things I want to get on paper before I forget.*
>
> *First, you have always been loved. When you come to find out about your childhood, never question whether your parents loved you or not. We both did and still do.*
>
> *Second, I have never been so happy in my life as I was the day I found out I was pregnant and the day you were born.*
>
> *Third, when you are blessed with children of your own, you will understand how I was able to put my life on hold, yet still carry on without you. It's because finding you became my means of survival. You will hold your own*

babies and imagine my suffering, but just know that I
always knew this day would come.

    Fourth, I hope that one day you can forgive me for
allowing this to happen. I was never going to stop fighting
for you, and I've always had faith in God that we would
be together forever.

Just below the journal entry, there was fresh ink.

February 10, 2009
Love you so much, my sweet girl. I am so proud of you.
Together forever.

I close the book and gaze down at her string of pearls. It's astonishing how quickly she slipped through my grasp.

I drape the pearls around my neck and secure the clasp, allowing her energy and strength to seep into my skin with the weight of each bead.

A tiny smile emerges through my tears.

I have some big, fancy pumps to fill.

I will never know why bad things happen to good people, but thanks to my mother, I'll know how to deal with them.

ACKNOWLEDGMENTS

While this book is entirely a work of fiction, it was inspired by an extraordinary woman and her very real experiences. A profound thank-you to my friend for sharing her mother's harrowing and poignant life story with me as she grew from a headstrong young woman into a loving grandmother battling cancer. It's been an incredible and humbling honor to be trusted with her memories.

Additionally, I could not have told this story without the support and encouragement of the following people:

Brigitte Ghannoum—Since I've never been to Beirut, and certainly not in the 1970s, I am so grateful to Brigitte for her invaluable FaceTime session with me and her notes on the sights, sounds, and smells of this Lebanese city. Also, thank you to my Purdue University pal Raed Taji for the introduction! I can't tell you how many times I referred to the pages and pages of notes I was able to extract from her.

Christina Tracy—Speaking of Purdue pals, thank you to my Kappa Kappa Gamma sister Laura Tracy for introducing me to her real sister, Christina, who lives in Greenwich, Connecticut. Thank you, Christina, for the conversations and many, many, many wonderful texts and photos of that incredible town. Additionally, thanks to Christina's friend Brian Salerno for some added tidbits about the town and the food and the Stanton House Inn. I can't wait to visit someday soon!

Stephanie Bass—I seem to write a lot about divorce in my books, because I'm always turning to my friend of four decades (and former divorce attorney), Stephanie Bass. Her knowledge about the law is incredible, and her willingness to share it with me is equally amazing. Thank you for your time and friendship and generosity!

Badass Beta Readers—A massive shout-out to some beta readers who always give great, intuitive feedback: Erin Haase Budington, Beth Suit, Beth Schenker, and Meg Costigan. Reading a manuscript in its early unedited stages is no easy task, so thank you for that.

My mom and dad—Beta readers extraordinaire! I can't thank them enough for their support throughout the entire process—for this book and each one before.

My husband and son—Love you both so, so much. Once my novels are turned into movies, I know you're going to love them!

Sandra Harding—I was so blessed to be paired with Sandy as my developmental editor on this book. Her character insight and ability to interpret the story in a new way was such a gift to me during the editing process. I cannot thank her enough for helping me make this the best story it could be.

Danielle Marshall—Danielle is the editorial director at Lake Union Publishing, but to me she has always been my biggest cheerleader. Thank you so much for continually pushing me and believing in me after all these years. I'm eternally grateful for your unwavering support and for all those times you pick up the phone when I call.

Lastly, a general, but no less substantial, thank-you to my friends and family who have always supported me in everything I do.

ABOUT THE AUTHOR

Photo © Robin Miller

Dina Silver is an author, a wine lover, and an excellent parallel parker. She lives with her husband, son, and twenty-pound tabby cat in suburban Chicago. She'd prefer to live somewhere where it's warm year-round, but she's also a licensed real estate agent in Illinois, and she loathes the thought of having to take the broker exam again in another state. Dina is the author of five other novels, including *One Pink Line*, *Kat Fight*, *Finding Bliss*, *The Unimaginable*, and *Whisper If You Need Me*. To find out more about Dina and her books, visit www.dinasilver.com.